Introducing

Alert for t[…]
he knew was seldom penetrated by foreigners, who were too often robbed or even killed there, Webster kept to the middle of the street. But now there was trouble ahead too.

Three men, tough-looking characters in fezzes and striped shifts, were barring his way to the arch.

Webster looked swiftly around him. To his right, a narrow entry led for fifteen yards towards a high, blank wall with a gate in it. And behind him two more Arab thugs advanced. Both wore boots beneath their robes; one held a knife half-hidden in his sleeve.

The busy life of the street, scenting violence, was visibly melting away into shops and doorways. Webster ducked into the entry and immediately swung around to face his attackers. He was out-numbered now five to one, and he was unarmed . . .

KILLERS UNDER A CRUEL SKY

Peter Leslie

Hamlyn Paperbacks

KILLERS UNDER A CRUEL SKY

ISBN 0 600 20255 0

A Hamlyn Original
First published in Great Britain 1981
by Hamlyn Paperbacks

Hamlyn Paperbacks are published by
The Hamlyn Publishing Group Ltd,
Astronaut House,
Feltham,
Middlesex, England

(Paperback Division: Hamlyn Paperbacks,
Banda House, Cambridge Grove,
Hammersmith, London W6 0LE)

Printed and bound in Great Britain by
©ollins, Glasgow

This book is for Graham and Vera –
the real Major Webster and his lady.

'If the German had succeeded in perfecting and using these new weapons six months earlier than he did, our invasion of Europe would have proved exceedingly difficult, perhaps impossible.'

– General Dwight D. Eisenhower.

PROLOGUE

North Africa - 1942

The blade of the knife was nine and a quarter inches long. It was triangular in shape, fashioned from rigid tungsten steel trademarked *Rostfrei – Schweitzer Fabrikat*, and had once been used to disjoint the carcases of sheep in a Genoa butcher's shop. The point, honed to razor sharpness, slid easily between the Arab's ribs, slicing through the inferior vena cava to pierce the ventricle just below a tricuspid valve. With the circulation thus rudely arrested, the Arab died instantly.

Gottlieb Voigt allowed the body to slump from the chair to the warehouse floor, raising a small cloud of dust in the yellow light cast by the hurricane lamp. It was stiflingly hot in the airless corridor between the stacks of crated merchandise.

'I suppose that was necessary?' Benckendorff's voice queried from the shadows.

'Certainly it was.' Voigt pursed his thin lips and smoothed a non-existent crease from his jacket. A tall, stringy man, he was dressed in a grey suit with a white pinstripe and sported a duelling scar on his left cheek. 'Security is of the utmost importance in this operation,' he said. 'You know as well as I do, Colonel –'

'Not *quite* as well as you do, Herr Voigt,' said Benckendorff. 'I have to remind you that the overall responsibility for the project remains yours, even though some fool in Berlin has seen fit to transfer me here from Italy to organize our counter-espionage system.'

'And is not the suppression of security leaks, Herr Colonel, an essential part of counter-espionage?'

'It is,' Benckendorff admitted calmly. 'But there would have been nothing for this man to discover if the rules had been followed. Who is responsible for routing this material?' In the gloom, a hand tapped one of the packing cases.

'An Oberleutnant working for the Armistice Commission. I shall make it my personal business to see that he is shipped home to Germany and sent to the Eastern Front.'

'I should hope so! Top-secret supplies from the Reich among this so-called lease-lend rubbish of the Americans!' Benckendorff sounded scandalized. Gold-rimmed sunglasses gleamed as he stalked into the pool of illumination and stood looking down at the dead man. Twin highlights reflected the lantern in the polished toecaps of his SS jackboots. 'I would have welcomed an opportunity for further interrogation in depth,' he said. 'This fellow's claim that he was just a common sneak thief, prising open the crates in the hope of finding something he could pilfer ... the story doesn't really –'

'Nonsense!' Voigt interrupted in his turn. 'I know these Arabs. Dishonest, unintelligent, lazy. Believe me, this man told us everything he knew. His type lacks the wit for anything more than simple theft.'

'Perhaps. In any case, it is too late to do anything about it now. What do you suggest we do with the ... remains?'

'The harbour. One more dead man there will scarcely arouse the French from their apathy. More important, how can we ensure that this crate goes back where it belongs without attracting attention?'

Benckendorff hooked his thumbs behind the black belt of his uniform. 'I have already arranged for a truck to call here at midnight.'

'But ... ?' For the first time, Voigt looked uncertain. 'The port authorities? It will require a squad of men to shift this. A military truck entering a restricted area ... even at night ...' He compressed his lips. 'You have to remember, Colonel, that this is not an active service region. We are in an equivocal position here. France itself may be defeated, but colonies like this – and the French living in them – are supposed to be neutral. It is important that we do not in any way give the appearance of violating that neutrality.'

'I am perfectly aware of that; I know it as well as you do,' the SS man mocked. 'Do not worry: the truck is not a military vehicle; the squad will not be in uniform. Office equipment urgently needed at Commission headquarters has unfortunately been misrouted. All necessary formalities have been observed so that it can legally be removed from here tonight.'

'And the guards at the dock gates ... ?'

'... will be presented with the correct papers.'

'Very well.' Voigt pushed back a cuff and looked at his watch. 'Then we had best attend to this as soon as possible.' He leaned over the dead man. The dust had settled, and the Arab's eyes, wide open still with petrified astonishment, had already filmed over. There was surprisingly little blood staining the striped robe which had been pulled up around his waist.

'We had better untie his hands,' Benckendorff said. 'You don't think the marks of ... persuasion ... will make the French think this is the result of something more than a dockside brawl? If anyone knew, by some mischance, that he was coming to this warehouse ...' He left the sentence unfinished.

'I told you. They are always fishing bodies out of the harbour – vagrants, the victims of robbers, people who have been attacked in the casbah. Why should they bother with this one more than another? In any case, most of the marks are internal.' Voigt placed a foot on the Arab's chest and slowly drew out the knife. He took a small pad of cotton wool from the pocket of his jacket and fastidiously wiped the blade clean. 'It has provided me with a great deal of information, this,' he said conversationally. 'I should hate to be without it.'

'I should have thought it was rather a clumsy weapon.'

'My dear Colonel, I do not regard it as a *weapon*. It is an instrument.'

'Nevertheless, you can hardly walk through the streets carrying –'

'I don't,' Voigt cut in. 'I don't. Strapped to the inside of my leg, the knife neither shows itself nor causes me any discomfort. In its original use, it was designed for small and intricate manoeuvres, and, as you have seen, it still works efficiently in precisely that fashion. Inserted and then twisted in even the smallest orifice – the nostril, the urethra, an ear ...'

'*Wait!*' Benckendorff held up his hand. Far away down the darkened aisle separating the stacks of crates, something moved. A scraping noise, quickly stilled, followed by a subdued pattering. The SS officer drew his revolver and unclipped an electric flashlight from his belt. He gestured towards the lantern and then jerked his head at the neighbouring aisle. Voigt picked up the lamp and nodded.

Together the two men advanced along adjoining passageways. Light from the hurricane lamp sent gigantic shadows swinging and dancing across the corrugated iron walls of the warehouse and up among the girders supporting the roof. Somewhere in the darkness above them a bird, started from its perch, flapped noisily away.

Benckendorff lanced the flashlight beam in among the crates and containers, bales and sacks. Nothing moved. At the first intersection, where a broad alley at right-angles to the two main corridors cut a swathe through the stack of goods, he shone the beam on Voigt as he emerged from his aisle. Voigt shrugged and shook his head.

The two of them listened, holding their breath in the oppressive heat. Outside the warehouse, water lapped at the rotting piles of a jetty. A long way away, dance music blared thinly from a radio. Inside, there was silence. And then again that sibilant pattering sound, nearer this time, a little to the left. Benckendorff got there first, his forefinger curled around the trigger of the revolver. He saw corn falling, sliding from a rent in a bulging sack; a changing pattern of grains on the dusty floor.

'Rats!' Voigt exclaimed disgustedly. 'The damned place is alive with them. It's a wonder our distinguished Gallic hosts don't starve completely.'

Later, after they had carried the body of the Arab down rickety, weed-slimed steps and lowered it into the dark water, they helped the Germans who had brought the truck to manhandle the packing case off its trolley and over the tailboard. The case was about six feet long and three feet wide, as high off the floor as a man's waist. Despite the stencilled information on the rough wood that it contained office furniture and duplicating equipment, the crate was abnormally heavy and the characteristic, sour smell of machine oil could be detected between the slatted panels. Four men and a Feldwebel made up the squad, but even with the help of Voigt and the colonel, it took them over half an hour to load the container. Finally, however, it was done and the canvas cover lashed in place at the rear of the three-tonner. Benckendorff and Voigt rolled the double doors of the warehouse shut and walked towards the waiting truck. The stars were unnaturally bright in the sky. Somewhere beyond the outer harbour a tug bleated mournfully.

'I suppose he'll be washed ashore tomorrow?' Benckendorff said.

'Not necessarily. Even with the minimum tidefall here, it can take days, weeks.'

'All the same ...' The SS man plucked at his lower lip. 'I am still not convinced that it was the right thing to do, killing him. If he really did know nothing of Project Thunderbird (and with your permission I retain my doubts), he could still have –'

'It was the lesser of two evils,' Voigt said curtly. 'There will be less questions asked over a body in the harbour than there would be if we had maltreated him and let him go. Besides, he had told us everything he knew. Which was exactly nothing.'

Benckendorff was following a line of thought of his own. 'It might even,' he mused, 'have been worthwhile keeping him under wraps for a while, putting the fear of God into him, and then setting him free. With a tail, of course. Then we could have seen whether he just crawled home to his wife and family ... or whether he really was on to something and had somebody to report to. Then we would have known for sure.'

'He wouldn't have been much good to his wife, would he?' Voigt said.

Inside the warehouse, the bird had been disturbed again. The man who had inadvertently ripped open the grain sack with the safety catch of his revolver dropped on to a pile of crates from the girder to which he had been clinging. Sweat plastered his dark hair to his skull and soaked the shoulders of his alpaca jacket. Easing his collar with a damp finger, he climbed down to the floor and tiptoed through the breathless dark towards the pass door at the rear of the building.

PART I

Briefing for Death

They got a direct hit on one of the Heinkels soon after we crossed the coast. She went up slow and orange, like one of those arrested motion shots in a Leni Reifenstahl documentary – and the poor bastard hadn't even been caught in the searchlights. Schultz said he thought it was Rudi Schmeisser's plane. It must have been a freak shot; we don't usually get much trouble from flak on the milk run. Just after that we were jumped by a night fighter and Schultz lost his guts on the floor of the turret. The Englander swine blasted away half the starboard aileron: I had to jettison and turn back before we had even flattened out for the bombing run. That's a thing you learn about the Dornier flying pencil – if the trim's not one hundred per cent, you're in dead trouble all the way home.

Chapter One

Webster was in bed with a girl from War Office Records when the sirens went. Her nipples were hot and hard under his palms and her hips swung savagely against him as the wolf wail rose and fell in the cold night air.

A few minutes later they heard the thwacking detonations of anti-aircraft batteries firing from each side of the Thames estuary, and then the crump-crump-crump of exploding bombs. Emergency fire service bells clanged in the distance. Soon the sinister, familiar drone of synchronized motors throbbed between the roars of high explosive. 'Third time tonight,' Webster said thickly into the girl's dark hair. He was still a little drunk. 'Can't catch me, though. I'm the king of the bloody castle!'

The girl said nothing. She was panting in the blackness, though not from fear. Webster was an accomplished lover.

'Bloody nerve!' he said. 'Trying to ruin my last night in London!'

The sound of German planes was suddenly very loud in the small flat. A stick of bombs burst with metronome precision, advancing towards them from the east. Glass jingled on the bedside table as the last one shook the block. In the silence that followed they heard bricks and slates showering back on to the roofs of the surrounding buildings. Six floors below, air-raid wardens' whistles shrilled in the street.

Later Webster rolled on to his back and groped for his cigarettes and lighter. He sucked in a lungful of smoke before he felt for the girl's mouth and placed the last Balkan Sobranie between her lips. In the faint illumination from the glowing tip, twin spots of fire burned in her eyes and there was an unfathomable depth between her breasts. 'I like it when you do that,' she said soon afterwards. 'Darling, I think this cigarette's gone out. Could you ... ?'

'You have to keep drawing on the black Russian ones,' Webster said, propping himself on one elbow. He thumbed the Ronson again. The flame trembled in the dark.

'Sweetie,' the brunette said, 'that one was very close. Don't you think that maybe we ought to –?'

'Slope off to a basement shelter? Not on your bloody life. Not unless you want an audience or something,' Webster said coarsely. He took back the cigarette and drew on it, watching the subtle curve of her hip etch itself against the dark as she lay beside him.

'Just as you like, darling. Do you want another drink?'

'Never been known to refuse,' Webster said, 'and the hell with Jerry and his squibs.'

They say you never hear the one that hits you. Either they're wrong or somebody forgot to do his homework on the science of acoustics. Webster heard the express train screech in time to pitch away the cigarette and fling himself across the bed to cover the girl's naked body with his own. The girl had time to gasp, 'What again ... ?' before the night erupted.

Through a tornado of flying glass and plaster, brick powdered, boards split, girders bent. The explosion was too shattering to be appreciable as sound. Webster and his brunette shot off the bed, plunged through a gap where the floor had been, and landed in a hurricane of cement dust somewhere in the flat below.

Choking, Webster stumbled to his feet. 'Christ!' he panted, cawing with hysterical laughter. 'Don't be alarmed, folks ... we just thought we'd drop in!' And then: 'Darling – are you all right?'

'I think so.' The voice came shakily from a point below him and to his left. 'I ... my elbow hurts and I've bruised my left leg. But otherwise I seem to be all right. How about you?'

'Never felt better, old girl. Stay where you are until I take a shufti here and there to see what the form is.'

Flames across the street spilled red light into the room through the shattered windows. She watched Webster's lean shadow flicker across the walls. A moment later, astonishingly, she was screwing up her eyes against the dazzle of an electric lamp. He had found a switch, and a wall bracket on one of the circuits was still working!

Almost everything else in the place was ruined. The apartment had been the twin of her own upstairs. Now wicked fragments of glass lay everywhere, studding the flock-sprayed walls, scythed into the furnishings, strewing the floor. The carpet was littered with picture frames, smashed ornaments and papers from a desk whose drawers had been sucked out by the blast. Through the yawning hole in the ceiling, fractured joists crossed by laths still hung with plaster sagged towards a mound of soot in front of the fireplace. From the middle of this, one of her own pillows absurdly protruded.

'Liz! Come out here: the bedroom's hardly touched! But watch those pretty feet on the glass.' Webster was on the far side of the splintered door, exploring. From the street outside came the confused sounds of running footsteps, shouts, more whistles, the crackle of flames, the clangour of approaching fire engines. An angry voice called some obscenity about lights.

'My God, darling, the wardens!' the girl cried. 'There's no blackout here and you switched –'

'Sod the wardens! Do they think the krauts are going to notice one sixty-watt bulb among this lot? Half of bloody London's on fire, for Christ's sake! Come on out here.'

'What for?'

'What do you think?'

'*Ian!* Surely you can't ... ? You're out of your mind!'

A salacious laugh, exaggerated to the point of caricature, came from the far side of the door. 'I'm telling you the room's untouched,' Webster said. 'Clean sheets on the bed, at that. It's all laid on. Hurry up, or you'll catch cold.'

'Honestly!' Liz was trying her best to sound outraged. 'You are the *end*!' Suppose the owners –?'

'Place is empty. I checked.'

'But they may come back. Perhaps the building's on fire.

Maybe it's not safe. Shouldn't we report to the wardens and tell them we're unhurt? If we went back to my –'

'There's no bedroom left in your place. Besides, the owners here are *away*. No food in the fridge. No clothes in the jolly old wardrobe. Letters piled up on the hall floor. Probably belongs to some black-marketeer sitting out the blitz in bloody Torquay.'

'But the block may be –'

'Safe as houses!' Webster cackled with laughter again. 'Only blast damage. You can see out of the window: direct hit on the office block across the road. And if you think I'm going out starkers to report to some insurance clerk in a tin hat at four o'clock in the morning, you want your pretty head examined!'

Liz shrugged helplessly. Giggling a little, she scrambled to her feet and trod cautiously towards the door. From the passage she heard a cry of triumph. Splendid in his nudity, Webster appeared with a dark brown bottle grasped in one hand. 'Scotch!' he exulted. 'In the po cupboard beside the bed. Damned near full too! I told you they were black-marketeers.'

'Ian ...'

'The guest room is waiting. My invitation.'

'Darling, I'm on duty at eight!'

'Not tomorrow, you're not.' Advancing into the shattered room, he scooped her up in his arms and carried her, still protesting, towards the door.

'Ian, I *am*. I must be. I can't just take the day off as if I was a ... a secretary or something. I'm in uniform, even if you aren't. Put me *down*: that bottle's hurting my back.'

'You don't *look* as though you were in uniform,' Webster said mildly, setting her down beside a single divan draped in pink candlewick. 'And there's no need to get snooty because the work I do keeps me in mufti. You'll be handing out the white feathers next!'

'Darling, you know I didn't mean that. Engineering's just as important to the war effort as –'

'All right, old girl, all right. No offence.' He was looking at a low cupboard beneath the blacked-out window. One of the doors was slightly ajar, and through the gap a gleam of metal was visible. 'My goodness,' he said, opening the door wide, 'this bugger certainly does himself well, doesn't he? This is a pretty expensive wireless he has in here . . . and look, there's some sort of home recording gubbins on the lower shelf, discs and all. Probably switches it on while he's counting the money, so that he can play it back to his chums in Torquay.

'Ian,' the girl said, 'if you meant what you said about the use of this bed . . . well, I don't want to sound unladylike, but I *am* getting cold now.'

'Frightfully sorry.' He was at once contrite. 'Only two ways to make amends and warm up the inner girl. First, I think, a touch of the old Highland dew . . .' He paused in the act of unstoppering the bottle. 'That's funny,' he said slowly.

'What's funny?'

'Just that . . . I don't know. With everything else put away so neat and tidy, it's funny they should have left a dirty glass on the bedside table.' He sniffed. 'It still smells of the old firewater, at that. Perhaps the sirens went as they were clearing up . . . or clearing out, what?'

'Darling, come on. It won't be the first time I've drunk out of a bottle.' Liz was suddenly impatient. 'And I told you before – I do have to be at the War House at eight.'

'And *I* told *you*' – Webster was jubilant – 'that you can forget it. If you can't take a day off, at least you can go in late. And your boss can jolly well like it or lump it.'

'Ian . . . Please . . .'

'He has to, duckie. He has to.' He was lying beside her now, offering the bottle. 'You just got yourself bombed out, remember?'

The Gestapo brought in this Belgian soon after midnight, a great big fellow, as strong as an ox. They'd actually caught him with the radio, transmitting. And of course the SS wanted the details of the rest of the network. We tried the usual tricks – lifted his nails, burned off his pubic hair, stuck knitting needles through his eardrums, beat him on the belly with rubber hoses – but he wasn't talking. After that we went back to the old bucket routine. We were holding his head under for the third time when – would you believe it! – the pig managed to snap the chain of the handcuffs behind his back and lay out Kessler with one of the steel circlets. He was a tough one all right. Then Klaus had a brainwave. We brought in the Belgian's 8-year-old son, stripped him, hung him up by the heels, and started to flog him with an electric flex. In no time at all, the father was blubbering like a kid himself, spilling everything we wanted to know.

Chapter Two

The long buff OHMS envelope had been pushed through Webster's letterbox two days before the Luftwaffe had so rudely disturbed his night with Liz. He read the contents without surprise. For Webster – Major Ian Lindsay Webster, DSO, MC, to give him his full name and rank – was something of a madcap, and after the life he had led nothing astonished him any more. In the Crimea, his superiors might have dubbed him a Caution. To fellow officers in the Great War he would undoubtedly have been a Card. But in the desperate days of 1942, his particular brand of reckless courage was considered more of a liability than an asset. That bloody man Webster, they would say; what in Christ's name has he been up to now?

Some of the things he had been up to already made discouraging reading for the chair-bound wonders masquerading as Staff at his regiment's permanent headquarters in Rutlandshire.

He had missed the boat at Dunkirk, for example, because he had been in bed with a blonde and he was determined to get his money's worth. Alone on a hostile continent after the last small vessel had departed, he had made his way to the nearest German forward airstrip, stolen a Stuka, and flown himself home in that. In Norway with a special task force a little later, he had been too fatigued to blow up the heavy-water plant he had been briefed to destroy (there had been another blonde in Bergen), so he swanned in a Nazi HQ, captured a colonel and a dozen men single-handed, and forced them to do it for him. Back in England during the post-Dunkirk lull, he had pestered his own colonel to recommend him for some offbeat, death-or-glory posting while his off-duty exploits with bottle and glass were drawing unfavourable attention elsewhere.

For Webster was a drinking man. He was also a whoring man and a fighting man – a man for whom the end was all that mattered, and who gave a damn for the means? As for justification, the word was simply not in his vocabulary. He had won his MC cleaning up a German machine-gun nest that was harrassing the Allied retreat through Belgium (though the citation didn't mention that he was wearing a looted Nazi uniform belonging to an officer of the Waffen SS at the time). The DSO was the result of a disreputable incident involving a one-man raid on Occupied France which the newspapers had got hold of and blown up before the censorship was properly established. In fact Webster's principal aim had been to replenish his dwindling stock of Calvados.

To such a man therefore – a man who had flown private planes from Brooklands before the war and made a living selling racing cars on commission – to such a man, a curt request that he report in civilian clothes to an address near Liverpool Street station was in no way surprising, buff envelope or no buff envelope.

He showered, shaved, shut the kitchen back into the wall, and left the one-room flat in Nell Gwynn House that he kept for forty-eight-hour passes and periods of leave. It had rained during the night but now a pale, wintry sunshine varnished the wet streets with gold. Webster walked down to the King's Road and joined a queue at the Number 11 bus-stop – a lean, rakish figure with an Errol Flynn moustache and the kind of face that looks faintly dissipated even when its owner is not hung-over. Ten minutes later (there was still no bus in sight) he spotted a cab turning out of Bywater Street and flagged it down from the middle of the road before anyone else in the queue had time to move. 'Black-marketeer, I shouldn't wonder,' a fat woman in ATS uniform said audibly as he settled himself on the threadbare upholstery. Webster grinned. 'Why can they never look *smart* like the Waafs or the Wrens?' he remarked to the driver.

The office to which he had been summoned was in a dingy building off Commercial Street, near Spitalfields market. The neighbourhood had suffered in recent raids, and fragments of brickwork still littered the pavement. At the far end of the street, a roped-off slant of rubble marked the site of a direct hit.

Outside, there was nothing to distinguish the place from the tailors' workshops and manufacturers' agencies surrounding it, but a WD notice on the frosted glass of a second-storey door announced cryptically: *War Office: Special Services A.F.C. (Liaison)*, and underneath, in more discreet lettering: *All Passes To Be Shewn.*

Webster turned the brass handle and went in. He found himself at one end of a long corridor loud with the clacking of typewriters. On each side, numbered doors led into offices separated by steel partitions with more frosted glass criss-crossed by anti-blast paper. At the far end, a commissionaire in a blue uniform stood guard over a polished mahogany wicket. Beyond this was an open space housing a middle-aged blonde at a desk.

'Your pass, sir, if you please?' said the commissionaire.

'No pass,' Webster replied shortly. He hated red tape. 'I had a letter ordering me to report here.'

'Yes, sir. If you were to show me the letter, sir ...'

Webster produced it, tapping his foot impatiently while the man read it carefully through. At length he folded it, handed it back, and said: 'Very good, sir. If you would just come this way ...' Holding the wicket open, he called to the blonde: 'Major Webster.'

The blonde got to her feet, favouring Webster with a professional smile. The corners of her mouth stretched a half inch at either side. A colonel, Webster thought, would get three-quarters of an inch, a lieutenant a barely perceptible twitch, a brigadier the full treatment, including teeth and gums. 'Please take a seat,' she said. 'We shan't keep you a tick.' She disappeared through a door, oak this time, bearing the legend *Armed Forces Cooperation: Colonel Chard.*

Two minutes later, the door opened and she beckoned him in. Colonel Chard was sitting behind a large desk, holding an open file. He was about fifty years old, and almost (Webster considered) too good to be true. His face was seamed and grey, and his neat, short hair was grey too – but everything else about him positively sparkled. From the brass buttons securing his red Staff tabs to the buckle of his Sam Browne, from his teeth to his piercing blue eyes, he gleamed and shone in the light from the green-shaded lamp hanging low over the desk. He looked as though he took a cold bath before every meal . . . and the meal would contain precisely the right amount of vitamins, too. Over his ears a sufficient number of grey feathers had escaped from the rest of his hair to indicate that he was intellectual as well as efficient.

'Morning, Webster,' he said, the voice dry and rather light. 'Been having a dekko through your dossier. Had a word with your CO on the blower yesterday. He said you keep badgering him for some kind of one-off job, cloak and dagger stuff, so forth. That right?'

'Yes, sir,' Webster said. 'Anything rather than countersigning movement orders back at base.'

'Want to be up and at 'em – the Hun, I mean. That it?'

'Well, yes. I mean they're giving us quite a battering from the air, aren't they? And we seem to be doing nothing in return. Nothing at all.'

'Archie Wavell didn't do too badly in North Africa a while ago,' the colonel said mildly.

'Yes, sir, I know. But here. Now. Today.'

Chard chuckled. 'I get the picture. But you haven't exactly been a model soldier, have you?' He tapped the open folder in his hand. 'Not what you might call the reliable type, eh? What makes you think an officer who won't accept discipline is suitable for special work?'

Webster grinned. 'I get results,' he said.

'Yes. Well. I see.' The older man leafed through the typed sheets in the dossier, frowning slightly. 'I think we'd better have a bit of a chinwag. What about a cup of tea? You'd like some tea, I expect?'

'Thank you, sir,' Webster said unenthusiastically.

The colonel flicked up a switch on an antique-looking intercom at one side of the desk. 'Pottie? Could you come in?'

The faded blonde appeared in the doorway. 'Yes, Colonel?'

'Oh, Pottie – a nice cuppa for Major Webster, please. And the usual for me.'

'Yes, sir. Milk and sugar, Major? You can have up to two lumps: we didn't use all our ration last month.'

Receiving the regulation smile reserved for officers of junior field rank, Webster replied sourly: 'Neither, thanks.'

While the woman was away, he looked curiously around the room. Green metal filing cabinets flanked a casement window affording, between two warehouses, a view of the bomb damage in Aldgate. A light misting of spring leaves veiled the branches of an elm beyond the shattered walls. On the far side of the office there was a chart table, with large-scale maps of various theatres of war hanging from batons above it. The fireplace was of white marble, with scrolled consoles supporting a mantel loaded with reference books. Among them, Webster was surprised to notice, were André Simon's *A Wine Primer*, Horvath's *Drinks For The Connoisseur*, and lavishly illustrated works by Brillat Savarin, Curnonsky and other masters of the gastronomic arts.

'Wonderful woman, Miss Potter,' Colonel Chard was saying. 'Can't for the life of me think how the place would run without her.'

'If it's not indiscreet to ask, sir,' Webster enquired, 'what exactly *is* the place anyway? I mean I've heard of the Special Services, of course – but I'm damned if I ever heard anyone mention A.F.C!'

'What? Armed Forces Cooperation? No, don't expect you would have.' Chard gave his dry chuckle. 'Just rolled off the production line, as a matter of fact. Collaboration between our chaps, the Navy and the RAF to provide the right personnel for a series of specialized, tough, self-contained fighting units and raiding parties. Kind of unit that doesn't have to keep referring back to base, just as long as the objective's gained, what?'

'Sounds just my cup of tea,' Webster observed as the blonde returned with a mug of black canteen liquid and a glass of milk which she put on the desk in front of the colonel. 'You mean you're picking the men for these units?'

'Not to say picking. Sort of preliminary screening, mostly

– then liaison between the three services if they *are* picked. Know what a *kommando* is? Ever heard the word?'

'I don't think so.'

'You will. It was originally an Afrikaaner term to describe the more rugged kind of scouting party in the Boer War. We plan to adopt it. But we also lay on a few ops on an even smaller scale. One-off jobs, you know.' He paused, and then asked abruptly: 'Know anything about Algeria?'

'Algeria!' Webster echoed, caught off balance by the sudden change of subject. 'Well, yes – the wine's frightful, for one thing.'

'Only the rubbish we get here. Stuff you drink out there is superb, just as good as burgundy or claret. But they don't export their best: people would never pay the price, not for something that was labelled Algerian.'

'Am I to have the chance to prove you wrong, sir?' Webster asked.

'Perhaps. But you won't, you know.' Chard permitted himself a frosty smile. 'I was in the business before the balloon went up.' He rose from behind his desk and walked across to the wall maps. He was about five feet eight, and he limped slightly. 'Now listen carefully: the situation there is hellish complex, and you have to understand it if you're going to be chosen to do the job.'

Chard pulled out a huge sheet showing the northern coast of Africa and hung it in front of the other maps. He cleared his throat. 'Here you are, then,' he said, tapping the chart with the back of one finger. 'On the Atlantic coast: Morocco; on the Mediterranean: Algeria. Both neutral, both French-run, both full of Arab rebels who want to chuck the French out. And both, of course, chock full of refugees who managed to get out of France before Pétain capitulated.'

He eyed Webster for a moment, as though he suspected that he might not be paying attention, and then went on: 'But there's one big difference: Algeria's next door to the desert war in Tunisia and Libya. And there's over a hundred thousand trained French troops in the country, with twice as many more in reserve.'

'But I thought they were disarmed,' Webster objected. 'I mean, they have no weapons or ammunition, have they? Wasn't that part of Hitler's armistice terms?'

'Yes, it was. It's an army that's completely neutralized. Not allowed to wear uniform, officers only let out of prison camps if they gave their parole not to take up arms, that sort of thing. But they're *there*, Webster. That's the point. They are there.'

Webster waited in silence. If that was the point, he didn't get it.

'I say neutral,' Colonel Chard explained. 'But one day we're going to have to invade French North Africa, the Yanks and us and the Free French. We've got to throw Jerry out of Africa before we get back into Europe – and the only way to do that is to biff him from both sides at once, Egypt and Algeria. See what I mean?'

'Yes, sir,' Webster replied doubtfully.

'The *colons*, the French settlers, are unpredictable buggers, more fascist than the bloody Germans, half of 'em. How do you think they and those hundred thousand defeated soldiers would react if we did invade?'

Addressed thus abruptly, Webster sat up straight like a pupil in class. 'Er ... haven't a clue, sir,' he said. 'I should think they would object.'

'Damned right they would object. And one of the things exercising the General Staff at this moment is how to prepare the ground, how to change the climate, as it were, so that they *don't* object. I don't mind telling you, it's a damned ticklish problem.'

'Yes, sir. I can see that.'

'If we just knew they were with us in spirit, that they'd stand back and do nothing and let us walk through and get on with the job, that'd be enough. Better still if we had an assurance that they'd come in on our side. But what we have to avoid at all costs is chivvying them into a state where they could team up with the Boche.'

'The French? Fighting with the Nazis?' Webster was amazed. 'You're not serious, sir!'

'I am indeed,' Chard said soberly. 'It could easily happen. Think, man. Pétain was their god and he collaborates. All the Vichy lot are Frenchmen, after all. Most of those who are genuinely anti-fascist are over here already with de Gaulle. The ones in North Africa are trying very painfully to get back on their feet after a humiliating defeat. Like anyone who's been knocked out of the ring, they're touchy and on the defensive. They feel we let them down in Europe, they blame the Americans for staying on the sidelines until Pearl Harbor, they're bitter as hell because we sank the French fleet at Mers-el-Kebir in case the Jerries got hold of it and used it against us. Twelve hundred French sailors lost their lives there ... and most of their families live in Algeria. My God, it wouldn't take much to swing them into Hitler's lap, you know!' As if unexpectedly convinced by his own argument, the colonel limped back to his desk and sat down heavily. He sipped his glass of milk.

'The thing is,' he resumed finally, 'the show we may be asking you to put up could do exactly that ... if it went wrong.'

Webster leaned forward in his chair. At last the subject was beginning to interest him.

'Because, you see,' Chard added, 'Mark Clark is actually planning an invasion of French North Africa at this moment.'

'Wacko!' Webster exclaimed involuntarily.

The colonel winced. He stared with disfavour at Webster's rollneck sweater and tweed jacket. Even in mufti – Webster could read his thoughts – the done thing would surely have been to wear a collar and tie! 'Because of Mers-el-Kebir,' he went on, 'the planners thought it best for us to stay out of it, at least in the initial stages. That's why the Yanks have been given the job. Your show would have to be pulled off some time before Mark Clark's plan is operational ... but as I say, if you're rumbled you could jeopardize the whole shoot and have Clark's landings opposed by the Frogs as well as the Jerries.'

'That's quite a responsibility,' Webster said with enthusiasm. 'Just what *is* my show, Colonel?'

Chard shook his head. 'Not my job to tell you,' he said. 'Security an' all that. I make my report on you, and then the powers-that-be will do the rest ... if you're selected to do the job. In the meantime, I'm instructed to tell you: no more uniform.'

'No more uniform?'

'You're to remain in civilian clothes, until either you hear from us again or you're recalled to your unit.'

'Good-oh!' Webster was interested. 'And how long is that likely to be, sir?'

Colonel Chard smiled. He allowed himself the luxury of an Americanism. 'Don't call us,' he said impishly. 'We'll call you.'

They called him in fact only two days later. The doorbell rang soon after nine, and there was a dispatch rider with goggles pushed up over his crash helmet standing outside when Webster had sufficiently emerged from his hangover to answer it. The man saluted and held out another buff OHMS envelope. 'Mr Webster?'

For a moment Webster was caught off guard by the loss of his rank. 'Who?' he enquired blearily.

'Mr Ian Lindsay Webster?'

'Oh. Yes. Of course. That's me all right.' He reached for the envelope.

'Excuse me, sir. I was instructed to ask for identification.'

'Quite right, quite right. Moment.' Webster stumbled to his bureau, opened a drawer, and fished out a movement order. That should blow this civilian lark sky-high, he thought wryly as he showed the man the paper.

'Thank you, sir. Excuse me, sir. Orders are: report at twelve-fifteen sharp.'

'What? I don't quite ...' Webster began. But the dispatch rider had saluted again and turned on his heel. Webster heard his booted feet clattering down the concrete emergency-exit stairs. He shrugged and slit open the envelope with his thumb.

The single sheet of paper it contained carried no letterhead, no date and no signature. An address was neatly typed in the centre of the page, and then the words, underlined: *Memorize and Destroy*.

Webster sighed and shook his head. He repeated the address to himself a couple of times, tore the paper into small pieces, and flushed them down the lavatory.

At ten thirty he walked down the five floors to the back entrance. It was a Sunday, and behind the doors of the apartments rented by prostitutes on the third and fourth floors he could hear the usual babble of male voices accented in Polish. American, North Country and Scots. He went to a café in the King's Road called the Bar-B-Q and swallowed two cups of vile, black, scalding wartime coffee. By the time he arrived at the address he had been given – it was in one of the elegant

Nash terraces overlooking Regent's Park – he felt that his brain and body were functioning normally again.

The waiting room into which he was shown was in complete contrast to Colonel Chard's headquarters. It was comfortably furnished, with leather armchairs and magazines on a low table. Between the strips of blast paper latticing the lofty bow windows, a grassy slope fringed by trees was visible. A young man wearing the uniform of a captain in the Royal Engineers lolled in one of the chairs. He was slightly built, fair-haired, blue-eyed, and even the huge moustache on his upper lip could not make him look a day over twenty.

'What-ho!' said the young man. 'Another candidate for Cosy Corner, eh?'

Webster stared. 'Cosy . . . ?'

The young man gestured towards an inner door. Attached to the shining white paintwork was a small notice which read: *Combined Operations (Security) Executive Captain S. M'P. O'Kelly, RN.*

'C.O.S.E . . . Cosy. Cosy Corner,' he explained. 'As you're togged up in the jolly old civvies already, I imagine they'll be launching you pretty soon.'

'What *is* this place, anyway?' Webster asked. 'Some kind of C-and-D outfit, obviously. But what do they *do*?'

'Oh, I expect they'll tell you in there,' the young man said vaguely. 'But you mustn't mind O'Kelly. Bark worse than his bite an' all that.' He pushed himself upright and murmured confidentially: 'Besides, he's never been nearer the Emerald Isle than Mooney's pub in Piccadilly!'

Webster shrugged and turned his back. His headache had returned and he was in no mood for the enigmatic pleasantries of a junior officer who sounded like a silly-ass character from an Aldwych farce. Through the window, he could see a YMCA mobile canteen serving tea to the crew of a sandbagged anti-aircraft gun-site in the park. The spring green on the trees here, he noticed, was further advanced than it had been in the East End.

'Might as well introduce myself, I suppose,' the lazy voice drawled behind him. 'Name of Fortune. Charles G. Fortune.'

Webster nodded and said nothing.

'The G stands for Goode,' Fortune said helpfully. 'With an E at the end. It's almost a pun: good fortune, don't you know?'

'Very droll,' Webster said coldly.

The young man sighed. 'Can't win 'em all, can you?' he said.

A small pilot-light above the white door suddenly changed from red to green. 'Will Major Webster please come in?' a disembodied voice called from a loudspeaker fixed to the wall.

Major Webster strode to the door and went in. The room beyond was even less like a military office than the one he had left. Although the day was quite mild, a real coal fire crackled in the grate. New, low leather chairs surrounded a drinks table on the white fur rug in front of the hearth. Behind a desk between the wide windows sat a large pink-faced man with thinning silver hair. He had a prominent nose, a strong, resolute mouth, and very bright blue eyes. Four wide gold bands encircled the sleeves of his naval jacket.

'Webster,' he said. 'Come in and sit down by the fire. So far as your personal file is concerned, the most important item I can recall at the moment is that you prefer vodka to gin. Is that right?'

Webster raised his eyebrows, 'Er – yes, sir.'

Captain Seamus M'Phee O'Kelly levered himself upright and walked ponderously over to the drinks table. 'What do you like with it? Tonic? Lime?'

'Just ice, if that's possible, sir.'

'Almost anything's *possible*,' O'Kelly said. 'If it wasn't, you wouldn't be here and I wouldn't be doing this blasted job.' He removed the lid from a Georgian silver teapot, plunged his hand inside, and withdrew it holding two cubes of ice. 'Fortunately,' he said, 'some rather good Polish stuff has come my way this week. Having this kind of show to run does have its advantages, after all. My chaps are very good when they're in the field.' He picked a small bottle from the collection on the table and gazed at the silver lettering on the label. Most of the words, Webster saw, seemed to be formed of consonants at the end of the alphabet.

A moment later he found himself grasping a wide, short glass of heavy Waterford crystal filled with the most generous measure of vodka he'd ever seen. 'I'll not bore you with too many details,' O'Kelly said, 'but it seems that Hitler's pulled something of a fast one in Algeria.'

'It wouldn't be for the first time.'

'No.' The naval captain held up his own glass and scrutinized the midday sunlight slanting through the pink gin it contained. 'In this case the Germans have evidently bribed, browbeaten or blackmailed the Vichy authorities into turning a blind eye towards the illegal use of neutral territory for military purposes. Somewhere out in the desert, they've built a secret base to develop an even more secret weapon.'

'By Jove!' Headache dissipated by the ice-cold spirit, Webster suddenly looked alert and interested. 'What kind of weapon?'

'It appears to be some kind of radio-controlled pilotless plane.'

'Pilotless?'

'Right. Fill it with explosive and you have all the advantages of a bomber and none of the disadvantages. You steer it on to the target, crash it there . . . and you don't have to worry about getting the bloody thing back, or about the possible loss of a trained and expensive crew.'

Webster whistled. 'But the cost of the thing itself . . . ?'

'Apparently they're pretty small – less than half the size of a standard fighter. Probably pretty crude as well: you don't need all that sophisticated instrumentation and equipment if the crate's only going to make one straight flight and then . . . *bang!* So the cost could be relatively low.'

'What are they using as power units?'

O'Kelly scowled, as though the question had been out of order. 'We don't know,' he grunted. 'Such gen as we have is third-hand anyway. One of my chaps in Oran, Willis, had an Arab contact – one of these nomad johnnies who's always hiking up and down the Sahara. And this Arab told him about an oasis in the desert where infidels had built a camp and said they were trying out some newfangled miniature flying machine. They couldn't be very good machines, the nomad said, because every one that he'd seen had crashed in flames! Well of course my man started ferreting around among his other contacts, and pretty soon he cottoned on to the fact that the infidels were German and that what the bloke had seen was some kind of firing range. The rest came partly from deduction, partly from guesses and partly from the odd snippet of intelligence.'

'Your man didn't actually see the planes for himself?'

'No, he didn't. Couldn't locate the damned oasis. How the hell can you pinpoint a couple of square miles of desert in a huge area like the Sahara?' O'Kelly demanded angrily, as though the question had been a personal affront. 'When your informant never saw a compass in his bloody life and wouldn't know a map co-ordinate from a leave chit? All he could say was that it was very far away – far, far beyond the mountains in the interior.'

'Couldn't your chap have paid the Arab to lead him there?'

'Of course he could, you fool. I don't employ halfwits.' The pink face had flushed darker still. 'But they must have been on to my chap – nothing stays secret for long out there, and the place is stiff with Nazi agents.' O'Kelly sighed. 'His body was found floating in the harbour three days ago. Someone had shoved a knife between his ribs.'

'And his replacement?'

'Replacement? Replacement? Well *you're* his replacement, of course. Can't waste any more time messing about. Not with Mark Clark's landings due later this year.'

'And you want me ...?'

'Locate this base and eliminate it, naturally. We'll give you a small, hand-picked sabotage and assassination squad and leave the details to you. Bearing in mind your record – and Colonel Chard's report on you – we think you're probably the man for the job.'

Webster smiled crookedly. 'What the Yanks call "Seek and destroy"?'

'Exactly.' O'Kelly drained his glass and reached for the bottles of Angostura and gin. 'The weapons are not in production yet: those are just prototypes they're testing in the desert. But if they were to *go* into production ...' He paused and shook his head. 'Suppose each one carried a ton of H.E. with an impact fuse. Imagine the blast! Think of the havoc a score of them could cause on a beach crowded with landing craft!'

He glared accusingly at Webster while Webster thought of that.

'Clark wouldn't have to worry about his hundred thousand Frenchmen if Rommel could protect his rear with that kind of armoury,' O'Kelly said grimly. 'Worse still, think of the invasion of mainland Europe – when the blasted planners get around to it. You need a build-up of troops and supplies lasting days, maybe weeks, before you can mount an operation of that size. Suppose these weapons were to be used against such a concentration in a crowded area like southern England? Help yourself when you're ready, man. The ice is in the teapot.'

Over the crackling of the fire, the thin wail of distant sirens rose and fell. Silver barrage balloons hoisted themselves into the sky beyond the green slope of park outside the windows.

'Not to worry,' O'Kelly said. 'It'll be the usual high-flying recce job that Jerry always sends over to photograph the damage the day after a big raid.'

'Better than a squadron of these pilotless flying bombs, what?' Webster said.

'My God, yes! Think what they could do to a city this size!'

Webster poured himself some vodka. 'You say that the French are actually conniving at the development of this weapon, sir?'

'Not to say positively conniving. Looking the other way would be nearer the mark. Officially, the base won't exist, that's all.'

'I see.'

'The important thing,' a brigadier in the Intelligence Corps told Webster an hour later, 'is that, officially, your squad won't exist either. You know the drill, I suppose?'

'The drill, sir?'

'If you succeed, you get another gong. If anything goes wrong, we disown you absolutely.'

'It sounds just like ordinary regimental service,' Webster said.

They were sitting now around a polished oak table in a windowless room beneath O'Kelly's cellars: Webster, the brigadier, a red-tabbed Staff officer from the War Office, an American colonel from General Mark Clark's headquarters and O'Kelly himself. A large-scale map of Africa covered most of the table. In an ante-room packed with a complex of electronic and radio equipment, a naval telegraphist wearing earphones sat below a battery of radar monitor screens, watching red and blue lights wink among the dials and switches of his transmitter.

'If a non-existent base is destroyed by a non-existent unit,' the brigadier said, 'then nobody can complain. Obviously. The Germans dare not, because they can't admit they were using neutral ground for warlike purposes; the French won't because it would mean admitting they'd let the Germans do that. But if the place is *seen* to be destroyed – if the chaps doing it are rumbled – then all hell will break loose.'

'My God, yes!' – it was the War Office man speaking – 'One of the belligerents invading neutral territory ... naked aggression by the Allies ... violation of the Geneva Convention ... rules of war chucked out of the bally window! You can see the headlines.'

'Plus the fact that the *colons* would probably allow Hitler to march into Algeria, or at best oppose our landings themselves,' the American colonel said.

O'Kelly swivelled the map around on the table. 'That's why a commando-style army assault by one of the long-range desert groups based here' – he tapped the section of the map representing Libya – 'is out of the question. Same thing applies to a bombing raid: even if we knew where the oasis was, no raid could be one hundred per cent certain of wiping out all the researchers, destroying the paperwork, and totally wrecking the base.'

'Yeah, and that's what has to be done,' Mark Clark's man said. 'The installation must be taken out and the eggheads working on the project eliminated before they can transfer their equipment and repeat their experiments some place else. This whole deal has to be pushed back to the starting point.'

The Intelligence Corps brigadier was studying the map. 'Algeria's twelve hundred miles deep and over a thousand wide in some places,' he observed. 'If this base is right down in the south, it'd be far out of range of any bombers based in the Med theatre anyway.'

'Right,' O'Kelly concluded. 'We are agreed, then, that the job must be done clandestinely, and that Webster here is the man to do it.' He looked around the table and when the officers had all murmured their agreement he continued: 'We can't give any preliminary training to the unit he'll lead because we know nothing about the terrain. They'll have to go into Algiers openly under some civilian cover: British nationals have a right to be in a neutral country in time of war so long as they don't wear uniform. Webster can work out the details with my Number Two, Archie Lang. But for the moment all we can say is that they'll hang around until they get a lead on the precise location of the base; only then can they go underground and make their way there to take care of it.'

'Secretly!' the brigadier emphasized. 'Anonymously. If they're identified, we might as well send in the marines with a band playing.'

'And quickly,' the American added. 'We want to know these weapons have been gotten out of the way, that the danger is effectively over, before we finalize plans for the landings.'

'But it'd be as well if they could make some observations first, and report on the performance of the bally machines before they blow them up,' said the Staff officer.

'And make an extract of the main design points, obviously,' the brigadier put in. 'And perhaps bring back a couple of blueprints.'

'And try to find out whether or not the French really do know about the project,' O'Kelly said.

Webster smiled. 'Is that all?' he asked. 'No other little commissions you gentlemen would care to mention? Some halvah, perhaps? A nice oriental rug? Brassware from the *soukhs*? They tell me the Arabs make a spot-on fig liqueur.'

'Now that,' said Captain O'Kelly, 'I could fancy.'

* * * *

The All-Clear was sounding when Webster emerged from the back entrance of the C.O.(S).E. headquarters and found himself near the White House in Albany Street. It was then that he saw Liz Macnamara for the first time.

He was cutting across the diagonal drive-in at the front of the block on his way to Great Portland Street underground station. She was paying off a taxi by the sandbagged entrance doors, standing with one foot up on the running board, and Webster paused in mid-stride to admire the shapely calf, the voluptuous swell of her hip against the tightened material of her skirt, the promising bulge of the khaki jacket above a trimly buckled belt. He was about to draw level when the girl, searching for change, allowed her handbag to fall open and a shower of small objects cascaded to the pavement.

Webster was on his hands and knees collecting cigarettes, coins, lipstick cases, a compact, a lighter, almost before the girl's cry of annoyance had died away. 'Madam,' he said with exaggerated gallantry, 'I owe you a thousand apologies.'

'Oh, but it wasn't your fault,' she said. 'Really. You didn't knock into me: it was my own clumsiness. Thank you ... thank you.'

'That's not what I meant,' Webster said shamelessly. 'I was apologizing because I told a cab driver a couple of days ago that it was impossible to look beautiful in an ATS uniform. Clearly, I was never more mistaken in my life.'

She repressed a smile. Wide mouth, large hazel eyes, soft dark hair curling beneath the officer's cap. 'I think you're kneeling on my pay-book,' she said.

He sprang to his feet, handed her the thin folder, dusted off the trousers of his charcoal suit and paid the cab driver before she had crammed all her things back into the handbag. 'Do you live here?' he asked.

'No, no. Just visiting a friend.'

'Then the very least I can do is offer you a drink. As it happens I know rather a jolly little club. It's just across the road in Fitzroy Square. We could go there until they open and then –'

'But you don't have to offer me anything!' the girl protested. 'I mean, you haven't –'

'Oh, but I do, I do. Got to make amends, dash it all! Unjustified slur on members of His Majesty's armed forces ... slandering a fine body of women. A very fine body,' Webster said meaningfully.

'Honestly!' She shrugged helplessly, still trying not to smile. 'I don't know ... Really, I shouldn't ...'

But she did. And such were Webster's assurance and powers of persuasion that the road from the jolly little club led first to the Cheshire Cheese in Fleet Street, then to Scott's restaurant for dinner, on to the Captain's Cabin, and finally to an ill-lit table at the Orchid Room where, over a bottle of black market champagne, he talked her into taking him home with her.

She lived in a block of flats off Chancery Lane. The cabbie

who took them there an hour and a half before Hitler's bombers blasted them out of bed stayed parked by the kerb after they had gone inside. A few minutes later, an anonymous-looking Ford V8 slid to a halt on the other side of the street. The hooded headlamps flashed once, twice, three times. The taxi driver climbed from his cab and crossed the road. He leaned in at the open driver's window on the offside of the V8. 'If you ask me,' he said in a low voice, 'you'd be safe enough to grab a bit of kip now. From what I heard – and what I could see in me mirror – he ain't goin' to leave before breakfast.'

The driver of the Ford nodded. He was a short, spare man wearing horn-rimmed spectacles. With two companions, he had been shadowing Webster ever since he left Colonel Chard's office two days before. 'After tonight,' he said thankfully, 'the rest will be welcome.'

They shot the ten hostages against the wall of the church soon after dawn. It was still raining and there were pools of water all over the cobbled square. The shutters of the town hall were nailed up with planks across them. One of the hostages was sick; there was a lot of influenza about that year. Two soldiers carried him up from the cells and out into the rain. They tried to prop him up against the wall but he sat down in a puddle of water. The other nine stood very quietly on the wet leaves that had drifted against the wall. Finally the Oberleutnant told the soldiers it was useless trying to make him stand. When they fired the first volley he was sitting down in the water with his head on his knees and the rain splashing up all around him. Afterwards bulldozers knocked down the church and the town hall and pushed the rubble over the bodies. 'There'll be no more German patrols ambushed in this village,' the Oberleutnant said.

Chapter Three

Archie Lang was a commander in the Royal Navy. He met Webster in a fifth floor bedroom at the Regent Palace hotel early in the morning on the day after the raid – a tall, thin, lantern-jawed man with piercing blue eyes. (My God, Webster thought wildly, they've *all* got blue eyes: Chard, O'Kelly, this fellow, even that absurd kid in the waiting room at Regent's Park!).

'Algeria!' Webster complained. 'I must say, that's a hell of a place for the krauts to choose for their blasted experiments! The place is crawling with refugees, there's a food shortage – and can you think of a more difficult place to get around in, for a start?'

'That's probably why the Germans chose it,' Lang replied in his slow, deep voice. 'After all, where else could they find a suitable firing-range for a secret weapon of that kind? The North Sea? The Baltic? With spotter planes all over the sky? No, I should imagine the Sahara looked pretty good to Hitler's planners: spies there are not exactly thick on the ground; they knew, once they had forced the French to agree, that they could go there and work undisturbed. Now it's up to you chaps to breeze in and disturb them.'

'Quite. When we know where to go. And I can tell you the answer to that question now: smack in the middle of six hundred thousand square miles of trackless desert! God, how do we even *start*?'

'It may not be as bad as you think,' said Lang. 'As you can imagine, Algiers itself is what I call a hotbed of intrigue. There's a Nazi Armistice Commission and an Italian one, to check that the peace terms are observed. The Americans have a Military Mission, and so do we. There are embassies and consulates from here and there. And you mustn't forget the PPA – the Arab liberation fellows holed up in the mountains in the interior. The place is seething with agents and informers: German spies trying to find out what the French think and what we're doing; French spies watching the French; Arab spies trying to locate supplies they can pinch and pass on to their rebels in the mountains; and of course our spies spying on their spies. With all that lot to work on you should be able – if you listen in the right places – to get a line on this oasis somewhere.'

'Yes, of course,' Webster said dubiously. He was a man who liked action.

'In any case, not to worry, old boy. We have it all worked out.'

Webster stared unbelievingly. 'You have?'

'Certainly. You do the job in two stages. A or One, you listen, as we said, in the *soukhs*, in the casbah, in the dives and bars and joints where foreigners meet. From what I hear' – Lang smiled faintly – 'that shouldn't be too arduous a task for you. Then, when you've checked the info you get with certain contacts you'll be given, you pass on to B or Two. Once you've worked out roughly where the place is, you pinpoint it accurately from an aircraft and—'

'An aircraft?' Webster exclaimed. 'But we were told this was absolutely undercover. How can we—?'

'Not a military plane, man. It's a neutral country. They have an airport there. There are private aerodromes. I imagine an Irish film crew could hire some kind of plane for a couple of hours to look for locations?'

Webster stared again. The subtlety of the plan was getting

beyond him. He needed a drink.

'Look,' Lang said patiently, 'the most difficult place for you and your chaps to be inconspicuous will be Algiers itself. You'll have to stay there some time too, until you get a fix on this base. Your unit's got to be small – but even half a dozen Englishmen arriving at the same time would look pretty suspicious to the people out there who are paid to be suspicious of everything. So we split the group into two lots, each arriving at a different time, each with a different cover, each staying in a different part of the city – and never, never making contact except through a link man.'

Webster nodded slowly. 'Jolly good. I like that.'

'We fly the film crew in on some commercial line with connections to Dublin. We'll find you an Irishman to act as director, a pilot, and some lad who can make a convincing PR type. All they need then is a hired plane, and they're in business.'

'And the other lot?'

'That'll be your pigeon. You'll be mining engineers. Prospecting. The southern part of Algeria is stuffed with natural gas and oil. You're after concessions for development once the war's over – and naturally you want to look over the terrain. We'll send you in on an American liberty ship delivering lease-lend supplies to the French. Put you aboard from a helicopter somewhere off Gibraltar.'

Lang tapped an Abdullah on a silver cigarette case, placed it carefully between his lips, and flicked his lighter. 'Once you have a lead on the approximate position of the testing range,' he said, blowing out a cloud of smoke, 'you contact the film crew through the link man, they'll pinpoint the base and take photographs from their hired plane – and after that the two teams can join up and go there.'

'Suppose there are parts of the country where they won't let us go?'

'Then you'll have a pretty good indication where you'll find your base, won't you?'

'Wacko!' Webster enthused. 'When do I meet the rest of the team and when do we start?'

'Since we don't even know where the target is, as you know, there'll be no sand-table briefings or assault rehearsals. And the less you are seen together outside Algeria, the better.

So, for security reasons, we're not bringing you together until the last minute. You'll meet your Number Two and the other members of the unit in Gibraltar. You'll leave from Southampton on a Sunderland flying boat at dawn tomorrow. Report to the RTO at Waterloo station at midnight tonight. Any questions?'

'Just one, sir. How and where do I get in touch in Gib?'

'You'll be contacted.' Lang reached into an inner pocket and produced a sealed envelope. 'Here are your new papers and one or two letters, official and personal, that should help establish your cover identity. Now – you have the whole of the afternoon and all of this evening as embarkation leave. But don't forget: you're *not* in the army now!'

Once the Commander had gone, Webster phoned down to the desk to retain the room and then hurried back to his flat in Chelsea. There were one or two arrangements to be made, and he wanted to keep the latter half of the day entirely free. He packed a grip with lightweight tropical kit suitable for a mining engineer in the Sahara, checked the grip into the left-luggage office at Waterloo, and strolled back over the bridge in the direction of the Strand. Overhead, barrage balloons gleamed like silver fish in the translucent sky. It was just after high tide, and the river raced silently under the arches towards the sea.

Webster looked at his watch. They were already open. He turned right beneath the railway at Charing Cross underground station and walked up Villiers Street to a pub near the Watergate Theatre. Two pink gins later, he produced a couple of pennies from his pocket and shouldered his way through the crowd to a pay telephone at the back of the bar. 'Commandant Macnamara in Movement Control, please,' he said when the switchboard had answered and he had pressed Button A. 'Hallo? Darling? I'm in the saloon at the Black Horse. Come and drink. Maurie promises real steaks in the back room, with chips and a bottle of something red, if we can wait until two.'

'I'm only supposed to take an hour for lunch,' Liz said. 'I'll see you at half past one.'

Every man in the bar turned his head when she came in. Webster made room for her at the bar, and a stool appeared as if by magic. She put her handbag and the matching leather gas-mask container on the polished counter. 'How did your interview go?' she asked.

He grinned. There was the light of battle in his eye. 'Spot on!' he said. 'Tell you all about it when we eat ... Another pinkers and a large gin and lime, please.'

They ate in the small dining room that the landlord reserved for favoured customers. (A favoured customer, Webster once remarked unkindly, was anyone who had paid for six doubles of any spirit). 'All right, Ian, let's have it,' the girl said. 'You've been posted somewhere, haven't you?'

He was thankful that she had never seen him in uniform. He had told her when they met that he was a European representative for Standard Oil, and that the call-up people regarded this as a reserved occupation. Hesitating only a fraction of a second, he said: 'Too bloody right, old thing. Meet Mister Cinderella.'

'What do you mean?'

'I have to leave town tonight at the witching hour,' Webster said. He leaned back in his chair to allow a waiter to pour, with suitable ceremony, from a bottle of Vosne Romanée.

Liz was on her second glass when she asked: 'Where are you off to, Ian? Or is it a state secret? I don't want to tempt you into Careless Talk!'

Webster thought quickly. In his kind of work, security was everything. This time, on the other hand, he was going in openly, as a civilian. And a civilian would have no reason to hide his destination. Telling her his cover story might even strengthen it, if only in his own eyes. 'You could tempt me into anything,' he said finally. 'But it's no secret: I'm off to French North Africa tomorrow.'

'God, poor you! What are you going to do there?'

'Make a geological and mineralogical survey, actually. If we should strike it rich there, we hope to open the place up after the war. I've been hanging around, waiting for my visa.'

'Just my luck!' she said with mock despair. 'I meet an oil man from Texas ... and he leaves immediately for Africa!' She reached across the table and took his hand. She looked very beautiful, very desirable in the sunlight slanting through the window, very feminine in her subtly re-shaped ATS officer's uniform. 'I shall miss you, Ian. You'll be coming back, won't you? You won't marry a sloe-eyed belly-dancer from the casbah, or get carried off to a desert stronghold by a sheikess on a white charger?'

'If I knew of a desert stronghold,' Webster said, 'I'd be asking Maurie to call me a camel . . . and I'd be throwing you across my saddle! Of course I'm coming back. I'll phone you in a couple of weeks. Maybe I'll even bring you a box of Turkish Delight.'

'Smashing!' said Liz. 'In that case, I'll be generous too. I'm going to give you the address of a girlfriend of mine, and if that isn't self-sacrifice, I don't know what is. Her name is Céleste Harari; we were at finishing school together in Lausanne. Tell her you're a friend of mine and she'll show you the town.'

'You mean she lives in Algiers?'

She nodded. 'Céleste's half French and half Moroccan. Her father's a doctor. They used to have a super flat overlooking the yacht harbour. Of course they may have moved: I haven't heard from her since the beginning of the war. But you can always try.'

Webster chuckled coarsely. 'I always do,' he said, 'and right now—'

'Ian!'

'Finish your coffee. We have a date with a double bed at the Regent Palace.'

'Darling, you're mad. I've got to get back to the—'

'Balls! You were suddenly taken ill. Woman's complaint. You suffered from delayed shock after you were bombed out. Anything. You can phone later.'

'You're impossible. In any case, why a hotel? Even if I was bombed out last night, you have a perfectly good flat of your own in Chelsea.'

'Too far away,' Webster said. 'And the beds at the Regent P. are . . . palatial. Wait till you see!'

'We've no luggage,' she said weakly. 'They'll turn us away.'

'Serving officer in mufti. Kit being brought by my driver later. Anyway, I've all the luggage you need,' Webster leered.

The girl blushed. 'I don't know why I should fall for a man who's so vulgar,' she said. 'And take your hand off my knee: the waiter's watching.'

Still protesting, she allowed herself to be led away. A short, spare man with hornrimmed glasses folded his paper, pushed some coins across the bar, and followed them into the street.

Towards the end of the afternoon, when she had fallen asleep exhausted with her head on his lean chest, Webster lay for a long time staring at the gap between the blackout curtains, watching the light fade. He was always like this before the action started – tense as a coiled spring with suppressed energy, ready to explode into movement at the slightest touch. As the sirens wailed the first of their nightly alarms, he rolled over and entered her again, pounding into her soft body as if he would rid himself of some demon clamouring for release in his blood.

Five floors below, the short, spare man moved to a chair nearer the reception desk. He settled his glasses on his nose and re-read the front page of the *Evening News* for the fourth time. The Afrika Korps, in their latest advance, were drawing dangerously close to the Egyptian frontier. Java had fallen to the Japanese. In the United States, RCA scientists had perfected something called an electronic microscope.

PART II

Assignment in Algiers

Willi Kunstler scooped a shallow depression out of the soft shale and lay as flat as he could when Montgomery's artillery barrage swept through the wadi. 'Holy Mary, Mother of God, get me out of this,' he prayed. 'For the sake of Our Lord Jesus Christ let me live. Blessed Virgin, keep me safe. Please, please, please, please let me be saved. I know good Nazis shun the Church, but I believe in You. If only You'll stop me getting killed, I'll tell them all that You are the One. Just this once, and I'll do anything You say. Please, Holy Mother, please.' The bombardment crept further down the wadi and then the Panzers roared through. After that there was no more shelling. The next day, the unit was withdrawn and sent back to Darah. That night, Willi took a girl upstairs at Fatimah's, but he didn't tell her about the Virgin Mary. He never told anybody about either of them.

Chapter Four

The first thing that struck Webster about Algiers was the fact that there were lights everywhere. After months of war-time blackout in Europe, he took an innocent pleasure in the long loop of street lamps garlanding the esplanade that curved along the waterfront, the flashing neon of cinemas, the oases of brilliance marking boutiques still open for business here and there beneath the colonnades. He was fascinated by the light escaping across dark pavements through shutters and half-open doors, intrigued by the Christmas-tree complex of illuminations that rose, behind the new city, where the ancient houses of the casbah leapfrogged up steep lanes and stone staircases into the night.

In the daytime, under a hot and humid sky overcast with grey clouds, the place was less magical. No traffic jammed the promenade below the tiers of sugar-cake balconies barring the tall white buildings above the port. Petrol was scarce and only diplomats, members of the Armistice Commissions and city officials could command cars. There were very few buses; most of the transport was provided by carts and cabs drawn by bony horses flogged twelve hours at a stretch through streets strewn with litter and filth – for the city sanitation department, along with other civil amenities, seemed to have ground to a standstill. The stepped alleys and squares were crowded with Algerians in dirty European clothes and fezzes, milling from the doorways and porches where they had spent the night towards the wealthier neighbourhoods where they might with luck touch some newcomer for the price of a meal. The general air of apathy and disintegration was heightened by a growing crisis in the supply of food and clothing: Berber women in the mountains were said to have to wait for their husbands to return from work before they could fetch water from the village wells because they possessed only a single burnouse per family.

Webster and the three men posing as his fellow prospectors found rooms in a *pension* which lay to one side of the old Arab seaport, in a quarter projecting out into the sea on the first of the small islands that encircled the harbour. The supposed advance party from the Irish film unit were to be lodged in a hotel nearer the centre.

There had been trouble – the nearest Webster ever got to open mutiny – over the selection of this group in Gibraltar. It was Lang himself who made contact after the passengers in the Sunderland, mainly diplomatic staff returning to Spain after leave, had been ferried ashore. It was Lang who delivered himself, with great lucidity, of a further run-down on the current situation in Algiers. And it was Lang who said, on the morning after Webster's arrival, 'Now I think it's time you met your Number Two – a young man called Fortune.'

'*Fortune?*'

Lang raised his brows at Webster's tone. 'Why, yes. C. G. Fortune. He'll pilot the hired aircraft and head your second unit as well as being your lieutenant.'

'Whiskery type with blue eyes, looks about fifteen? Speaks like something out of *Jeeves*?'

Lang smiled. 'I suppose you could say that.'

'Saw him outside O'Kelly's office the day of my interview? Made some damfool joke about his name?'

'He was at HQ that day, yes. And he does throw in the odd pleasantry about his last two names. Goode, Fortune.'

'Bad luck.'

'What do you mean?'

'I'm not taking any three-pip sapper clown as my Number Two on this show,' Webster said. 'Absolutely not.'

'Fortune is not in the Royal Engineers.'

'Bully for them. But he was wearing—'

'He wears a lot of different uniforms,' Lang interrupted, 'at one time or another. As a serving officer, you have been seconded to this outfit for one specific operation. Fortune is a professional.'

Webster grunted non-committally. 'What does that mean?'

'Sometimes he ferries planes for the Air Transport Auxiliary. That uniform's a good front for someone who needs to move around. He is entitled to wear a squadron-leader's uniform in the RAF: he joined up in 1939 and shot down fifteen Hun planes in the Battle of Britain. And he holds, as it happens, a rank equivalent to your own in the Intelligence Corps.'

'What, that little pipsqueak?'

'Fortune is one of the best men we have,' Lang said coldly. 'It hasn't occurred to you, I suppose, that an apparently naïve, even foolish, manner could be a pretty good cover for an intelligence man?'

'I don't care. I'm not having that idiot on my show.'

The blue eyes were suddenly steely. 'I'll remind you that you're under orders, Webster,' Lang said. 'This is not *your* show: it's a team effort. And unless I have your undertaking, instantly, that you will carry out those orders and co-operate to the very best of your ability, I'll have you posted straight back to England and hand over the leadership to Fortune himself. Is that clear?'

Webster sighed. 'Yes, sir,' he said.

It was nevertheless with a marked lack of enthusiasm that he met Charles G. Fortune again at the first of several briefings given to the entire seven-strong unit. The young man's opening remark was not calculated to improve matters. 'Let cornets blow and cymbals clash,' he crowed: 'here comes the Galloping Major!' Webster noticed, however, that the handshake which accompanied the inane words was quite unusually muscular. And there were moments during their meetings when he surprised in Fortune's eyes an expression that was both shrewd and purposeful and completely at variance with his normal demeanour.

'There's a Cierva C.3 that can drop you and your chaps

on to a liberty ship scheduled to pass through the straits tomorrow,' Lang said to Webster when they had been in Gibraltar three days. 'Fortune and his two will have to wait until the flight from Lisbon on Friday.'

'Quoth the jolly, jolly sailorman,' Fortune said irreverently. 'Heavenly violins, please, for Jack Tar as he flies into the sunset.'

'It's high time you learned not to cheek senior officers – or the Senior Service for that matter,' Lang said. 'It won't be so jolly for you when you come under the orders of a real disciplinarian.' And later he drew Webster aside and said: 'You do realize, I hope, why you're so anti-Fortune? You pride yourself on your refusal to toe the line, militarily. Now you're up against someone who's more of a rebel, even more disrespectful, than you are – and subconsciously you resent the rivalry. You're both good men, so why don't you snap out of it, accept him for what he is, and behave like an adult?'

Was it just pride that stopped Webster accepting the rebuke?

In any case, he was happy enough with the three men billeted at the *pension* with him. Sergeant Hawkins, tall, blond and massively taciturn, could have passed for a typical German ... until he opened his mouth. But the few words he did utter were unmistakably Anglo-Saxon. Chilton, a Cockney corporal from the Royal Electrical and Mechanical Engineers, was a radio and electronics wizard. In complete contrast to Hawkins, he was a wiry, parrot-faced little man with an overhung lower lip and crooked teeth. Between the two of them was a curious mutual wariness that could almost pass for respect. The third member of the trio, Zygmund, was an expatriate Pole whose hatred of the Nazis showed only occasionally in a flash of the eyes behind thick-lensed spectacles and never on his pale, stolid features.

The *pension* was pleasant enough: a collection of balconied rooms arranged around a central courtyard which was reached through an arch leading from the street. But the fountain was rusted and waterless, the white walls were discoloured, and the tree geraniums hung brown and listless in their cracked urns. Through a small window in the back wall of his room, Webster looked down on the yacht harbour, crammed with rows of tarpaulined pleasure craft, and on the main port beyond. Apart from the liberty ship which had brought them in, a small tanker just arrived from Marseilles, and three merchantmen tied up for the duration, the docks were empty. On the far side of the water, shuttered luxury hotels closed nineteenth-century Gallic eyes among the pines.

Hawkins, Chilton and Zygmund had gone to the British and American consular offices with accreditation papers forged by O'Kelly's backroom boys. This was the first step in the laborious series of manoeuvres which should ultimately result in their getting permission from the French authorities to prospect the interior. Webster, meanwhile, called at the U.S. Control Bureau to introduce himself to the first of the contacts given him by Lang.

This was a lease-lend inspector by the name of Seymour Weiss. 'Very rum job he and his mates have,' Lang had said. 'Before Pearl Harbor, the Yanks arranged to send lease-lend supplies to French North Africa. Help the *colons* get on their feet again economically, and that kind of thing. As neutrals, they agreed that none of this stuff would fall into the hands of belligerents – and especially that it wouldn't fall into Rommel's hands or get re-exported to Germany. Weiss and his boys were sent to see the agreement was kept.'

'How the hell did they do that?' Webster had asked.

'By following through each shipment from the dockside until it was actually used in the factories or displayed on the market stalls. Once they were in the war, the Americans continued to send the supplies, only now the inspectors act as unofficial undercover men as well.'

'And this chap Weiss ...?'

'Weiss was checking on a consignment of raw cotton when he came across a crate that had apparently been misrouted. He passed the information on, but our fellows didn't realize at first that the crate could be connected with the secret weapon in the desert – spare parts for the pilotless planes, or something like that. By the time they did cotton on, of course, the bloody thing had gone.'

Seymour Weiss was a fleshy, blue-jowled man of about forty. He looked more like a successful businessman than a minor diplomat. 'I *was* a successful businessman until I talked myself into this racket,' he confided lugubriously when Webster had explained the reason for his visit. 'Now I'm what they call a non-career vice-consul – "non-career" because we're not part of the regular diplomatic service and our jobs end with the end of the war. Non-anything, boy, if you ask me! As control officers we're ignored by the Germans and Italians, suspected by the British, who think we shouldn't be helping Vichy France anyway, resented by the *colons*, and regarded as a goddam nuisance by the Arabs because we could louse up the network of bribery in which they work. Oh, yeah ... and our own consular people are jealous of us because they figure they could do the job just as well. Or better still. It's a great life, I'm telling you.'

'At least it must be more rewarding now that you have the undercover work as well,' Webster offered.

'Rewarding, he says! Filling in forms, forms, forms! And having the professionals mad at us because we're horning in on *their* preserve. Are you a professional in that line, Major?'

'I'm a professional soldier,' Webster said. 'Though out here, for this job, it might be better not to mention the rank.'

'Thank God for that! Are you a drinking man?'

'You could say that.'

'Then we have no problems, you and me.' Weiss closed a file that had been lying open on his desk and rose to his feet. 'So we'll move our asses to the Place Bugeaud and take the temperature of the town, okay?'

'The Place Bugeaud?'

'An open space with palm trees and sidewalk cafés. In the evening you can hear a military band. Daytimes there is gossip from all over North Africa that is twice as loud and about as accurate. It's near the harbour, just around the corner.'

'Just the job,' Webster said. 'Shall we go – if it's not messing up your inspection round, that is?'

'The only rounds you should worry about today is who pays for the next pair of Jack Daniels,' said Weiss, 'and can we get them without moving to another dive. The liquor shortage here is something else! No, they don't unload your liberty ship until tomorrow: for the rest of today I am, like they say, at your disposal.'

Ten minutes later they were sitting at a minute table over two large bourbons. 'So this mysterious crate you discovered ... ?' Webster prompted.

'Mysterious is right,' said Weiss. 'There it is in a warehouse along with the cotton bales and binder twine and sacks of tea and sugar that come from the U.S. There is no consignee marked but it is labelled 'Office Equipment' and the waybill says it's for the German Armistice Commission. The stencilling is unmistakably German too. It has come from a freighter just in from Bremen, so I figure it for what it says: something that some *schmuck* he misdirects it to the wrong warehouse. But I report it as a matter of routine.'

'And then the crate disappeared?'

'Damn right it disappears. I happen to mention it to Captain O'Kelly's man here and he sends one of his agents, an Arab, to check it out. The Arab does not come back. So O'Kelly's man goes to the warehouse himself and finds there are Germans there ... and the Arab dead of a knife wound at their feet. He gets out without being tumbled and wises me up on what might be in the crate.' Weiss shook his head. 'Not only does the crate vanish – there is no trace of it at the docks, no record of its arrival or despatch, nothing. But zero. Also, although the goddam thing has been lying in this warehouse a day and a half, there is not one lying sonofabitch who works there will admit he has even seen it!'

'Somebody's got the thing sewn up all right,' Webster said. 'Kraut efficiency?'

'Kraut and pro-kraut. There are plenty of collaborators around.'

Webster nodded. 'Tell me, old boy, d'you think all the supplies for this proving range come this way? In ships from the Fatherland? The components for the secret planes and all?'

'Absolutely not.' Weiss was decided. 'It would be much too noticeable – especially when they shipped the stuff on, out of Algiers and into the interior. Too many curious eyes. There are plenty of non-collaborators also, and the Nazis couldn't risk it getting around that they were abusing the country's neutrality. My guess is that they run it in overland, in convoys across the desert from Rommel's headquarters. Tunis is in German hands, after all. Or maybe they fly it to some West African country and take it from there. This crate was probably something urgent – some replacement they wanted in a hurry. A one-time deal.'

'That makes sense. Especially since there isn't a soul who

has the ghost of an idea where the place is. Regular caravans from here would be as good as a bally signpost, what?' Webster drained his glass and signalled a waiter. 'Now this stuff that's *supposed* to be in your warehouse: do your inspections really stop it falling into German hands?'

Weiss laughed bitterly. 'What do *you* think? Of course not. But we have to go through the motions – and it probably keeps the leakage down to respectable proportions. To be one hundred per cent certain here would be impossible. Just look around you, friend.'

Webster looked around him. The cast-iron tables covering the broad pavement were jammed with a crowd as diverse as any he'd seen. There were Algerians in white ducks and tarbooshes; Arabs in Western suits and moslem headdresses; Bedouin in robes and Berbers in stripes; French and Italians and Americans in crumpled lightweight clothes; even a group of Germans perspiring around their duelling scars. At the back of the crowd, where a narrow gangway had been left for pedestrians, half a dozen over-painted girls in white dresses and platform-heeled shoes sat nursing their cheap aperitifs.

After London and the near-siege atmosphere of Gibraltar, two things particularly struck Webster as bizarre: there were very few accompanied women, and no uniforms at all. 'Where in blazes are these hundred thousand trained soldiers everyone keeps talking about?' he asked.

'All around you,' said Weiss.

Webster frowned. He turned and stared at the seated crowd. 'You mean ...?'

'The army is disarmed ... and in this case uniforms come under the heading of arms,' the control officer explained.

'You mean the whole damned lot are here in the city, in mufti?'

'Not in the city, no. Not all of them. There are plenty in the other towns, plenty on the big fruit and vine estates. Out there in the country they may even be in uniform again. And drilling for all I know. This place is feudal: the big landowners pay no attention to what Vichy says, like they paid no attention before to what Paris said.'

'Is that what you were getting at? When you said your job was an impossible one?'

'Partly. The deal giving us the right to go where we want

and inspect what we like was signed by Robert Murphy and General Weygand after the capitulation. Half the folks here, they don't feel bound by anything Weygand fixed; they figure he ratted on them at the fall of France. The other half are shit-scared the krauts will object and walk in to take the place over. Either way, nobody wants to know us. But who dares to know anybody in such a town! Look...'

Weiss waved an arm at their fellow drinkers. 'The little guy in the pale blue suit – the one with the shell glasses – a sous-préfet from Oran, he is. In the pay of the Germans so they can keep an eye on any aliens registered in the city. Beyond him, two tables away, is a go-between for Abd-el-Kerim, the Arab nationalist boss.'

'Type in the red and black striped robes?'

'That's him. Here on our other side...' Weiss lowered his voice and glanced surreptitiously over his shoulder. 'You see those four guys with moustaches and sunglasses? Part of a cell from an extreme right wing of the army that's all for co-operating with Hitler and suppressing the rebel nationalists by force. That blonde with the fat man is the mistress of a colonel in the Italian Armistice Commission. She's earning the rent of her apartment.'

'How d'you mean?' Webster felt as naïve as a schoolboy.

'The fat guy is a black-marketeer – and the colonel likes to eat well.'

'Isn't there anyone on our team?'

'Oh, sure. Five to be exact. But it would be indiscreet of me to point them out right now. After all, you could be on the other team, couldn't you?'

Webster laughed. 'What-ho the cynic!' he said.

The Arab in red and black rose to his feet and left with his companion. Their places were taken by a good-looking blond man and a wizened Algerian in a fez. 'Boche undercover man and one of his stoolpigeons,' Weiss observed. 'His job is to keep an eye on all newcomers who might be Allied agents. They're probably talking about you.'

'They didn't warn me I was going to meet an optimist,' Webster said. 'The type who's just left – the one crossing the street – you said he was a contact man for this rebel leader? What's the strength of the nationalists? Do they amount to anything?'

'Do they ever! The PPA's got one hell of a membership! Besides, when they want to, they can call on the entire Moslem population. To shove out the French, this is like a kind of holy war with them: nobody dares to refuse when he's asked to help. If he won't co-operate, he's liquidated by Kerim's strong-arm boys. But quick.'

'But what do they *do*, actually? Apart from terrorizing their own people?'

'Sometimes they bomb a restaurant or a bar, the kind of place where the diehard *colons* hang out. Sometimes they shoot up a rich man on his estate. Just to remind the French they are there. Mostly they wait, they plan, they stockpile any arms they can buy, steal or hijack.'

'What for?'

'For the bloodbath that's coming once the war's over. The *colons* wet their pants at the thought. Folks who've been here several generations and made their pile exploiting cheap labour – what the hell are they going to do back in France if Algeria gets to be independent and throws them out?'

'Your guess is as good as mine, old boy,' Webster said. 'My God! Look at that redhead over there ... under that palm across the street! What a pair of charlies!'

'*Vingt mille francs*,' Weiss said. 'And you'd be back at this table in fifteen minutes – and probably at the clinic on Friday.'

'I say, what a shame! I could really— Never mind. So what are our hosts doing about the nationalists? Cleaning them up?'

'Not right now. Too disorganized by their military defeat. They just quake and hope it'll go away. But the extreme right-wingers in the army – guys like those four over there – and the big businessmen, they're going to start shooting up Algerians in reprisal soon. And when that happens – watch out, Jack!'

Webster had turned in his chair to watch the redhead. 'And the big-shot – Kerim, is it? – where does he hang out?'

Weiss laughed. 'If I knew that, I'd be up at the Hôtel de Ville, claiming the fattest reward in North Africa! He has a hideout in the mountains, somewhere in the south. Exactly where is what every French security man would love to know.'

'In the south? Do you think *he* would know where our testing range is? Would he help if I could find out where he hides and go there?'

Weiss shrugged. 'He might. But he's just as likely to be in cahoots with the Germans, keeping snoopers away from whatever part of the desert the range is in. Especially if he was being paid to do it.'

'Talking of Jerry, how *does* he fit into all this?'

'He mixes it,' Weiss grinned. 'It suits him to have the French kept quiet by the threat of civil war. It suits him to have the Arabs anti-Allied. So although he can't afford to feed them arms, he does slip them a little quiet encouragement, a little moral support, from time to time.'

The red-haired girl had picked up a client. She was walking off, a bunch of keys swinging from her hand, with a florid man who dabbed continuously at his forehead with a wadded handkerchief. Webster followed her hungrily with his eyes. Half a dozen tables away, a short, spare, tan-suited man in dark glasses ducked his head suddenly behind a copy of the evening newspaper. 'Do Abd-el-Kerim's lot trust the Germans, then?' Webster asked.

'In this country,' Weiss said morosely, 'Nobody trusts anybody.'

When the Fascists caught up with Giancarlo Abba near Sologna, the river was in spate because the snows in the mountains were melting early. They took him to the crypt of an abandoned monastery and emasculated him, and then they put out his eyes. Towards the end of the following afternoon, the youngest one cut Giancarlo's throat. They lashed the body to a pole, fitted an inflated inner-tube around the waist, and floated it away on the swollen yellow waters of the Brenta. There was a notice tacked to the top of the pole on which they had printed the words: THIS IS WHAT HAPPENS TO PARTISANS. Fifteen miles away, the girls at the farm were preparing a special meal for Giancarlo Abba's eighteenth birthday celebrations.

Chapter Five

Webster had been at the *pension* three days before he saw the girl. He and his companions had got used to the conventions imposed by the war: the linen shortage reduced the issue of sheets to one single per bed, and on some days the water was only turned on for an hour. For those who needed it at other times, an open cistern was kept filled behind one of the staircases.

It was to replenish an earthenware jug that he had come down to the courtyard late in the afternoon: a day with Seymour Weiss exploring the *soukhs* of the old town had left him exhausted and craving a wash. And in the evening it was to be the bars and the night-spots again with Hawkins and the others. It was a hell of a way for a soldier to pass the time, Webster reflected as he dipped the jug into the tepid water: pretending to be a civilian, striking up conversations with strangers, and listening, listening, for the stray word, the telltale phrase that might be a clue to the location of a place you had never seen – when all the time you were mad keen to go, seething with impatience to get out and blow that place to smithereens! It wasn't the way he was used to working. Find out about the objective, get the gen on all the obstacles, and then go on in and fight – that was the way he played it.

Pussyfooting around like some military Lord Peter Wimsey was really getting on his wick!

And it wasn't as though it was getting them results. In three days, separately and together, they hadn't had the smell of a clue. Following Lang's instructions, Webster had gone to the cocktail lounge of the Miramar hotel at noon that day and installed himself at the end of the bar nearest the door. To his surprise, the 'contact' who arrived a few minutes later and slid on to the next stool was O'Kelly himself. In the apparently casual conversation they had struck up, the old man told him that Fortune and his men had arrived safely, but they had had no better luck in the plushier haunts where film people might be expected to go.

Tomorrow, Weiss had told him earlier, the Bedouin who had actually seen the German range should be back in town. He had promised to put Webster in touch with the man. It looked now as if they would have to waste time bribing the Arab to lead them there before they could make any plans at all, Webster said in exasperation.

O'Kelly signalled the barman. 'Then you could all go together and save the cost of hiring a plane,' he said mischievously. 'But it may not be too bad. Wait until you hear from our man here: he could have better news.'

'Frankly, I expected to meet him here today,' Webster said. 'It was a bit of a surprise, seeing you, sir.'

'Yes, well, there's a flap on, actually,' O'Kelly said. 'He ran into a spot of trouble. But he'll get in touch as soon as he can. As for me ... well, let's say that at my age it's a relief to get away from the English weather for a spell, what?'

Fetching water at the *pension* that afternoon, Webster shook his head at the memory of the encounter. He straightened up with the dripping jug in his hands ... and then suddenly became aware of a movement in the shadows to one side of the stairs. Evidently the girl had been about to draw water herself when she had heard him coming and stepped back.

'One excuses oneself,' Webster said in French. 'I did not see you. I did not mean to take your place.' She was no more than a blur in the dusk.

'It is nothing,' she said. 'One is not pressed for time. And today, for once, there is plenty of water in the tank.' Her voice, lacking the husky quality characteristic of so many

Frenchwomen, was pitched rather low.

'Bad show, just the same, shoving a member of the fair sex out of the way!'

'I am sorry. I do not very well understand English.'

'My fault again, Mademoiselle. I was saying that you must forgive me the gaucheness typical of my race.' Webster was heavily gallant in French.

She laughed – a small, soft sound in the gloom. 'It seems in fact that you are being unusually courteous.'

'Not at all— Here, let me fill that.' He took the brass pan from her hands and scooped it below the surface of the water in the cistern. 'Can I carry it somewhere for you?'

'You are very kind, Monsieur. Perhaps ... the first floor on the other staircase. It always spills over when I try ... The third door on the left.'

When they had climbed the stairs, he saw in the light flooding through the landing window that she was rather beautiful. She looked as though she might be a Moslem, although her clothes – a white linen suit and high-heeled straw sandals – were almost Parisian in their chic. Her hair, night-dark and silky, was gathered on the nape of her neck in a loose chignon. Her body appeared soft and pliant beneath the severe lines of the jacket rather than taut and reined-in like most of the European women he had seen in the city. A light down shadowed the flesh at the outer edges of her upper lip.

Webster lowered the pan carefully on to a marble-topped table beneath the window in her room. Stifling the desire to date her there and then, he murmured a few conventional phrases and withdrew. Later, if he could wangle a few hours off ... At the moment, however, there was work to do. Regretfully, he returned to his own room, splashed water over himself, shaved, and went to see Sergeant Hawkins.

But the image of the dark girl haunted him all night. 'There's something about her,' he told Seymour Weiss the next morning. 'She's got the biggest brown eyes I ever saw on a girl. What a bint! D'you know, I could hardly keep my blasted hands off her!'

'Professionals should take their pleasure where they find it,' the control officer said. 'But they should never take it home. Which is to say, don't get serious, huh? Especially in Algiers.'

'Crackerbarrel philosophers,' Webster said in what he

imagined was an American accent, 'I can do without.'

Weiss laughed. 'Can you do without a pre-lunch drink? If not, friend, we'd better get going. I have to check out the market before we can get down to the serious business of the day.'

The market was a large open space high above the harbour in the old town. On two sides, flat-roofed houses rose in rectangles of white and pink above colonnades of Moorish arches sprouting from the tangle of bivouacs sheltering the merchandize. A battlemented mosque with three domes and five minarets blocked off one end, and at the other a tall, dun-coloured wall pierced by a single gateway shut out the view of the sea.

Webster's first impression was of the noise – a Babel of a hundred dialects arguing, bargaining, gossiping and joking among the shouts of the merchants crying their wares. Beneath the sprawl of umbrellas, awnings and rattan shelters cramming the open space, fruit, vegetables, garments, pots and pans, brassware and sweetmeats tempted the huge crowd eddying among the stalls. There were Algerians and Moroccans in modern suits, *fellaheen* wearing robe and fez, white-gowned Bedouin from the desert with fierce, proud eyes beneath their burnouses, Berbers and Touaregs with black headdresses and flowing blue aprons – and, milling around the sellers of food, the soft-footed Arab women marketing behind their veils. Here and there Webster saw Europeans. Some of them he recognized – the red-haired prostitute from the Place Bugeaud; a Dutch sea captain he had met in a waterfront bar; the four extremist army officers Weiss had pointed out on the day of his arrival, striding arrogantly through the multitude.

As the control officer worked from stall to stall with his clipboard, checking invoices and bills of lading and manufacturers' code numbers on boxes and cartons, Webster drifted away on his own. He had seen it all before, and if Weiss did hear anything that sounded like a lead, he'd call him back soon enough. Hawkins, Chilton and Zygmund were at some government office, trying to hurry along their permits. O'Kelly had ruled that not more than one of the team should be seen in public with Weiss, in case his undercover activities were too well known.

In one corner of the bazaar, behind a rampart of cane shelters displaying figs, dates, halvah and pastries decorated with honey and nuts, there were rows of circular wooden vats brimming with scarlet, ochre and green fluid. Intrigued by a curious rancid smell he couldn't identify, Webster went to investigate. He found that the liquids were dyes and the smell came from hundreds of newly cured skins that were destined to become the brightly coloured belts, purses and slippers characteristic of the region. Further on, musicians strummed oriental melodies around a whole kid roasting on a spit.

Hearing his name called, Webster turned and saw Weiss in a crowded alcove hung with hardware and copper. 'I think I may have a lead,' the control officer murmured excitedly. 'I just heard one of the Berbers talking about a battle way down in the south. Explosions in the sand, flames in the sky – you name it. It's a thousand miles from the nearest fighting. Ten to one he saw your testing range from a distance!'

'By Jove, I rather care for that!' said Webster. 'Lead me to him, O wise man.'

'Okay, just let me finish here, and I'll be with you. The guy had a stall over on the other side. In the meantime, here is the address of the Bedouin who tipped off your man in Oran. He'll be back there tonight.' Weiss handed over a folded slip of paper.

'Come on, hurry up with that damned bumf: I want to see this bloke before he dies of old age.' Webster found it hard to conceal his impatience.

The American chuckled. 'I like a man he should be an enthusiast!'

At that moment a furious argument broke out behind them. Someone had knocked into a small brazier and spilled the contents of a cooking pan on the ground. The air was heavy with the cloying smell of the hot sweetmeat now coating the cobbles. The stallholder was demanding compensation; the Touareg responsible wanted to claim damages for his singed robe. A crowd gathered around the two men.

Webster watched for a short time and then turned back to the alcove. Weiss was no longer there. Frowning, he looked at the neighbouring stalls, made several casts in each direction, and scanned as much of the bazaar as he could see between the bivouacs. There was no sign of the control officer.

Webster grunted in exasperation. Where could the fellow

have got to? He must almost have finished his inspection: he had said so. Could he have gone to see his Berber contact on his own? It didn't seem likely – not when he had just spoken about it to Webster. Would he have gone back down to the centre then? Not without seeing the Berber first. So why the hell should he have wandered off to some other corner of the market? Christ, he'd only been ten yards away!

Suddenly, the sun came out from behind a cloud. Earlier, rain had lashed the esplanade, threshing the palms and bouncing up from the empty sidewalks, but the sky had been clearing ever since they climbed up into the casbah. Now the crowded square was vibrant with colour, tiger-striped with dense shadow between the stalls.

But there was still no sign of Seymour Weiss. Where *could* the bloody man be?

The Berber's stall, he had said, was over on the other side. Webster threaded his way across, almost knocking over a short, tan-suited man in dark glasses in his haste. He searched the stalls along by the arches bordering the bazaar. No luck. He walked through one of the arches, in case Weiss had gone that way, and found himself in a long passageway stretching off to left and right. It was empty.

As he turned to go back into the square, somebody pushed him violently in the small of the back. Webster stumbled, tripped over a kneeling figure that had suddenly materialized at his feet, and fell headlong. He felt the practised fingers twitch the wallet from his hip pocket before he hit the ground.

He was on his feet again in an instant, shouting angrily – but they were already far down the passageway under the arches: two urchins about ten years old. One of them was clutching the wallet openly in his hand.

Furious at being tricked like any greenhorn tourist, Webster gave chase without thinking. The boys scampered out into the open air – a blazing white courtyard barred with shadow – and then pelted down a narrow lane between windowless stucco walls. The alley twisted, ran through a gatehouse pierced by a pointed arch, and ended in a steep flight of steps curling upwards between the mud-walled houses. Panting, Webster pounded up in pursuit.

At the top of the staircase there was another courtyard. There were people in this one – prostitutes with kohl-fringed eyes and sticky red mouths sitting by an open doorway; men in striped shifts and men in robes. He heard guttural murmurings and Arab expletives as he clattered past. Hands plucked at his clothes and an out-thrust foot almost tripped him again. Then he was through and gaining on the thieves along another narrow lane. Now he could hear the sound of running footsteps behind him too.

The alleyway turned a corner and divided. The two urchins separated, each taking one branch. Webster followed the one with the wallet. He was less than twenty yards behind, his feet striking echoes from the cobbled roadway. A long way above, sunlight slashed a white wall and struck fire from a pot of geraniums on a windowsill.

The boy plunged through an open gateway with Webster at his heels. The Englishman had a confused impression of flagstones, a small fountain, and sun-browned foliage behind iron railings – then he was in semi-darkness, chasing the boy down a corridor inside a tumbledown house.

The end of the corridor was a black rectangle: an open doorway with a lightless room beyond. The boy turned and stopped, holding up Webster's wallet with an impudent grin. Webster snatched it back – and as he did so, the boy leaped nimbly aside. At the same time Webster felt himself pushed again. He went staggering forwards through the doorway, stumbled down a short flight of steps, nearly fell, and was finally brought up against a wall on the far side of the room.

Behind him, the door slammed shut.

Webster opened his mouth to curse. But before he had voiced his rage, there was a scraping noise in the dark and then the abrupt flare of a match. A moment later, the serene light of an oil lamp widened and spread over the room.

It was a small room, hung with rugs. There were two divans, cushions, a low table with coffee cups on it, and a shuttered window embrasure. In front of the table stood a middle-aged man in bush jacket and shorts – a slight, wiry figure with close-cropped black hair and a tanned face against which the network of wrinkles showed white.

'Major Webster?' he said, shaking out the smoking match in his hand. 'Sorry about the unconventional intro, but it was unavoidable. O'Kelly tells me I may be able to help you.'

There were soldiers resting on the bank below the Gasthaus at Siegsdorf when the two telegrams came for Frau Stebel. Below the bank, on the far side of the lane, was the single-track railway, and then the river, the village and the peaks of the Bayerische Alpen very white against the blue sky. The soldiers whistled at some women washing clothes on the flat stones below the bridge. Frau Stebel came to the gate of her cottage to take the telegrams from the boy. He went away quickly because he knew what was in them. One told her that her son, Helmut, who was with the Afrika Korps, had been awarded the Iron Cross, 3rd Class, for gallantry; the other regretted to inform her that Helmut Stebel, Private 1st Class, was missing, believed killed in action. She stood looking at the two pieces of paper for a long time, then she went back into the yard and began to feed the hens. A Feldwebel called the soldiers to attention and they marched off. 'It was funny,' the boy said later, 'the two telegrams arriving at the same time. Perhaps the department dealing with decorations works more slowly than the one dealing with death.'

Chapter Six

His name was Mackenzie, Alastair Mackenzie, although there was no trace of Scottish accent in his clipped army voice. 'Dam' nuisance, having to bring you here like this,' he said to Webster. 'Melodramatic, don't you think? No other way, though. I'm blown, you see. Well and truly blown. Can't leave the quarter. Risky to put my nose outside the door, even. They're waiting for me, somewhere out there.'

'Who's waiting for you?' Webster asked. 'The krauts?'

Mackenzie smiled faintly. 'Oh ... odds and sods. A Boche undercover man. Kerim's assassins. Four unsavoury-looking frogs I seem to have upset. It's enough.'

'The Frenchmen – are they all about the same height? Dark glasses and army moustaches?'

'Those are the ones. Army officers in civvies. They're pro-Nazi and I managed to put a spoke in the wheel of a plot they were hatching up with the Hun. Why? Do you know them?'

'They were pointed out to me soon after I arrived. I saw them at the bazaar half an hour ago.'

'Nasty,' Mackenzie said. 'Decidedly nasty. They were arranging a nice little anti-Arab riot to get the moderate French elements in bad and give Hitler the excuse to march in and take the place over. Jerry already has wind of the landings – only in a general sort of way, of course – and it would suit his book if he could forestall us. Still, that's nothing to do with your show.'

'Why are the Arabs after you? They weren't in on the plan, were they?'

'Absolutely not!' Mackenzie chuckled. 'I shopped one of their top men to the French to buy a little co-operation on the other thing. So now the word's gone out: wanted, the Mackenzie head! Deuced inconvenient.'

'Couldn't you sneak out at night and lie low somewhere else?'

'Possibly. Have a shot at it anyway. The thing is, O'Kelly told me to stay put until I'd contacted a couple of bods and genned them up on the situation here. One's a Free French johnnie who's just been smuggled out of the old country via Spain. The other was you.'

'Well, you nobbled me all right! What price the frog?'

'Hoping to see him tonight. So far as you're concerned, I think we may have a lead on the location of this range.'

'Fair enough.' Webster dropped on to one of the divans with a sigh of relief. 'About bloody time too! We've been running into dead ends all the way. I say – you wouldn't have anything to drink, would you?'

'My dear chap!' Seeing Webster seated, Mackenzie was suddenly contrite. 'Frightfully sorry. Should have offered you something before. Most remiss of me. Would you like some coffee?'

'Er . . . yes. Of course. Coffee would be super. Thanks.'

'Sorry I can't offer you anything else,' Mackenzie apologized. 'Dare not send out for alcohol. Moslem quarter, you see: the buggers don't drink. Be like a signpost saying "Bloody Foreigners Live Here".'

'Not to worry. Coffee'd be spot-on.'

'Ali brews a fair cup. I'll get him to make us some.'

'Ali?'

'The lad who decoyed you here. Smart little beggar. I use him as a messenger, houseboy, cook, the lot. He's been a godsend since I was obliged to hole up here. Don't know what I'd have done without him.' Mackenzie opened the door and clapped his hands. The boy appeared, grinned at Webster, and then listened respectfully as the Scot spoke to him in Arabic.

When Ali had gone, Mackenzie lowered himself to the other divan. Only then, in the droop of his shoulders, in the lines of fatigue around his eyes, did the strain under which he was working show itself. 'As I was saying ... a lead on the range. There's a Berber merchant who reported what he thought was a desert battle in—'

'Yes, we heard about him,' Webster cut in.

'You did? Oh, well, maybe you're clued up already?'

Webster shook his head. 'We were on our way to talk to the bloke when I lost contact with *my* contact. An American called Seymour Weiss. Know him?'

'Of course. Most helpful man. It was he who tipped me off about that damned crate. Too bloody bad it was too late to do anything about it. Still – he wasn't to know, was he?'

'What did happen about the crate?' Webster asked.

'It was just routine at first. Weiss said there was something rum about it, didn't believe the contents were as specified on the label, and so forth. So I thought we'd better take a shufti. I sent a fellow down – good type, loyal, intelligent, comes from over the border in Morocco. His instructions were to prise open the crate, check what was inside it ... and, if he was rumbled, to pretend he was just a sneak-thief on the make.'

Mackenzie sighed. 'As you know, he was rumbled. I went down myself when he didn't show up at the appointed time. Too late. He'd been nobbled by a couple of krauts. Caught in the act, tortured – but he didn't say a bloody word! I was hiding among the sacks, waiting for a chance to play the giddy St George, when ...' Mackenzie swallowed. He blinked and shook his head. 'Nothing I could do,' he said huskily. 'It was cold-blooded murder, over in a flash. They just stuck a knife into him and that was that. I kept mum, hoping to get a closer look myself, but they ran in a squad and took the crate away while I was still there. I suppose I was lucky they didn't spot me.'

'Who were the krauts?'

'An SS colonel in uniform and a little shit from the Armistice Commission called Voigt. Poisonous bastards, both.'

'You didn't get any kind of clue from their conversation ...?'

'About the range? Not a sausage.'

'Or about the contents of the crate?'

'Not really. They said it was secret and it had to be got out of there quick – but they were talking about it as though it actually *was* office equipment, only kind of in quotes. Know what I mean?'

Webster nodded. 'Nothing else?'

'Nothing ... Oh! Wait a sec! There *was* a reference that seemed to me as if it could tie in with the pilotless plane, or flying bomb or shell with wings idea. Just before they left, one of them said he hoped Ahmed – the Arab they killed – he hoped Ahmed really did know damn-all about ... what was it? Yes! "Project Thunderbird".'

'Project Thunderbird?' Webster sat up. 'I say, that does sound as though we were on the right track! And it certainly links the crate with kites falling out of the sky and big bangs in the desert and what-not. Did you mention it to Weiss?'

'As a matter of fact I didn't. It escaped my mind when I was giving him a run-down on the events at the warehouse: I was so choked about Ahmed that I forgot everything else. And I haven't seen him since. To tell you the truth, I rather thought he'd have tagged along when Ali pinched your wallet.'

'Probably would have done, if he hadn't got himself lost in the bloody bazaar two minutes earlier. I looked everywhere. Not a sign of him – and he was standing beside me a second before.'

'Always happening in the markets,' Mackenzie said. 'Maybe you don't know the local rule: if you lose contact with a mate in a bazaar, don't waste time looking for him. Go straight back to the Place Bugeaud and order him a drink. He'll soon be there!'

The boy Ali came in carrying a brass tray laden with fresh figs, dates, and two long-handled copper pans brimming with steaming, fragrant coffee. Webster reached for his wallet, took out a banknote, and tucked it into the youth's hand. 'Cheeky little bugger!' he said. Ali grinned again and withdrew.

'Anyway,' Mackenzie resumed, pouring into two frail cups supported in filigree metal cradles, 'this Berber was able to give me a rough idea where the so-called battle took place. It's about eight hundred miles due south – between the Plateau de Tinrhert and the Mouydir mountains, slap in the middle of the bloody Sahara!'

Webster shook his head ruefully. 'Doesn't mean a thing, I'm afraid. The local geography's a closed book to this pupil.'

'I'm not surprised, laddie. It's an area of shale and sand desert a hundred miles wide and half as deep again, with bare mountain ranges on either side. But there are one or two small oases, and Jerry must have built his base in one of those. Wherever it was, he'd have forty or fifty miles all around that he could safely use as a range.'

'How far away is the nearest town?'

'According to our Berber, about sixty miles. A mud-walled city called Hamadiyah. Now that we know the approximate area, it should be easier to cross-check with other sources and perhaps even identify which oasis. There's a Bedouin who contacted poor old Willis in Oran before he was knocked off, and—'

'We heard about him too,' Webster interrupted. 'Back in town tonight, so they say. I'm hoping to breeze round and see him.'

'Good. You'll know he's illiterate, then: can't show you on a map where he saw his pilotless planes flying. But he can jolly well *describe* the place. And if his description can be identified, so to speak, with a particular oasis, by the Berber or some more knowledgeable bloke, then you're halfway there, aren't you?'

'M'hm. This desert city – Hamadiyah? – how accessible is it? I mean, is it one of these blasted strongholds, sort of sacred spot and all infidels shot at sight? Or can you actually get there by road? Openly, I mean, with your head still on.'

Mackenzie smiled. 'It could be worse,' he said. He went to a carved table beneath the window and brought back a large-scale map of North Africa. 'Look,' he explained, spreading it out on the floor between the two divans, 'Algeria's roughly diamond-shaped, with Algiers at the highest point. From here, a series of mountain ranges runs to the southern tip, dividing the country like a spine. The general area we are discussing is about two-thirds of the way down, and a bit to the right of the ranges ... about there.' He pointed to a region just north of the Tropic of Cancer.

'Quite a spin for the old two-seater,' Webster observed. 'I say – this is wizard coffee!'

'Glad you like it. As I said, Ali's a treasure. Now, as you can see, there's a road climbing up through the cultivated coastal belt to Djelfa, on the first of the high plateaux. You cross the Atlas range to Ghardaia, and after that it's desert ... mountain desert, what's more. But the road goes on as far as El Golèa, about four hundred miles from the coast. And then there's a track only, a caravan route leading to In Salah, Hamadiyah, and south through the Mouydir mountains.'

'The oases you were talking about are not marked?'

Mackenzie shook his head. 'There could even be a track running east from Hamadiyah, but you'd have the devil of a job finding it amongst the shale. Much better to rely on radio bearings from your flying friends.'

'What are these?' Webster indicated a series of red symbols dotting the map to the left of the route pointed out by the Scot.

'Natural gas deposits,' Mackenzie answered.

'Ah! Then, at least as far as Hamadiyah, we could justify our cover as mining engineers prospecting for mineral sources?'

'I should think so. Most of the oil's over to the east, near the Tunisian border, but ... yes, I should think so. There's always the possibility of hydrocarbons on the fringe of a geosyncline, after all, and you could credibly be looking for the heavier elements outside that.'

'I'll take your word for it,' Webster said.

'Didn't mean to blind you with science. Used to work as a geologist in Saudi Arabia before the balloon went up. But the desert here is much tougher. I wish you luck.'

'Thanks, it looks as if we may need it.' Webster rose to his feet. 'And the same to you. Is there anything we can do to help? Provide an escort to get you out of here, or something like that?'

Once more the Scot shook his head. 'Good of you. Appreciate it. But best not run any more risks. Once you're tied in with me you're blown. Not sure that it wasn't a bit dicey letting Ali lead you here anyway.'

'You mean the place may be watched?'

'Not the actual building. They know I'm somewhere in this neck of the woods, but they haven't located the house yet. That's largely because they don't know there's any connection between me and Ali.'

Webster remembered the footsteps he had heard behind him when he was chasing the boy. 'Christ!' he said. 'I hope I didn't lead the buggers to you!'

'Not a chance, old man. They might see you chasing a boy. They might even know who you are. But they don't know who *he* is, you see. So they can't connect me up with you. Now piss off, there's a good chap: I have to get all this bumf ready for our frog friend. If there's any more news, I'll send Ali to you with a word.'

Webster shook hands and left. Following instructions given to him by Mackenzie, he took a different route back to the centre from that followed earlier by the boy, dropping down staircase by staircase, alley by alley, towards the boundary separating the casbah from the new town. As he descended, the lanes grew wider but more crowded, so that sometimes he had to shoulder his way through the throng to make any headway. And even here the thoroughfares were still too narrow to permit the passage of a car.

He was in sight of an arch through which, far below, he could see the blue of the harbour, when the first sign of trouble appeared.

For some time he had been aware – or thought he had been aware – of crisper, European-style footfalls behind him among the anonymous shuffling of the Arabs. It sounded as though he was being followed by a man – or was it two men? – wearing heavy leather-soled shoes. When he glanced behind him, he was unable to single out any individuals from the crowd, but he was almost sure now: he varied his pace and the footsteps quickened or slowed down in time with his own.

Alert for the sudden attack in a quarter he knew was seldom penetrated by foreigners, who were too often robbed or even killed there, Webster kept to the middle of the street. But now there was trouble ahead too.

Three men, tough-looking characters in fezzes and striped shifts, were barring his way to the arch.

Webster looked swiftly around him. Hole-in-the-wall stores lined each side of the lane, tiny *caves* in which carpet sellers, tinners, vendors of sweetmeats and jewellers plied their trade. To his right, a narrow entry led for fifteen yards towards a high, blank wall with a gate in it. And behind him – yes, he had not been mistaken! – two more Arab thugs advanced. Both wore boots beneath their robes; one held a knife half-hidden in his sleeve.

The busy life of the street, scenting violence, was visibly melting away into shops and doorways. Webster ducked into the entry and immediately swung around to face his attackers. If you're outnumbered, he had always advised the men in his private raiding parties, hit first and hit hard – as soon as you know the buggers are after you, or even before. If you strike first, you may take them by surprise and reduce the odds against you, apart from which it gives you a psychological advantage and it gives them a false idea of your strength. If you've made a mistake, you can always apologize afterwards. On the other hand, if you leave the initiative to them, there may not be any afterwards! Well he was outnumbered now, five to one, and he was unarmed. Here was a chance to put his theory to the test!

Webster leaped at the nearest man, who was running into the cul-de-sac ahead of his companion. The three who had been guarding the arch were still some yards away.

He slashed the thug across the throat with the edge of his right hand, slammed a short left into the robes at belly level and then, before he could as much as raise his arms, seized the man's head and brought it crashing down to meet his jerked-up knee. The Arab hit the ground like a felled tree, blood from his broken nose spraying the cobbles.

Webster stamped on the back of the man's head as he crouched to meet the attacker with the knife. This one was a professional, a killer – the wicked blade held hip-high, the point jutting upwards to rip the guts. But Webster knew about that one. His toe flashed out to connect with the thug's knuckles. The fingers opened involuntarily. The knife clattered to the ground ... and Webster sprang in to close quarters. Savagely, he hauled the man's shift up and forward, pinning his arms and half stifling him.

He jammed the attacker against the wall, kicked again with

all his force, and thudded three murderous rights to the dirty under-vest he had exposed. The man rolled away screaming, his hand pressed between his legs.

Only with the first two thugs down could the remaining three move in. This was why Webster had chosen to fight in the entry – you lose the advantage of five to one odds if the space available only allows two to advance at a time.

But the second wave was bigger and tougher than the first. One carried a stick weighted with lead and the other two had knives. The stick man and one of the others moved forward shoulder to shoulder, leaving the third man in reserve. Their plan must be to drop him with the cosh and then slash with the knives. Webster had no illusions about their intention. This was no rolling in an alley for the cash in his wallet – the aim of the operation was death. His death.

He looked desperately around him. He couldn't use the kick technique again on the knife – the man with the stick would cripple his leg before he connected. He turned abruptly and ran back to where the cast-iron bracket of a street lamp projected from the wall above his head. He leaped upwards. His outstretched fingers touched the rough metal, almost slipped, and then held firm as the assassins dashed in.

Swinging like a pendulum, he brought up his knees, straightened his legs, and then slammed his heels as hard as he could into the chest of the leading thug. There wasn't enough force behind it to do any damage but the man was caught off balance and lurched back to collide with his companions. For a moment they staggered between the walls of the alley.

It was the opportunity Webster had been waiting for. He swung hard back ... harder still forwards ... back again ... and then, lifting his legs once more, he launched himself up and over. His body lanced through the air above the heads of the attackers. There was a confused blur of activity as he hurtled over. Something struck his thigh. A razor-sharp blade sliced through his sleeve and pierced his forearm. Then he had landed on the cobbles with a jar that shook him from head to toe. He was in the street again, facing his attackers from the rear.

In the instant before they grasped the situation and whirled to meet him, he acted. Fear and anger and surprise, added to the past frustrations of enforced inactivity, lent him a formidable strength. Seizing the nearest thug by the shoulders, he spun him forcefully sideways.

There was a tinsmith's shop on the corner, with a brazier outside. The man cannoned into this, knocked it over as he fell, and received its cargo of glowing coals in his lap. His cheap cotton robes blazed up instantly, choking his screams into silence as he threshed on the ground in a holocaust of fire.

Webster's eyes were glittering in a face now twisted into an expression of malevolent glee. 'Three down and two to go,' he snarled. 'All right, you fuckers – come on!'

They were already coming. He twisted a tall pyramid of cooking utensils off its display stand and shoved it towards them. The remaining knife man charged into it, staggering aside as the pots and pans clanged to the roadway. Webster raised his arms to ward off a crippling blow from the club. There was a numbing impact that paralysed his left shoulder, and then he was at close quarters again, grappling with the assassin, pulling the man across his body as the thug with the knife recovered his balance and stabbed viciously upwards. The club wielder stiffened suddenly, gave a curious choking gurgle, and then slid limply from Webster's grip.

Before the last attacker could bend and pull his knife from the flesh of his unintended victim, Webster picked him up bodily, raised him above his head, and hurled him down on the overturned brazier. In a moment he, too, was ablaze, rolling frantically on the cobbles in a futile attempt to extinguish the flames devouring his garments.

The tinsmith was yelling blue murder, but the other denizens of the quarter had gathered in groups on the far side of the lane, where they stood respectfully watching the action unroll. Among them was a European, a short, tan-suited man wearing gold-rimmed sunglasses. Further away, Webster thought he glimpsed one of the four neo-fascist French officers.

Straightening his ripped bush shirt, Webster bound a handkerchief around the gash on his forearm and walked briskly through the arch and down towards the sea. Ten minutes later, he was sitting over a bourbon in the Place Bugeaud.

But there was no sign of Seymour Weiss. Webster went the

rounds of the sidewalk cafés. The control officer wasn't at any of them. He walked to the office. Mr Weiss hadn't been back since he left with Webster early that morning. Frowning, and by now a little alarmed, Webster returned to the *pension*.

He climbed the stairs and went to his room. Weiss was lying on the bed. His eyes were closed but there was an expression of faint surprise on his fleshy features. The knife that had gone into his back and pierced his heart had left only a small stain crimsoning the white shirt beneath his jacket.

By sunrise, a merchantman and an elderly tanker riding low in the water had fallen behind the rest of the convoy, outside the protective screen of destroyers. The flotilla leader raced back, his bow wave creaming against the dark, to find out what was holding them up. On the periscope viewing screen of the U-boat, the sea gradually lightened until the short steel-grey slopes of the waves could be distinguished beneath the paling canopy of sky. There must be quite a breeze blowing up there, the U-boat commander thought as he hauled on the rubber-covered handles positioning the screen. The image of the merchantman slid slowly into the centre of the viewfinder and then steadied as the crossed wires settled on her after hold. 'Now will my hand the multitudinous seas incarnadine,' the commander misquoted. He had taken English Classics as a subsidiary at Heidelberg. The helmsman looked worried. 'A quotation from Shakespeare,' the commander explained. 'You would not understand. Are all tubes ready to fire?' The gunnery officer clicked his heels. 'All ready, Herr Kapitan.'

Chapter Seven

The French official poked at the folder on his desk with the point of his pencil. He was a bulky man with brilliantined hair and a clipped moustache. 'In principle, Monsieur Fortune,' he said, 'it should be possible for you to hire an aircraft for the survey you mention. But fuel is scarce. I have to satisfy my superiors that the allocation would be justified. Can you in fact produce cogent arguments to support your application?'

'Sure I can.' Fortune's accent, Trinity College, Dublin, overlaid with a veneer of Mayfair motor car salesman, was beautifully judged. 'This is going to be an epic, a motion picture that will make cinema history. Isn't that right, Joe?'

'You can say that again, boy. With all the weight of Consolidated behind it, it'll put Cecil B. in the shade. But completely.' Joe Constantine was a Canadian, seconded to the assault party from an Air-Sea Rescue crew, but his voice was sufficiently transatlantic to pass muster as that of a Hollywood film publicist. '*Birth of a Nation*,' he said earnestly, '*Ben Hur*, *Gone with the Wind* – you can forget 'em all. I tell you, sir, *The Alien Corn* will be the biggest blockbuster of all time. With Bette Davis as Ruth, Lana Turner as Potiphar's wife, and Errol Flynn playing the key role of Elijah . . . ! We expect to gross sixty million in the first three months alone.'

'Er . . . yes.' The French official looked dubious. 'But aren't there . . . isn't there a certain amount of anachronism in that—'

'All history is an anachronism,' Constantine cut in, warming to his task. 'Mr Grossbreitner – that's our prodoocer, Curtis J. Grossbreitner – he aims to telescope all those biblical legends you heard at your mother's knee into one blistering story. The whole explosive drama of the Old Testament in a single searing three-hour epic! Just think of it!'

The Frenchman thought of it. 'But why,' he said after a moment, 'do you want to make this picture in Algeria? Surely . . . ?'

'For the locations,' Constantine said. 'You gotta lotta desert in this country, sir. Indispensable for Mr Grossbreitner's vision of *The Alien Corn*, desert.'

'You have, I believe, deserts in your own country. Utah, New Mexico, the Kansas dust bowl.'

'Not with the breadth of yours. And there's the emotive angle. We must never forget the emotive angle. Put yourself in the place of the audience. The story of the Bible, shot in the places where it actually happened! I'm tellin' you, it'll be sensational!' Constantine, Fortune thought to himself, had missed his vocation.

'There is a geographical disparity of some thousands of miles,' the official began. 'If you are looking for authenticity—'

'What's a thousand miles here or there? Mr Grossbreitner thinks big. Mr Grossbreitner is a person of imagination. Mr Grossbreitner is a great man.' Constantine paused and shook his head admiringly. 'They don't come any greater than Mr Grossbreitner,' he said.

'I still do not see—'

'Think of the publicity!' the Canadian enthused. 'All shot in your country, sir: the expulsion from the Garden of Eden, building the tower of Babel, the flight into Egypt, arrival in the land of Canaan, the Flood—'

'There is not a great deal of water in the Sahara,' the official said.

'Mr Grossbreitner will fix that. You can use the water afterwards to irrigate the desert.'

'I can see that there may be advantages to your company in using the Sahara as a ... location?' the official conceded. 'But you have not made out a case for the allocation of fuel. What would be the advantages to *us*?'

'Economic advantages. We'd spend a lotta dough here. We'd give employment to your people. We plan to staff the second unit with French personnel. The Children of Israel scenes alone call for three thousand extras. And as for the battles ...'

The official tapped his teeth with the pencil. 'We could perhaps provide motor transport?' he offered. 'A jeep or an ex-army truck?'

'No dice.' Constantine shook his head decisively. 'It has to be from the air.'

'Why? A desert is a desert, whichever way you look at it.'

'Not the way Mr Grossbreitner looks at it,' Fortune said swiftly. 'Sure, this isn't one of your cheap domestic dramas, panning from one room in an apartment to another, now. We aim to pan from one *army* on the east of a mountain range to another on the west, following them as they get nearer and nearer, building your suspense. The battle scenes and all the emigration sequences will be *shot* from the air; we will have camera crews in helicopters, for God's sake. But Mr Mullen can explain more clearly than myself.' He turned to the dark, saturnine Ulsterman who was sitting beside him. 'Is that not right, Mr Mullen?'

'Surely,' Mullen agreed. 'It's essential to see the locations from the air. Else how can we tell what kind of composition a shot might be? We could choose a place that'd look whicker from the ground ... and then find she was no bloody good when we came to shoot.'

'Mr Mullen's our director,' Constantine said. 'He's a famous director who trained under Bergstrøm in Sweden. He made *Winter Heat* and *Thunder in the Blood*, and now he's up for an Academy Award on account of *Frozen Blossoms*. In the motion picture industry, Mr Mullen's *the* coming man. They don't come—'

'Yes, yes, I understand,' the official interrupted hastily.

'They don't come any greater than Mr Mullen.'

Constantine settled his lanky body in his chair and narrowed his eyes. He had been chosen for the unit partly because he had been brought up in Quebec and his French was fluent, partly because he was a tough individualist, but mainly because he was a persuasive salesman. In any business operation, he knew precisely when the iron was hot enough to strike – and in this particular discussion he judged that now was the time to play his ace. He glanced at Fortune, who nodded imperceptibly. 'As I told you, sir,' Constantine said to the Frenchman, 'Consolidated aims to spend a great deal of money on this project. A very great deal. The production company may be Irish but the budget's American, and that means thinking big. As publicity director for the motion picture, I have access to a portion of the front money – a special allotment for advance promotion.' He raised his eyes and stared steadily at the official. 'And, in certain circumstances, I would be authorized to dispense some of that money now.'

The official coughed. He opened the folder and shuffled the papers inside it. 'You have made out a persuasive case, Monsieur,' he said. 'I will see what I can do. I cannot promise the fuel allocation but I will do my best. You understand, there may be certain administrative expenses—'

'I understand perfectly.'

'Very well. Perhaps if we could meet again tomorrow? I – er – I do not wish to inconvenience you gentlemen to come all the way here again. Shall we say the Hotel Aletti bar at noon?'

* * * *

Webster stood at the window, staring down at the pleasure boats laid up in the yacht harbour. 'It can't have been anything to do with my visit to Mackenzie,' he said bleakly. 'Weiss disappeared before the kid pinched my wallet. They must have knifed him and taken him away just after he spoke to me. That means the bastards must be on to me, whoever they are.'

'That's the way it looks, sir,' Hawkins said behind him. 'Any idea who the bleeders are?'

Webster shrugged. 'Your guess is as good as mine. People who didn't want me to talk to Weiss's Berber. Which means people who don't want anyone to hear that story about a "battle" in the south. And that means Boche undercover agents or their French collaborators. I saw those four fascist army officers up there – the ones Weiss pointed out to me himself. Perhaps they had a hand in it. I don't know.'

They were meeting in Hawkins's room – Webster, Zygmund, Chilton and the big sergeant himself. Weiss's body, locked in a huge colonial wardrobe in Webster's own room, was to be smuggled out of the *pension* after nightfall. In the meantime, Webster thought it prudent to hold a council of war and solicit ideas before he determined their next move.

'The men who are jumping you on the way back from Mackenzie's hiding hole,' Zygmund said. 'They are part of the same team?'

'I would think. I imagine they put the kybosh on Weiss and were just about to hand out the same treatment to me when the kid pulled off his stolen-wallet stunt. So they followed me – dammit, I *heard* people following me! – and waited until I left Mackenzie's place before they had another go. The only good thing is, they don't seem to know it *was* Mackenzie's place. That was a good wheeze, to use the boy that way.'

Sergeant Hawkins was thinking. His low brow was furrowed in concentration. 'If you ask me,' he said slowly, 'the thing is: were the fuckers out to get you because you was with Weiss ... or were they layin' for Weiss because *he* was with *you*?'

'Good point, Sergeant,' Webster said. 'You mean if they were after me simply because I was hanging about with Weiss, the reason could have been no more than we were suspected American undercover men. Fullstop. But if Weiss was killed because of his association with me, that implies that the purpose of my visit is known. Right?'

'Yes, sir.'

'I don't see how they *could* know why we're here.' Webster's tone was decided. 'Not yet. My guess is that Weiss was suspected of being a Yankee spy. He was seen talking to this Berber who had some gossip about the Nazi base, and he was killed because he *might* put two and two together and want to find out more. Same scenario for me: I was in their bad books because I'd been seen around with him. I reckon the murder was preventive rather than a cure, if you see what I mean.'

'I tell you what,' Chilton put in. 'I wouldn't like to be in that bloody Berber's shoes – if he wears any!'

'Shoes he wears,' Zygmund said. 'Made of cement and put away nice and tidy at the bottom of the harbour.'

Webster grinned. The Pole's sardonic Central European manner, allied to his somewhat personal approach to the English language, had already enlivened several tedious evenings spent in the city's dives and bars. 'Right you are, Ziggie,' he agreed. 'No point trying to follow up that lead now. But there's still this Bedouin I have to see. And I should think that from now on it'd be better if I steered clear of you chaps. My cover's blown to the extent that I'm now tagged as *some* kind of agent. No need for you to be up on a charge too. We'll stay apart until the permits come through. And, Sergeant, you'd better take over the daily rendezvous with Captain O'Kelly at the Miramar. If he got tied in with me, that would tie in Fortune and the others too, and the whole bang shoot'd be blown.'

'Very good, sir,' Hawkins said. 'You want us to keep on friggin' around in the boozers – about the base, I mean?'

'Good Lord no,' Webster replied emphatically. 'Too risky now. Just hang about and play the jolly old prospectors cover for all it's worth. We know to within fifty or sixty miles where the place is: you wouldn't get anything closer than that in bar gossip. We've got to get closer, just the same. But I fancy I may be able to pull it off on my own – find out the exact location, how to get there, how it's defended, alternative routes, the lot.'

'Christ, how in hell are you going to do that?' Chilton blurted out.

'Just a hunch, lad. Now all you fellows have to do for the moment is shift poor old Weiss's body out of here in the middle of the night – and then go on playing miners.'

'Play miners!' Zygmund echoed mournfully. 'I know about miners. A lot of money they make ... and know how to spend it too.'

'You can spend money. You know that. We have to make the cover convincing and the Captain'll stump up. Spend whatever you like.'

'Spend, the Major says. But what do we get for all this Special Services money we fling around, tell me that?'

'Come off it, Ziggie,' Chilton began with a chuckle. 'You fuckin' hung one on last night that —'

'I will tell you what we get,' Zygmund cried passionately. 'When I am coming here, I think of French cooking. Fish poached in herbs and wine, I tell myself. Plump chickens on a spit. Tournedos Rossinis sizzling on their bed of pâté. Maybe even a little delicatessen. And you know what we get – soup you can see through to the design on the plate; some noodles or pasta; maybe a watery stew made from God knows what animal; a lettuce leaf with a plastic tomato – and to finish a lovely water ice! And you say that this is the life of Riley?'

'It's not that,' Chilton said. 'What gets my bleedin' goat is that some days you can't get no booze. What kind of a balls-up is that?'

'Pétain,' Zygmund explained. 'Because France loses the war, he thinks there should be some kind of national mourning, like a bad boy he stands in the corner. So, no drinking on certain days and no dancing in public. A real mining man, he would weep.'

Webster laughed. 'Play the same scene over again in public,' he said. 'It'll strengthen the image of mining men no end! In the meantime, I'll push off and play my bally hunch.'

The hunch was based on something Mackenzie had said just before he left the house in the casbah. The Scot had told him that although the French neo-fascists were bitterly opposed to the PPA Arab nationalists, the Germans working undercover in Algeria were likely to be dealing with them both. There was even a possibility, he had said, that the Nazis at the experimental firing-range were paying Abd-el-Kerim to police the region and discourage unwelcome visitors. Certainly, Mackenzie had added, there had been a large number of deaths and disappearances in Kerim's territory recently – although most of them had so far been dismissed as guerilla excesses, examples of anti-French gestures by the Arabs.

If this was so, Webster reflected, it should be possible to get a much better line on the German base if he could somehow penetrate the Arab chieftain's mountain stronghold that everyone was talking about. And it was then that he recalled the man pointed out to him by Weiss as Kerim's contact. Would it be worth a try? If the bribe was large enough? If he could keep his interest in the secret base dark and invent some other excuse for wanting to get there?'

Webster decided it was worth a try. He sat at the café where he had talked with the American and scanned the crowd of early-evening drinkers. The sky was shading from blue to a limpid green, and there was a single star glittering above the roofs to the west.

Even if the man was here, of course, it would be a difficult stunt to pull off. It was hard for a European to strike up an acquaintance with an Arab he didn't know personally; the more important they were, the more they withdrew from any approach. Also, even if he did manage to engage the man in conversation, there was the difficulty of communication. He remembered his final briefing from Lang. 'They will speak French, of course,' the Commander had said. 'But that's not what I mean. You can talk to them but you don't communicate. An Arab is never specific, you see. The information exchanged in a conversation bears no relation to the actual words used. Your Arab loves the mental chess game: he's got time for it, after all. So you get the upper level of the talk – what anyone listening in might think was the subject of the meeting – and below the surface two, or even three quite different subjects on which the chap is communicating by hints and inferences. That's why it's useless taking notes of a conference with a Mahommedan. It's what I call the *impression* that you take away from the talk that counts.'

How the devil, Webster wondered, did you imply that you wanted to bribe somebody to smuggle you into a secret stronghold? At that moment, he saw the man he was waiting for: a wiry Arab of medium height with a hooked nose and a pencil-line moustache who looked exactly like a Hollywood casting director's idea of the typical Middle-Eastern intriguer. Still wearing his red-and-black striped robe, he was walking past on the far side of the square – and the young woman laughing and chatting beside him was the dark girl Webster had met over the cistern at the *pension*.

Swallowing the remainder of his vodka, Webster flipped some coins on to the saucer and followed them.

They went down to the esplanade, turned away from the harbour and followed the curving line of the waterfront for half a mile. Webster kept to the opposite sidewalk, looking down over the railing at the moored barges and the darkening sea beyond, watching them out of the corner of his eye. It had been a hot day and there were crowds of strollers in the dusk, so it wasn't difficult to do this without running any risk of being noticed himself. Perhaps this was why he failed to see the short man in dark glasses and lightweight tan suit who was tailing him.

Eventually the couple turned away from the sea and walked up a side street between the tall white buildings to stop outside the double doors of an apartment block. Webster crossed the patched macadam of the roadway and bought some cigarettes he didn't need at a corner kiosk. The Arab and the girl were still talking at the foot of the steps leading to the apartment building. They seemed to be on friendly, though by no means intimate, terms. The girl was laughing a great deal, but when finally she turned to leave, she shook hands quite formally and then walked away without a backward glance. The Arab hurried up the steps and disappeared inside.

While Webster was wondering whether to follow the girl or stake himself out near the building, the man reappeared and, after glancing up and down the street to make sure she was out of sight, walked swiftly off in the opposite direction.

Webster let him go. Even if he was able to find out where the Arab lived, he would be unlikely to succeed in forcing an acquaintance. And, judging from his behaviour with the girl, it seemed that the fellow didn't want anyone to know where he lived anyway. Now that he knew the connection, Webster thought, it would be better to cultivate the girl and hope to arrange a meeting through her. A hell of a sight more interesting too!

Almost absentmindedly he began to follow her now, keeping a long distance behind in case she turned and saw him. When it was evident that she was returning to the *pension*, he wheeled away and walked up past the Admiralty towards the Place Bugeaud.

After a solitary *couscous* in an Arab restaurant, he took up the now familiar round of bars and night-clubs – only this time he was concentrating on places likely to be sources of gossip about Kerim and his headquarters. But although he heard many oblique comments on the PPA and its activities, and many references to the Arab leader himself, none of the people with whom he got into conversation knew any more than he did about Kerim's supposed hideout in the mountains. Or if they did, they weren't letting on. It could be a dangerous piece of information to have, as Webster knew; he himself was forced to keep his apparently casual questions extremely discreet and indirect to avoid raising suspicion among the hordes of spies and informers with which the city teemed.

Just before midnight – and he was getting quite drunk now, with all the stuff he had taken – he was back in the Place Bugeaud, sinking his ninth vodka at the street café where he had first gone with Weiss, before moving on to the address where O'Kelly's Bedouin informer lived. Half a dozen tables away and three rows behind the short man in dark glasses ordered a mineral water and shook an indigestion powder into it with a martyred expression.

Webster allowed the babble of conversation to wash over him. There were arguments and heated discussions on either side, but none of them had any relevance to the information he was seeking. A group of *colons* bewailed the blockades which had ruined the market for the citrus fruit harvest. Behind him two Moroccan businessmen exchanged inane pleasantries with a couple of flashily dressed girls. The red-haired prostitute was standing beneath a lamp on the far side of the street.

He was draining his glass when he heard the German phrase, *das Vogel-Donner Projekt*, somewhere behind him. Startled, Webster swung around involuntarily in his chair. Project Thunderbird! That expression was the key to the whole mystery! But although he scanned the faces feverishly, straining to catch the words spoken by the several parties of Germans at the café, he was unable to tell from which table the telltale phrase had come, or identify anyone who could have spoken it.

A poorly dressed Arab shoeshine boy was threading his way between the tables, offering his box of polish and brushes to the indifferent drinkers. By God, Webster thought, they work the poor little beggars as hard as the cab horses! After midnight, still working – and the kid can't be more than nine or ten years old!

He was waving the urchin away from his own table when he saw that it was Ali, the child who had stolen his wallet. 'Hey, sonny!' Webster called. 'Here – go and buy yourself a square meal, for goodness' sake, and drop the shoe-black stunt until tomorrow.' He peeled a note from the roll in his hip pocket and pressed it into the boy's grubby hand.

'The *effendi* is very kind,' the boy said. 'Allah be with you, sir.' To the Englishman's embarrassment, his own hand was seized and kissed. When Ali darted away, Webster found that a ball of crumpled paper had been left in his palm. He reached into his pocket for cigarettes and stowed the message there. Behind him, a small man in dark glasses weaved between the tables and walked off in the same direction as the boy. Webster frowned. Surely he'd seen that fellow somewhere before?

In the evil-smelling men's room at the back of the café, he smoothed out the paper and held it up to the dim light from the 40-watt bulb. The two lines of pencilled script read: *K is holding a meeting at his H.Q. More positive news perhaps if you could somehow find your way there Sunday. M*

Webster shook his head. A message from Mackenzie confirming his own hunch that the key to the exact location of the range lay with Kerim was good news. Better still was the information that some kind of conference was planned at which this fact could be revealed. But it seemed that the location of the meeting was just as difficult to establish as that of the range itself. The more he plunged into this blasted affair, the more complicated it became.

Today was Tuesday – well, Wednesday now: it was long after midnight. That gave him four clear days in which to discover the whereabouts of Kerim's hideout, get himself there, and work out some way of gatecrashing the meeting. If Mackenzie was right and there *was* a meeting. In any case, what kind of meeting was it? A PPA conference to work out measures against the French? A discussion with the Nazis? A clandestine parley with some French faction?

Even if he got there, Webster reflected, how the hell could he, a foreigner, operate in what was probably an exclusively Arab enclave? Most important, where was the bloody place and how could he find out? It might be hundreds of miles away! The unanswerable questions multiplied in his head. With a curse, he put a match to the crumpled paper and watched it curl away to ash in the wash-basin. There was no point, he thought, turning the tap and swilling away the blackened fragments, putting himself and Mackenzie at risk by returning to the house in the casbah: if he had known any more, the Scot would have said so in the message. It still looked as if his best bet was to approach the contact man through the girl.

Before that, though, he must approach the Bedouin who had made the original report on the secret base. Allowing for unforeseen delays, the man should certainly have arrived at his lodgings by now. Webster decided to go there right away, even if it meant waking up the whole neighbourhood to find him.

The neighbourhood was adjacent to the market where he had been with Weiss. Webster took a taxi, one of the few motorized vehicles available in the city at night. 'The street itself is too steep, Monsieur,' the cabbie told him. 'Also there are steps and it becomes very narrow nearer the top. But I can depose you at the corner below, and you will have less than two hundred metres to walk.'

'That's fine,' Webster said. 'And you don't need to wait. I may be some time, and I can find my own way back.'

It seemed, however, that there might be some difficulty getting there. A crowd of Arabs milled around a police car angled in to the kerb at the foot of the steep, stepped lane. Beyond them, the red lamp on the roof of a fire department salvage truck pulsed rosy light over the dun walls of the buildings. Webster paid off the taxi and got out.

Half-way up the slope, mobile floodlights illuminated a waste of rubble slanting from the breached wall of a flat-roofed house. White helmets glinted as firemen played hoses over the steaming debris. Even at the foot of the hill, Webster could smell the acrid stink of cordite tainting the humid air. He tried to push his way through the crowd, aware of angry murmurs and hands plucking at his clothes.

A uniformed *agent de police* barred his way. 'I wouldn't go any further, Monsieur,' the man advised, saluting. 'The crowd is hostile to Europeans. I couldn't be responsible . . .'

'What happened?' Webster asked.

'A bomb. In the entrance to a Bedouin lodging house. It is feared that all the inmates were killed.' The crowd was pressing closer, the angry voices growing louder and more threatening. 'It seems that two men of European appearance were seen walking away just before the explosion,' the policeman said. 'Your cab is still manoeuvring to turn around, Monsieur. It would really be much safer if you were to get back inside before he leaves.'

Webster had no need to ask the street number of the savaged house. Once again, he thought bitterly, as he fought his way back to the taxi, his unknown adversaries had stolen a march on him.

'Germany calling ... this is Germany calling ... You are listening to the stations Hamburg, Köln and DJA. Here is the news in English. The sea war swings more and more in Germany's favour. One hundred and sixty-two thousand tons of Allied shipping was sunk by German submarines last week – over ten thousand tons more than in the previous week. Germany is winning the sea war. It is the same in the air. Fifty-seven British aircraft were shot down during the terror raid on the Rühr last night, making a total of two hundred and three in the past three days. The Americans lost thirty-nine Flying Fortresses in the daylight raid on Wilhelmshaven yesterday. In the same period German fighter losses were only seventeen. Strong forces of German bombers last night destroyed large areas of London, Bristol and Hull. Sixteen British night fighters were shot down. One German bomber failed to return. Germany is winning the war in the air. On land, the British army is reeling under General Rommel's attack in Libya. The British people are asking themselves how long these losses can go on. But there is worse to come, Britain! Soon, the secret weapon will be in use ...'

Chapter Eight

Webster found out from the aged concierge at the *pension* that the girl worked as a clerk at the British Mission in the old consulate building near the Admiralty. At noon the following day, he was walking past as she came down the steps with the rest of the staff for lunch. 'Mademoiselle!' he exclaimed with a show of astonishment. 'What a surprise!'

'Bonjour, Monsieur,' she smiled. *'Comment ça va?'*

'Chaudement!' Webster replied. It was a scorching hot day, and the flat roofs and domes of the old town trembled in the haze above the city. 'May I ... that is to say, would you allow me to offer you something cool and refreshing to drink?'

She smiled again and shook her head. 'I am sorry. I already have a rendezvous with friends.'

She was walking towards the city centre. He fell in step beside her. 'I am sorry too. Another time perhaps? Tonight?'

This time the smile spread to her huge dark eyes. '*Volontiers*,' she said, turning towards him. 'Willingly.'

'It would give me great pleasure, Mademoiselle ... ?'

'Harari,' the girl said. 'Céleste Harari.'

'Good Christ!'

'*Pardon?*'

'You won't believe it! What a wild coincidence!' In the complexities of the mission, Webster had completely forgotten about the name and address Liz had given him on his last afternoon in London. 'We have a friend in common ... in England! You remember Liz Macnamara?'

'Liz Macna—? But of course! Liz! We were at school together!'

'In Lausanne,' he finished for her. 'She told me. She asked me to look you up ... only I thought you lived in an apartment with your father. In a block overlooking the harbour.'

'I did,' she said. 'Once. But things are not so good now. My father was killed at Mers-el-Kebir. And of course I have not heard from Liz since before the war.'

'I am sorry,' he said again. 'But look here – you simply must have dinner with me tonight. I insist.'

'I should love to. Where do you suggest?'

A marked man in the midst of spies and intrigue, Webster did not wish to call for her at the Mission a second time. For the same reason, he was unwilling for the people at the *pension* to see him taking her out (coming back would not present the same problem: he could have met her by chance, and it would be normal to escort her home). 'I have some work on the other side of the city,' he lied. 'And I believe you have to dine early around here to make sure of a place. Could you perhaps meet me out? The Tabarin, halfway along the esplanade, isn't too bad. We could sink an apéritif there and then eat wherever you fancy.'

'Yes,' she said. 'That would be fine. I can walk there from the *pension* in about fifteen minutes. What time? About seven?'

'Seven o'clock would be spot-on. Er ... let me offer you a cab, since I can't collect you in person. As my guest, of course.' Webster knew what a small salary she must be getting.

'It is not too easy to find one at that hour of the evening. But we shall see. In any case, it is courteous of you to offer.'

Webster spent the rest of the day in another fruitless search for meaningful gossip. The name and location of Kerim's hideout remained a secret, although this seemed less aggravating now that he had a chance of some contact through Céleste Harari. Over an unappetizing sandwich lunch near the central railway station, he read the local newspaper. The item he was looking for was in a small panel on the back page, though it was not in the form he expected. Hawkins and the others had evidently succeeded in smuggling Seymour Weiss's body out of the *pension* and on to the quay, as he had instructed them. But the headline read: TWO CORPSES IN HARBOUR MYSTERY. With increasing bewilderment, he read on:

Guardians of the law on patrol in the pleasure harbour area at dawn today discovered the bodies of two men outside the *chef du port's* office. Each had perished from knife wounds in the back. Police at first thought the victims had killed one another in a dockside brawl. But the mystery deepened when a police surgeon told our reporter that one of the men, later identified as an American consular official, Seymour F. Weiss, had been dead for at least 18 hours, whereas the other had left this life no more than three or four hours previously. The second man, about 40 years old, with dark, short hair and blue eyes, is of the type categorized as Anglo-Saxon. The police anticipate an early solution to the mystery.

'My God!' Webster breathed. 'Mackenzie! He must have known they were on to him at last, poor sod, and got that message out to me just before he was jumped.'

It was clear that the people who had killed Weiss and who had tried to kill him must have been the same as those who had assassinated the Scot. But were the three motives linked to the fact that they were all, in their different ways, involved with tracking down the German experimental base? Or were they simply assuming that any foreign agent is better out of the way, whatever his work may be? In the latter case, the murders of the Arabs would appear to be somewhat excessive as a reaction; but if the whole lot were connected – as seemed most likely – then the killings could be tied through the first warehouse death directly to the Germans in Algeria. This in turn implied that Webster's mission might no longer be secret.

And yet ... and yet ... He thrust the folded newspaper savagely into a waste-basket and strode from the brasserie. There were specific reasons why the three groups Mackenzie had mentioned should wish to revenge themselves on him – but why, then, should Weiss and Webster himself have been involved? How did the killers know there was a connection between them, when Mackenzie had been so completely convinced that this was impossible? Most important of all, *how the hell did they know Weiss's body was going to be on the quayside, so that they could leave Mackenzie's beside it?*

They couldn't possibly have known, and that was the truth of it, Webster told himself fiercely, for he had told nobody but Hawkins and the others, and they had stayed in the *pension* with the body until it was time to smuggle it out. Yet it had happened. Was it a coincidence, the disposal of Mackenzie's body in that particular place? That was even less believable. And, assuming it was deliberate, what was the point of the exercise? Was it a warning? A gesture of some sort? A message, even?

The more he thought about it, the more insoluble the problem became. Finally he gave it up and continued his round of the bars in a desultory fashion, though all his hopes now centred on his date with the girl and the meeting he wanted her to arrange.

At seven o'clock he was sitting over a large vodka among the faded red plush and gilt of the Miramar. She was only five minutes late. He saw her climbing out of the ancient horse-drawn carriage through the glass doors of the bar. He was beside her before she had time to open her white calf handbag, thrusting the greasy pre-war notes into the cabbie's hand, ushering her into the bar, seating her with her back to the wall. 'I am so delighted that you could make it,' he said truthfully. 'Now what can I order for you?'

Céleste Harari chose a whisky sour. She was looking beautiful. The chignon had moved: her hair was now piled softly on top of her head like that of an Edwardian belle. She was wearing white again – a draped cocktail dress in tiny pleats whose cross-over top subtly emphasized the depth and the separation of her breasts. Her white, high-heeled shoes were decorated with oversize buttons in carved jet, and there were antique jet earrings swinging from her small ears. She wore no other jewellery.

They had two drinks at the Tabarin and then they walked along the promenade to a place she knew at the far end of the harbour. After the heat of the day, the evening was still very mild and stars already pricked the sky above the sea. The waves were so small that the thin line of foam rolling up the sand as they broke was only just visible in the dusk.

The entrance to the restaurant was down a flight of steps: a wide door faced with copper beneath a green and white awning. In the centre of the metal sheeting a narrow lip sheltered a Judas window. The girl exchanged a few words with the bouncer on the other side, and the door swung open.

From the minute lobby, carpeted stairs curved down again to a low-ceilinged dining-room layered with cigarette smoke. There was an American bar in an alcove, a savoury smell of food cooked in wine and garlic, and a piano-drums-clarinet trio playing quietly on a rostrum at the far end of the restaurant. From the balustrade at the top of the stairs, Webster looked down on women's bare backs, on gleaming white cuffs and uniform buttons that shone, on winking stick-pins and glittering rings. Over the discreet tinkle of cutlery and glass, waves of conversation ebbed and flowed. The war seemed suddenly very far away. He put his hand under the girl's elbow and they submerged themselves in the tide.

The food was better than anything he had eaten since he landed in North Africa: fillets of mostelle in a mayonnaise sauce made with real eggs, baby lamb chops baked in piecrust, crisp salad and genuine Camembert from the north of France. There was even a bottle of Bellet imported from the Côte d'Azur.

'Do you like the place?' Céleste asked.

'My pretty thing,' Webster said, 'I think it's wizard, absolutely topping. I haven't seen anything like it since I came here.' He had handed her the line about mineral concessions that he was using as a cover.

'I'm afraid that's because it's a little *marché noir*,' she said. 'You know. Black market. It's the only way to get real food.'

He nodded. 'Zygmund, thou should'st be here at this hour,' he said piously.

'Pardon?'

'I'm sorry.' He was at once contrite. 'Jolly bad form. I was thinking of one of my men. Chap's always complaining about the quality of food here. Privations due to the war, an' all that.'

The war nevertheless seemed now more remote than ever. The wine had brought a shine to Céleste's eyes. Her parted lips glistened. She looked like a child at a party and he found her enthusiasm irresistible. She was also well informed and well read, salting her opinions with that dash of pragmatic cynicism that is more French than Arab. He couldn't take his eyes off her.

They were halfway through the cheese course before he found an opportunity to broach the subject of Abd-el-Kerim's contact man. She had been talking about food again, saying that Zygmund was right: most of it was so bad that she preferred to spend her lunch hours out of doors and snatch a quick sandwich at a bar before she was due back at the Mission. 'Talking of which,' Webster said, 'I saw you at lunchtime yesterday.'

'Oh, did you? Where was that?'

'On the esplanade. You were turning up a side street by the *tabac*.'

'Was I?' She wrinkled her nose trying to remember. 'Oh, yes. So I was. Why didn't you come and say hello?'

'You were with somebody,' Webster said primly.

'With somebody? Are you sure?' She seemed genuinely to have forgotten.

'Absolutely. I remember because the man you were with happens to be somebody I'd like to meet.'

'The man I was—? Oh, but of course! How foolish of me. I know him so well that I had forgotten. That was Mahmoud Hassan. He used to be a patient of my father's. I've known him ever since I was a little girl in Morocco.'

'That must have been a hell of a long time ago,' he said gravely.

'Now you are teasing me. But if you wanted to meet him, why did you not come over? I could have presented you.'

Immersed as he was in a sea of trickery and deception, such a simple and straightforward idea had not occurred to Webster. It might even, he thought, have worked. But what the hell –

there was no use crying over spilled milk. 'Do you think you *could* possibly introduce me?' he asked.

'To Mahmoud Hassan? Well, of course, if you really want me to.'

'I really do! Does he live in the apartment house where you left him?'

'I don't know.' She looked puzzled. 'I imagine he does, simply because that's where I did leave him. But of course, come to think of it, he may just have been calling on a friend.'

'But you meet him quite often?'

'Well, yes. I *see* him two or three times a week. He must work somewhere near the Mission. Why? Is it important?'

'It could be,' Webster said carelessly. 'It's just that I'd like to pick his brains, ask his opinion on a matter of policy. He knows Abd-el-Kerim, doesn't he? At least, that's what I heard. My people wouldn't want to hurt the Arabs' feelings, you see. If we developed the mineral resources, that is. I thought Hassan might be able to advise me.'

'Abd-el-Kerim?' the girl repeated. 'The rebel leader? Does he? I wouldn't know. But I can certainly introduce you, if that's what you want.'

'I'd be frighfully grateful.'

'Very well,' she said. 'Leave it to me. Aren't you going to ask me to dance?'

He looked over his shoulder. The tiny floor was packed with couples. 'Nothing I'd like better, old thing. But I thought it was supposed to be sort of illegal here?'

'It is illegal to dance in public. Technically, this place is a club: you must have noticed that little charade at the door as we came in. And if it's a club, then clearly it cannot be public. There is an example of our fine French logic for you! Also, of course, the management pay heavy bribes to the administration and the police.'

Feeling her soft, supple body against him, Webster almost forgot Abd-el-Kerim and the German desert base, the spies and *agents provocateurs* all around them, and the members of his group waiting impatiently in the city for action. He forgot that he was a belligerent in a neutral country, a man whose trade was deceit, an officer seconded to a special unit with orders to kill and destroy. He was only aware of her cheek against his own, of the hand that cradled the nape of his neck with cool fingers in his hair, of his own hand on the small of her back and the way her thigh pushed between his legs as they danced. Her hair smelled faintly of almonds.

They went back to their table for coffee and brandy, and he forgot to let go of her hand. During the whole intermission their fingers traced arabesques on each other's palms in a dialogue that bypased a month of formal conversation. By the time they got up to dance again, Wesbster could think of nothing but how she would look without her clothes on.

A little later, as they were dancing, he leaned back from her and asked: 'Do you know who that is?'

'Who who is?' she queried in English.

'Who who is!' he mimicked. 'You sound like an owl! The softest and sexiest owl in the business!' He pulled her close and allowed his lips to slide around her cheekbone to her ear. A tendril of hair had come loose at the back of her neck.

'*Tu n'es pas gentil, toi!* No, but really – who do you mean?'

He leaned back again and looked into her large eyes. 'Behind you now. Beside the pillar to the left of the band. A small dark man with glasses, sitting alone. I've seen him several times in the past few days and I wondered if you knew who he was, that's all.' He swung her expertly around in the press of dancers so that she was facing the rostrum.

She looked, turned, and looked again. 'I don't remember seeing him before,' she said. 'But I think he is not French. See, he has left his knife and fork together on his empty plate like an Englishman or a German.'

'It doesn't matter,' Webster said. 'I just wondered; it's probably a coincidence.' But there was a frown on his lean face as he held her close to him again. She slung her belly against him and kept it pressed there provocatively all the way back to the table.

The bill was enormous. But what the hell, he thought as they walked out into the warm night: it was Special Services money anyway!

He kept an arm around her waist as they crossed the empty street and stood for a little staring over the railing at the sea. Half a dozen fishing boats with stern lanterns were just clearing the long breakwater embracing the harbour. There was a quarter moon low down in the eastern sky that silvered the waves beyond the jetty. A few hours away, the Malta convoys were ploughing through the dark waters, free for a short space of time from the fear of stalking subs and Stukas. And away to their right, around the corner in Libya and Tunisia, were the guns and the tanks and the moans of men whose entrails had spilled on to the hot sand.

'Sweetie,' Webster said. 'You know what I want to do, don't you? More than anything in the wide, wide world, I want to make love to you.'

She took his hand from around her waist and placed it on her breast. He could feel the warm weight of the flesh, the tautness of her nipple, through the pleated stuff of her dress. 'But of course, *chéri*,' she said. 'I also.'

His pulses were racing. He hadn't thought it would be that easy, that quick. In the Catholic countries, he had usually found that a good deal of sweet talk was required first. 'Where can we go?' he said hoarsely. 'The beds at the *pension*—'

'No, no. That would not be discreet.' She paused a moment and then added softly: 'I know a small hotel not far from here.'

It was up a side street off the esplanade, and it looked just like the apartment building where he had seen her with Mahmoud Hassan. Webster wasn't even sure that it might not have been the same one: there was no hotel sign outside and the entrée was on the mezzanine. There was a comfortable-looking woman with glasses reading the paper at the reception desk, and a plump, tired chambermaid to show them to the room. '*Merci, Mademoiselle Martine*,' she said as Webster dropped coins into her palm.

The bed was big. The room was clean and warm, and there was a bathroom adjoining it. He took her gently by the shoulders and drew her towards him. Her tongue, flickering between her lips like a small animal, was scalding hot in his mouth. 'Would you like to see me without my clothes?' she said breathlessly.

Webster's hands were shaking. 'What do *you* think?' he said.

She had surprisingly fleshy hips, with firm, round buttocks and a tiny waist that emphasized the double convexity of her belly. He gazed in fascination at the big triangle of dark, silky hair. 'By God,' he said thickly. 'You're the most—'

Seizing her by the hips, he buried his face between her thighs and began to kiss her passionately. She gave a small cry and disengaged herself. '*Chéri*, if you wouldn't mind ... It is customary ... Perhaps I could have my little present first?'

'Little present?' From his kneeling position, Webster stared at her uncomprehendingly. 'Customary ... ? I'm afraid I don't quite ... ?' And then, suddenly, as he did understand, for the first time since he was a boy he flushed a deep red. 'Good grief!' he exclaimed, stumbling to his feet. 'You don't mean ... ? You're not ... ? Oh, Christ, I didn't realize—'

'That you were dining with a *poule*? But my darling, how stupid of me. It was my fault. I should have made it clear, but I thought you would know.'

'It doesn't matter. Sweet Jesus, it doesn't matter,' Webster choked. 'It was just that, as you worked at the British Mission, I assumed ... God what a berk!'

'The money is not good and the prices are high,' Céleste said with a sigh. 'One has to live. But I do not go on the streets or in the bars. I choose, and I choose only occasionally, and only those I like.'

Webster didn't give a damn. He was embarrassed only because of his own ineptitude. Webster the great lover, Webster the World War II Casanova, Wicked Webster who had whored the world over from Wallingford to Wu-Yuan, not recognizing a business girl when he saw one! That would raise a laugh from the chaps in the Mess! What a twit he had been, as callow as a school kid on his first date! No wonder it had been such a snip; no wonder those tedious formalities inseparable from Gallic seductions had been so conspicuously absent; no wonder the world-famous Webster wooing technique had worked so well! And no wonder she knew a little hotel not far away: *Mademoiselle Martine* – that must be the name she used for business.

The girl was looking at him with a faint smile. 'You are angry?'

'God, no. It doesn't make any difference: I still want you just as much. It was just that I felt such a fool, such an unmitigated ass for not catching on ... it's so embarrassing for *you*.'

He reached for his hip pocket but she stopped him with a gesture. 'You are not to touch that wallet before you are out of this hotel,' she said. 'I could not possibly accept – not now. It would spoil everything.'

She lowered herself on to the bed and stretched like a cat, cupping the weight of her breasts in her own hands. 'Another time, perhaps,' she said lazily. 'But tonight ... tonight I want you as a man and not as a client.'

He cast himself down beside her, kissing her nipples, stroking the sculptured curves of her thigh. 'Holy smoke!' he murmured incoherently. 'Honestly, darling, you're so ... you're such a fabulous ... Hell's teeth, I want you *now*!'

Céleste gave a throaty laugh. She reached out a hand for him. 'In the words of your Hollywood movie stars,' she said, 'be my guest!'

The convoy pulled off the road and the troops spilled out of the personnel carriers to sprawl on the grass verge. It was only a half hour since they had left the camp at Papenberg, but it was 9.50 am and soldiers on the march always halt for a rest from ten minutes to the hour until the hour. That's the way they do things in the army, even if the march is motorized. There was a cold wind blowing across the marshes. High up in the pale sky five Messerschmitts in arrowhead formation caught the sun. Otto Preisser threw away the stub of his cigarette and asked why the unit was being moved. Special duties, the Feldwebel told him. He blew his whistle to call the men back to the carriers. 'We have a long way to go,' he said. 'Through Bremen, Hamburg, Celle, Hannover – all the way to a place called Dachau, just off the autobahn near München. Come on you lazy bastards – jump to it, or we'll never make it before nightfall and you'll have no time for beer!'

Chapter Nine

Captain Seamus M'Phee O'Kelly swung around on the bar stool and saw the monolithic figure with the low brow and the pugnacious jaw. 'Well, look who's here!' he said heartily. 'How's the mining business doing, Mr Hawkins?'

'Doin' a bleedin' treat,' the sergeant growled as he shook hands. It outraged his sense of decency, being ordered to act in a familiar way with a senior officer. 'What they call a fast-growin' industry. I wish I could say the same for the government fuckin' departments here what issue permits. We been hangin' around a week now, and do you think there's a sign of the bloody papers we need? In a pig's arse there is!' And then, remembering their cover relationship, he added with an attempt at joviality: 'An' how's the Military fuckin' Mission business, Captain?'

'Booming!' O'Kelly chuckled. He was officially attached to the British Mission as an ostensible reason for his presence in Algiers. 'All we need is a couple more belligerents and we could dream up a cricket team between us, umpires and all! Now what can I get you, Mr Hawkins?'

The big sergeant shifted his feet, staring at the fitted carpet. 'I don't s'pose they'd have a beer, would they?'

'Of course they would. And if they don't, I'll jolly well make them send out for one,' O'Kelly said, adding in a low voice: 'For God's sake stop standing to attention, man! We're supposed to be casual friends. Now sit down and offer me a cigarette.'

'Yes, sir. Thank you, sir.'

Hawkins perched himself gingerly on a stool and did his best to exchange banalities with his chief in the manner of fellow countrymen meeting in a foreign city. He bought a round. A few minutes later he looked at his watch and then slid from the stool. The old man had a cheroot between his lips. He slapped his pockets in search of a lighter. 'Here, let me . . .' Hawkins offered awkwardly. He struck a match and held the flame out as the old man sucked in smoke. 'Cheer-oh, sir. 'Ope to see you again soon.' He raised his hand and strode from the bar, leaving the matchbox on the polished counter.

Five minutes later, O'Kelly unfolded the message it had concealed in his room. *W. has organized a conducted tour to K's home ground*, he read. *He will need 5000 dollars American, in cash, by 1900 hours to pay for the ticket admitting him to the stadium. One of us will be at the low stakes table in the Aletti casino's roulette room from 18.30.*

Seamus O'Kelly swore. 'Low stakes table be buggered,' he growled as he burned the paper and flushed the ashes down the lavatory. 'They can save money as much as they bloody well like, arsing around the city, but with Fortune's bribe to get himself an allocation of aircraft fuel and now this, the Comptroller's going to have a heart attack explaining my expense sheet to the Treasury!'

* * * *

There was an airfield five miles away on the coast road to Bejaia, not the official airport where scheduled commercial flights landed and took off, but a private field that had belonged to a rich man's club before the war. Now it was used as an overflow landing ground for the smaller planes bringing VIPs and army chiefs from Italy and Spain and the Midi.

Weeds grew in the cracks of the single concrete runway, and the windows of the old clubhouse beneath the control tower were shuttered and barred.

Two CRS men with white helmets and blancoed belts stood guard by the doors of the big hangar that was screened from the road by a row of eucalyptus trees. As the ministry official led Fortune, Mullen and Joe Constantine across the parched, dusty earth from the gateway where they had left the Citroen, the men unslung their carbines and advanced a few paces towards them.

The official flourished a pass and produced a sheaf of impressively stamped documents from an inner pocket. He spoke rapidly to the two men in French, and they re-slung the weapons and rolled back the huge corrugated iron doors on the gantry framing the hangar.

The plane that was for hire – and it was, they were told, the only one – was an elderly Italian machine, a Macchi-Castoldi five-seater with three radial engines and a non-retractable undercart. It stood like a prim spinster aunt above the sleeker, slimmer shapes of the twin-engined Dewoitines and Dorniers parked beneath the French-truss roof. So far as they could see, however, it was in fair condition – and visibility from the cabin was good.

'What about the fuel?' Fortune asked from the pilot's seat, where he sat fiddling with the controls.

'It should be through by tomorrow,' the official replied. 'There are no permanent facilities here, but I can arrange for a tanker to come out some time in the afternoon. Then, once your flight plan is approved, you can carry out your survey whenever you want.'

'How much fuel?' O'Kelly asked later that evening, when they were leaning over the baccarat table in the Alctti's gambling rooms.

Fortune grimaced. 'The allocation's only enough for 750 miles,' he confessed. 'Unless Brother Webster hits the jackpot this side of the halfway line, we're stymied. In which case there are only two things to do: drop the ball out, count one stroke, and start again. Or wangle a larger allocation of fuel.'

'At the prices they charge here, that could be expensive,' O'Kelly said tartly. 'The plane itself's all right, though?'

'Tight as a goddam drum,' Constantine said. 'She's a bit like the Ford Tri-Motor, or maybe Lindbergh's *Spirit of St Louis*. You know – high-wing monoplane with the driving seat behind the central motor and a cabin under the wing. Struts here ... and here. And streamlined fairings covering the wheels. Old, but quite smart.'

'I don't want to put the blasted machine into a beauty contest,' O'Kelly snapped. 'All I want to know is: can you fly it?'

'I can so,' said Mullen. 'Both of us can. Isn't that right?'

'Piece of cake,' said Charles G. Fortune. 'Easy as falling off a bally log.'

* * * *

Not long before dusk, clouds rolled across the sky from the west and blotted out the setting sun. At the Hôtel de Ville, Hawkins heard at last that their application for a permit to visit the interior on a prospecting expedition had been provisionally granted. With the permission came the use of a three-ton half-track vehicle to transport them and their equipment over the desert terrain; but again the petrol allocation had been calculated on the basis of a round trip of no more than 750 miles – barely enough to reach the area in which, according to Webster's latest information, the firing range was located, let alone bring them back. And none of their arguments, pleas or promises of bribes could get the ration increased by a single gallon. There just wasn't the fuel available, the man at the Ministry of the Interior said apologetically.

'We'll have to play this one by ear,' Hawkins said as they drove to the Hotel Aletti for the rendezvous with O'Kelly. 'There may be no soddin' pilots in the secret kraut planes, but they still have to fuel the fuckers, don't they? So all we have to do is liberate enough aviation spirit to get us home before we blow the buggers to hell.' They were riding in a jeep borrowed from the British Mission – three tough and well-paid mining men out for a last flutter at the casino before they braved the rigours of the desert. Webster was holed up in the *pension* waiting for them to bring back the money from O'Kelly.

Chilton was driving sedately down a wide street lined with modern tenement blocks in stained, cracked concrete when a white Mercedes sports car driven by a middle-aged man in dark glasses overtook them with a snarl of chromed exhausts. 'This man is worried by the gasoline shortage?' Zygmund asked sourly. 'With nearly six litres of engine, 250 horsepower and 110 miles per hour? I should be so lucky: that's a Type 540K he's driving!'

'Bloody hell, Ziggie!' Chilton was amused. 'I never knew you were a bleeding sports car fan! You don't get much chance to put on the dog in this dump, do you? That's only about the third hotted up bus I seen since we got here.' He paused, idly watching the big convertible brake, blow its horn three times as it passed a driveway, and then accelerate away. Chilton swore and changed gear as a black Peugeot saloon shot out of the entry ahead of them and then balked the jeep at an intersection. Two men in the rear of the French car seemed to be having some difficulty closing the offside door.

'Ask me,' Hawkins said from the back seat, 'I'd say the fuckin' Boche has an edge in this town when it comes to bypass the bleedin' petrol— *Watch out!*' he yelled ferociously, seeing the heavy, squat package fall from the Peugeot and spin towards them as the car raced ahead.

He jammed his arm between the front seats and seized the handbrake lever, hauling on it with all his strength.

The cloudy weather had brought a trace of humidity into the air. The roadway was slightly greasy. The four-wheel-drive jeep, with two wheels suddenly locked, tried to pull up in a straight line. But Chilton, half-turning his head in astonishment, moved the steering and the little vehicle skated across the macadam with a screech of tyres. The back end broke away. Chilton over-corrected, and the jeep – with Hawkins still wrenching white-faced at the lever – turned completely around. It shot backwards across the street, clipped the high kerb, and then rebounded into a pedestrian refuge, where it slammed against a post and tipped over on its side.

The crash was drowned in the thunderclap of the explosion, which blasted a ten-foot crater in the road where they would have been if Hawkins hadn't grasped the handbrake. Miraculously, nobody was hurt.

They scrambled to their feet. The attack had taken place

just short of the boulevard leading to the station. People were running towards the cloud of yellow smoke blanketing the corner. In the distance, a police whistle blew. 'Come on,' Hawkins panted. 'Let's get the hell out of here before anyone starts to ask questions.'

Followed by the others, he sprinted for an alleyway that twisted between tall buildings towards the sea.

'That's it then,' he said grimly ten minutes later as he picked fragments of toughened glass from his hair. 'Whoever these buggers are, they have cottoned on to our connection with the officer ... before he started stayin' away from us.' He passed an oil-smeared forearm across his forehead and shook his head. 'The sooner we piss orf into that soddin' desert, the better I'll be pleased!'

PART III

Sahara Double-Cross

'It was in Byelo-Russia,' Klinger said. 'Somewhere between Bobrujsk and Zlobin. We were wheeling south to advance on Kiev, and the Russkis were scattering like ants when you lift a stone. Then the partisans lobbed a couple of grenades into a personnel carrier as we passed under a bridge at the entrance to this village. The colonel halted the column, rounded up all the men and women he could find, and locked them in the village jail. It was more like a cage than a jail, mostly iron bars the way you see the sheriff's office in a Western. When we put the flame-thrower on them, they began leaping about and jumping up at the bars like a cage-full of monkeys! And of course the bars were pretty well red hot, so they would let go and drop into the flames again. But they kept on jumping, right to the end. I never saw anything like it,' Klinger said.

Chapter Ten

Webster shielded his eyes against the blazing sun. Under the folds of his burnouse, the heavy Colt special had worn a sore place on his hip and he shifted the belt supporting its holster for the hundredth time. Beneath his aching thighs, the dromedary lurched and swayed, picking its way over the shale slanting up to a massive sandstone bluff a thousand feet above them.

The caravan was a large one – a long line of camels, horses, men and women, some mounted and some on foot, strung out for almost a mile across the desolate plateau. It had been five hours since they struggled up the steep valley from the last mud-walled village – five hours of sweltering torment for Webster. The sun had risen giddily in the sky as the caravan climbed inexorably south through barren foothills pockmarked with patches of scrub, along a crest of rock and sand where nothing but thorn bushes broke the monotony of the scorched terrain, and now across this bleak upland slope beyond which, he dazedly hoped, their route would at last tilt downwards again.

The furnace heat was insufferable, shrivelling the skin, hammering in the veins. He eased the belt once more, scanning the plateau with red-rimmed eyes. Below and behind them, the dead land dropped away in parallel ridges of bracken-brown and ochre. Above, some geological upheaval had left a thin vein of richer rock between the weathered shale and the sandstone, and here a streak of dun-coloured vegetation daubed the foot of the bluff. So much, Webster thought sardonically, for the innocents who believed the Sahara was nothing but sand!

He shaded his eyes and stared ahead. A few hundred yards further on, the line of stunted bushes followed the strata as they dipped towards a fault breaching the cliff. The leaders of the caravan were now moving in the direction of this pass.

Between the towering walls of the cleft, the relief from the assault of the sun was immediate. It was still stiflingly hot in the shadowed gorge, but the contrast with the blast of direct sunlight was as refreshing as a shower. Webster moistened his lips with tepid water from a padded bottle slung over his shoulder. He could scarcely believe that it was less than forty-eight hours since he had been sipping iced bourbon with Céleste at a sidewalk café on the Place Bugeaud! Algiers, the *pension*, the small hotel off the esplanade, the girl herself – they were like dreams from another existence. In the interval he had been introduced to Mahmoud Hassan, had shot him a line emphasizing that his company wished to co-operate with the Arabs over any mineral concession that might be granted, and had then been passed from contact to contact in a series of improbable meetings arranged at coffee houses and bazaars all over the city. Finally, having dispensed most of the money that Hawkins had obtained from O'Kelly, he had been informed that he could be conveyed to Abd-el-Kerim's stronghold, but that it would be up to him to gain an audience with Kerim and the other chiefs with whom he wished to discuss the matter: the contacts could guarantee nothing. There were a number of stipulations attached to the offer. Webster was to stain his skin and adopt Arab dress; he was to tell nobody, but nobody, that he was going; and he was to understand that the agreement to take him to Kerim's base did not imply that he would or could be back in Algiers on any specific date.

He had accepted at once. He was quite happy to play it by ear once he arrived – it was the way he worked normally, in any case. And he doubted if he knew enough about the country – or about mining – to carry off a formal conference on the subject. A messenger had contacted him at the central station at dawn, and taken him to the assembly point of the caravan on the outskirts of the city.

It was a mixed caravan, Hassan had told him. There were ivory merchants and dealers in ostrich feathers on their way to the Congo basin, traders leading pack camels loaded with bales of merchandise destined for Bahr-el-Ghazal and the Central African Republic, tribesmen from Kerim's own territory, and the usual supernumeraries – individual travellers and nomads who were tagging on for the ride, as it were. For this was dangerous country: small, isolated groups could easily fall victim to a marauding guerilla band or even to over-zealous members of the PPA.

The largest single group was a collection of pilgrims on their way to an obscure Moslem shrine near Agadèz in the Baguezane Mountains, and it was as one of them that Webster was disguised. The yellow and black robes were distinctive and the pilgrims were under a vow of silence until they reached their goal – which would, as Hassan pointed out, effectively take care of Webster's relative lack of Arabic. His guides, nevertheless, were taking no chances: he had been allowed to keep his gun, but the ammunition had been removed. And there was a surly-looking Touareg outrider armed with a machine pistol immediately behind him as he rode. Apart from his man and Hassan, he had no idea how many other people in the caravan knew that there was an infidel amongst them.

What the hell, Webster thought more cheerfully – things were moving at last; he was on his way. They were due to arrive at Wadi Elmira – this was the name of Kerim's headquarters, he had been told – at noon the following day. And at least this ravine was a change from the gaunt perspectives of the Atlas across which they had so painfully been riding. After those open wastes, the rock walls of the defile seemed to amplify the incidental noises of the caravan: the beasts' stony footfalls, the creak and jingle of pack stays and harness, an occasional whinny from an outrider's horse, and the guttural murmurs of Arabic in front and behind. Above them all rose the singsong voice of Abdul Mohammed, the camel-master, as he discussed the route with Hassan at the head of the column.

When they rode out of the gorge into the full glare of the sun, Webster saw with relief that the trail led downwards across a stretch of country dotted with huge sandstone boulders. The oven heat of early afternoon was now tempered from time to time by a puff of hot, dry wind; the sun was beginning to sink. Two hours later, in a flat wilderness of thorny scrub punctuated by rocky outcrops, they stopped for the night.

The caravan boasted entertainers, and as the western sky faded through vermilion to pale green above the rim of the *wadi* where they were camped, plaintive quarter-tones of Arab strings and pipes rose into the rapidly cooling air. Sitting, like most of the silent pilgrims, in the outer ring of figures squatting around the fires, Webster dipped his fingers into the aromatic mess filling the bowl before him and watched acrobats and tumblers as he ate. As a member of the faithful, he had to be rigorously careful that nobody saw him drink from the flask of whisky hidden in his bedroll. Soon it was the turn of the girl to perform. And as he had feared – for the same thing had happened the previous night – she sought him out again, apparently executing the greater part of her act for his private benefit.

She was a belly-dancer. Not a very good one, possibly – but the brown body with its lean shivering breasts and eloquent hips spoke as clearly as if she had tossed a card with her telephone number on it into his lap. Her name was Yemanja. She was probably, Webster thought, of mixed Arab and Negro parentage. Certainly the name was of Yoruba origin, and while she had the nubile figure and high-bridged nose of most Arabic women, the full-lipped mouth and smouldering eyes were pure African. She was the property of Abdul Mohammed, a sullen and muscular giant from Tunisia whose glowering regard had already been drawn towards the Englishman far too often for his liking. 'All I need,' Webster thought grimly, 'is to get involved in a punch-up with a jealous squire!'

He kept his rakish, predatory face – stained brown now and ornamented with the drooping moustache he had adopted for the journey – bent low over his food as Yemanja stopped for the third time opposite him. The soft, fleshy abdomen heaved and rotated and jerked as the tempo of the music increased; the haze of shaven pubic hair above the low-slung skirt writhed darkly from side to side. And then, with a final provocative flash of her eyes, the girl was gone and the dance was over. Webster heaved a sigh of relief. Desperate as he was to avoid attention of any kind, he found the girl's nightly attempt to entice him a hazard he could do without – especially as (he was forced to admit) he found her deucedly attractive! Watching a group dance begin on the far side of the firelit circle, he determined to keep well clear of her for the rest of the journey: if he found himself in close proximity with half a chance of making it, he couldn't answer for the consequences . . .

Fighting to keep his mind on the group dancers, he watched for a while and then, as the music grew wilder and the fires burned low, he slipped unobtrusively away to erect his bivouac beside his tethered beast. The night was cold. They had come a long way down from the pass, but the *wadi* was still more than four thousand feet above sea level. Rolling himself into his striped blanket, Webster eased into the low tent and reached for the comforting flask. Ten yards away, the Touareg outrider sat cross-legged on the hard earth, his machine pistol cradled in his lap.

They were under way soon after dawn the following day. Three hours later, they breasted a rise and looked down on an ancient Berber fortress village nestling in a ravine whose sinuous course through the highlands was marked by a line of stunted trees. There was even a trickle of water sliding yellow over the flat stones on the river bed. The village was a compact mass of dun-coloured battlements, walls, domes and watchtowers surrounded by terraced slopes of gravel on which nothing grew. With the life-giving belt of vegetation immediately below, it looked more like a medieval castle than an open community, but as they rode slowly down towards the huge gateway with its fortified arch, Webster saw it open out visually until the course of the narrow streets could be charted by the bands of shadow gashing the age-old stone in the morning sun.

They passed beneath the arched gate. There were soldiers on guard inside and outside – at least a dozen that he could see. And whereas most of the outriders in the caravan were armed with obsolete rifles or carbines, these men carried Stens, FN machine pistols like that sported by Webster's personal guardian, or Parabellums looted from the German army. Kerim was certainly security-minded!

Once inside the walls, Webster saw a scene of surprising bustle and activity. Isolated in its barren environment, the village had from a distance appeared deserted. But the maze of courtyards and alleys was thronged with armed tribesmen. Berbers from the High Atlas mingled with desert nomads, mountain farmers, Touaregs in exotic robes – a dense crowd of figures in white and grey, accented here and there by individualists dressed in brilliant orange, azure, citron or acid green. In a small central square unexpectedly fringed with olive trees, men and women chattered, joked, exchanged news and gossip or bartered the goods they had brought into the village while they applauded Bedouin tumblers, watched a snake charmer or munched hardboiled eggs with *couscous* and mint tea. As the caravan wound its way through, Webster saw a Berber warrior dictating a letter to a scribe sitting in a doorway exactly as his ancestors must have done a thousand years before.

They halted in an open space before the mosque. The beasts were watered, fed, and tethered in rows beneath a line of date palms, and then most of the travellers vanished into the narrow streets of the town. Only the women, a few old men, and the pilgrims sitting quietly among their bedrolls were left in the dusty square.

Mahmoud Hassan was talking to Abdul Mohammed, the camel-master, and the girl Yemanja by the entrance to the mosque. Beyond them, one of the outriders was having his head shaved beneath the wicker canopy of an itinerant barber. Webster saw the belly-dancer looking his way and turned his back. A few minutes later, Hassan began moving among the pilgrims. When he got to Webster he said in a low voice: 'Be sure not to show that you are replying when I address you.'

Webster, impassive, inclined his head.

'Lodging has been found for you with some of the other pilgrims,' Hassan said. 'They continue their journey the day after tomorrow. You had best complete your business before then, while this disguise' – he touched Webster's djellabah – 'is still valid. As you have been told, we cannot ourselves arrange a meeting with the *pasha*, but for your information there is a *diffa*, a ceremonial banquet, to be given at his house tonight. Some of the more illustrious pilgrims have, as a matter of courtesy, been invited – although their vows of silence naturally preclude them taking part in the conversations.'

'I suppose there is no chance of you smuggling me in?' Webster murmured.

Hassan shook his head. 'Impossible, my friend. It would be more than my life is worth. Abd-el-Kerim is a very important *pasha*. I will do my best to help you later, but I can promise nothing. In any case it may cost a little more money.'

Webster had retained a thousand dollars of the sum he had received from O'Kelly. Surreptitiously, he passed over a packet of five hundred that he had already separated. The bills disappeared into the sleeves of Hassan's robe. 'In the meantime,' the contact man continued, 'there is nothing to stop you seeking an audience on your own. The *pasha's* chamberlain is sometimes amenable to reason, and of course he speaks French.'

'How do I get back to Algiers?' Webster asked. The question was academic, since he cherished a hope that he could liaise with Hawkins and the others on their way south, once the German base had been located. But it was one that would naturally be asked by a genuine mining man in his position.

'A small caravan will be leaving for Djelfa and the coast in three days' time,' Hassan replied. 'Doubtless some suitable way for you to join it can be found. Once on the coast, you can discard any disguise that has been provided and make your own way back to the capital.'

'What about the gorilla?'

'Gorilla?'

'The guard. The man who has been riding behind me with his gun trained on my back.'

'He has already been relieved of that duty. Once in Wadi Elmira, you are no longer his responsibility. But you must understand,' Hassan said deprecatingly, 'that we are obliged to take certain precautions on the way here. Many people would like to know the route to the *pasha's* house; some might even leave the caravan and head back towards Algiers once they knew where it was going. You could after all be an agent in the pay of the French government.'

'What makes you believe that I'm not?' Webster asked.

'Your behaviour here will supply the answer.' Hassan was enigmatic. 'Come now: I will show you to your lodgings.' He moved away towards the other pilgrims.

Webster followed the party and found that he had been allocated a tiny room at the top of a tall building near the market place. The room – it was little more than a cubicle – was furnished with cushions, an earthenware bowl and a stone ewer containing water. Through the window he could see past a warren of old houses to the colourful awnings of the bazaar. He was closing the door when he heard Hassan talking in French to a tall man in black, white and saffron robes on the other side of the landing. It was clear from the conversation that this was one of the important travellers who had been invited to the *diffa*, and Hassan was telling him how to get there. Webster listened for a moment and then shut his door. He was smiling.

The black, white and yellow djellabah and burnouse fitted him quite well. Their owner was lying trussed up and gagged in his room. He would not return to consciousness for several hours, although unfortunately he had turned around just before the butt of the Colt struck him and got a good look at his attacker's face. Whether his religious vows would permit him to voice a complaint was a question that Webster was content to leave to the future. As with the clandestine visit to Kerim's reception that he planned, he would deal with the problem when it arose. He had no idea what he hoped to gain by the imposture, but the distinctive garments would confer on him the right to silence – and he might hear something of value.

Like all Moslems, Abd-el-Kerim followed the holy Koran, which instructs the faithful to keep the façades of their dwellings simple, lest they excite the envy of the less fortunate. The outer wall of his hideout was therefore nothing more than a row of sandstone blocks pierced by a central gateway and a few arrowhead windows at the upper level. But inside, as Webster found out when a slave admitted him with a crowd of other guests, it was a palace.

They were led along a twisting, high-ceilinged corridor to a kind of cloister edged with delicate, highly ornamented Moorish arches on slender pillars. Beyond this was the courtyard where the *diffa* was to be held. The waning moon flooded the place with pale brilliance, silvering the tiles, striking jewelled lights from the mosaic floor, throwing into relief the orange trees and pomegranates beyond which they could hear the splashing of a fountain. Somewhere in the background there was the jangle of a stringed instrument and the strange, alien yodel called the *yo-yo* which Arab women chant on occasions of great importance.

Abd-el-Kerim was seated on a low divan covered in furs. He was a tall man, dressed in white robes and a white turban, sitting as straight as a ramrod despite his sixty years. Centuries of power were implicit in the arrogant curl of his lip, the droop of his eyelids, the flare of his nostrils. Rings flashed on his fingers, but otherwise there was no external sign of his wealth or his eminence. It was all, Webster thought irreverently, in his mind ... or the minds of the millions who owed him allegiance.

He felt a twinge of apprehension when he saw that the guests were being presented individually by Mahmoud Hassan, who had changed into ceremonial robes. But he managed to sidle up behind two more pilgrims so that the three of them were presented together, identified by their distinctive dress. Since they were unable to reply to any courtesies, Kerim contented himself with a few perfunctory words of welcome and then turned to greet more interesting guests. Webster pulled the hood of his burnouse as far over his face as he could, bowed low, and kept his head down. He had no idea if Hassan had recognized him; if he did, the contact man gave no sign.

There must have been forty or fifty diners, Webster estimated, plus of course the empty place at Kerim's left, which was solemnly served with every dish – the place traditionally left for the unexpected guest who must always, according to Arab custom, be fed if he should arrive. They sat on deep cushions and ate course after course of admirably cooked food with their fingers. Behind them, servants in turbans and fezzes waited around the edge of the courtyard for a sign from the *pasha* to serve more food – chickens grilled with olives, succulent roast lamb aromatic with spices, pitchers of milk flavoured with rose petals, tiny birds on beds of rice, skewered *kebabs*, orange juice tasting of cinnamon. It was all exotic, unexpected and delicious ... but good grief (Webster thought to himself with an inward groan), what wouldn't he do for a glass of burgundy or claret! Kerim, a strict Moslem, would naturally serve nothing alcoholic. The hip flask secreted beneath the important pilgrim's robes had never seemed so far away!

If there was no stimulation internally, there was, however, plenty outside. Kerim had a great deal to say, in French as well as Arabic, and most of it was interesting. He spoke at length on the coming fight for independence and the problems it would bring with the French *colons*, he was knowledgeable and even amusing about local politics, contemptuous and amusing about the hotbeds of international intrigue in Casablanca, Marrakesh and Algiers. But it was when he came to discuss the war and its conduct that Webster was really impressed. Kerim knew the strengths and the weaknesses of the German war machine, fighting outwards from a blockaded centre; he had a shrewd and informed knowledge of the Allies' sea power, their industrial capacity, and the strategic geographical positions they held in relation to the coming battles; he predicted defeat with honour for Rommel – and a North African invasion which would lead to that defeat. He spoke not just as a mountain tribesman brought up on guerilla warfare or a nationalist fanatic, but as a world strategist, a soldier, and a statesman entirely familiar with the international scene. For the first time, Webster suffered a twinge of uneasiness. If he did manage to wangle an interview, would he, as a supposed mining expert, be able to keep his end up against such a keen intelligence?

At first the discourse was in the nature of a monologue. The guests contributed little, apart from an occasional murmur of agreement, to interrupt the flow of their host's opinions. But as the *diffa* progressed, he drew them more and more into the orbit of the conversation, until finally it reached the stage of a full-scale debate. It was while this centred on Rommel that Webster had his piece of luck – not before time, he thought wryly!

Kerim's Arabic singsong ceased for a moment and he addressed a few words in German to a man opposite Webster and a little nearer the head of the table. 'Unless,' he said, 'you are able to perfect your Project Thunderbird and put it into production in the immediate future, I fear its undoubted merits will be unable to save General Rommel the attack from the rear that he envisages.'

The man he was speaking to was about forty years old. He

was bronzed and tough and lined – and, like Alastair Mackenzie's, the wrinkles seaming his face showed white against the tanned skin. Although he was wearing Arab dress, his features were unmistakably European. He fingered a pair of gold-rimmed spectacles as he replied. 'There have admittedly been certain development difficulties,' he said in German, 'but they are inseparable from the nature of the project. It is with the accuracy rather than the efficacy of the weapon that we are now concerned. However, the scientists believe they have isolated the faults. A few more days' testing, and Flakregiment XII will be able to ship a prototype and blueprints back to the Reich.'

'You will forgive me, Colonel, but I seem to have heard a similar prophecy rather more than a month ago,' Kerim smiled.

Webster's pulse was racing. Project Thunderbird again! Flakregiment XII! This was the break he was looking for! Evidently Kerim and the Nazi had lapsed into German in the belief that none of the Berbers and Touaregs present would understand. But his own knowledge of the language was good, even though he was not a fluent speaker. Bending his head over his food, he strained to catch the Teutonic gutturals.

'If you do not believe me,' the colonel was saying, 'why do you not visit the range yourself? As you know, the oasis is less than forty kilometres from El Glouai, just to the east of the ridge. The troops patrolling the approaches – troops which you yourself so kindly supply – are due to be relieved in three days. Ride up with the fresh contingent, and you will see.'

'Perhaps.' Kerim was noncommittal. 'If Allah wills it. We shall see. And now you must excuse me: I must attend to my guests.' He turned courteously to the chieftain on his right and resumed his Arabic.

Webster could scarcely believe his good fortune. It wasn't the kind of pinpoint location given by map co-ordinates, but it was far more precise than anything he had learned so far. It was precise enough to communicate to Hawkins and his men as a target to aim for; it was precise enough to give Fortune as a centre for his aerial reconnaissance. Forty kilometres, after all, was scarcely more than twenty miles: from the air, they couldn't miss it! With luck, as he had hoped, he wouldn't have to make his way back to Algiers: Hawkins and the others could start right away and pick him up in the desert.

And, for the record, it was good to have confirmation that there *was* a German base in the desert, that they *were* developing a secret weapon and that the oasis *was* guarded by Kerim's men. It was nice to know that the whole show wasn't a wild goose chase!

Webster waited with mounting impatience for the *diffa* to end. There was music and dancing after the banquet. But at last the guests filed past their host, bowed, and went out into the night. Relieved to see that Mahmoud Hassan was no longer beside Kerim, Webster followed the example of the other pilgrims and then hurried back to his lodgings. The moon had long since disappeared behind the roofs of the palace, leaving a blue-black sky studded with an incredible brilliance of stars, but naphtha flares burned at street corners and flooded the market with garish yellow light and there were still townsfolk abroad in the narrow lanes radiating out from the centre. Once more Webster was relieved, for what he had to do now could not be done in the privacy of his room, and a single stranger in deserted streets would have drawn too much attention from the armed guards patrolling the walls.

The radio was concealed in his bedroll. It was neat and light and compact, but from this distance he would need extra power. He permitted himself a quick gulp from the flask, took a pencil flashlight and clipped it to the radio, hid both beneath his robes and left the room. At the stairhead he paused by the door of the man whose clothes he was wearing. Should he go in and check? No – the fellow should still be out for the count. In any case, there wasn't time if he was to call up O'Kelly; they had arranged that the old man would listen in for an hour every night and there wasn't too much time left. There was no sound from the far side of the door, no muffled appeals for help or drumming of bound heels on the floor. Someone was snoring loudly somewhere below. Webster stole out into the street.

It took him nearly twenty minutes to find what he was looking for. An ancient Renault truck fitted with half-tracks on the rear wheels stood by a clump of orange trees in a deserted *place* on the far side of the mosque. He crawled underneath and took out the flashlight.

The battery was housed on the footboard beside the driver's cab. Webster attached two lengths of wire to the terminals with bulldog clips and plugged the other ends into the radio. Then, placing his lips against the grille piercing one side of the bakelite box, he thumbed a button on top of the instrument. A faint, barely discernible whine quivered on the cool air. He turned a milled wheel set flush with the back of the box and the noise increased. He spun the wheel the other way. The whine faded, died away momentarily, swelled again. Patiently, he experimented until he had located the null point, the setting where the noise was tuned right out. As soon as he found it, he spoke very softly into the grille.

'ILW calling the Captain,' he breathed. 'ILW calling the Captain ... If you receive me do not, repeat do *not*, answer. Acknowledge with the signal we agreed.'

He paused. The radio was silent for a moment, and then it emitted three very faint pips in rapid succession. Webster spoke again. 'Good-oh!' he said. 'Listen, sir – I have news. The place we want is somewhere within forty kilometres of an oasis called El Glouai ... Have you got that: El Glouai? ... Take a circle eighty, eight zero, kilometres in diameter, with El Glouai as its centre. It's somewhere in there, just to the east of a ridge. There may be several ridges; if there are, it's east of one of them. Are you receiving me?'

The receiver emitted a single, prolonged bleep.

'Good show! As we thought, the base is an oasis too. Don't know the name. The approaches are guarded by troops provided by K. Don't know how many. Don't know the size of the garrison or its armaments. Suggest in any case that we now know enough for CGF to take to the air and pinpoint it. Once he's found El Glouai, it should be easy enough. At the same time, suggest that H. and the others set out at dawn tomorrow in the half-track with orders to head for El Glouai. Give them as much fire-power as you can.'

Webster paused. Hundreds of miles away, across the barren wastes he had traversed, he knew that Seamus O'Kelly would be covering pages of his notebook with words and figures in his neat, precise handwriting. 'I am at a Berber village called Wadi Elmira,' he resumed. 'It's in the southern Atlas. If I can find out which way El Glouai lies from here, I'll cut across and intersect the half-track's route, but I'll have to call you again to let you know where he can expect me. Is that clear, sir? I'll try to call you up again at the same time tomorrow, right?'

Again the single, sustained bleep.

'Wizard!' Webster murmured. 'Don't call us, and so forth. Over and out.'

He dismantled the leads and wrapped them around the radio. He had just scrambled to his feet with the incriminating box still in his hands when an armed patrol rounded the corner and marched into the *place*. Webster was in a quandary. It was late; he might be stopped; he might be searched. At this stage, anything was better than a guard-house interrogation. He would have to risk losing the precious transmitter, bet it against his own freedom of movement. Reaching swiftly up into the shadows, he thrust it hastily into the leaf-covered fork of an orange tree.

The tall, lean figure drifted towards the patrol out of the dark. The leader called his men to a halt. He stepped forward, his carbine at the ready. In the dim light flickering out from a flare at the corner of the *place*, Webster joined his hands as if in prayer, raised a finger and laid it across his lips, and approached the patrol. The guard looked at the black, white and saffron robes, grunted something in Arabic, and drew aside.

Webster glided past. Ten minutes later he was climbing the stone staircase to his room. He opened the door, fumbling in the blackness for the primitive oil lamp. He struck a match and held it to the wick. As the clear light dissolved the dark, he saw four tribesmen with machine pistols standing two on either side of the door. The German who had been at the *diffa* was in the centre of the room.

'Major Ian Lindsay Webster of the Combined Operations Security Executive, I believe?' he said in English. 'I am afraid I must ask you to come with us.'

The merchantman was down by the head, wallowing deep in the water and listing so far to port that the guard rails of her well-deck were submerged and waves broke across her fo'castle. The bridge and wheelhouse had disappeared in a tangle of buckled plates and twisted steel; behind them a huge hole had been smashed in the upperworks through whose jagged edges the rim of the sun could be seen hoisting itself above the horizon. Continents of cloud revealed in the fiery light of dawn now dimmed and vanished as the direct rays of the sun flooded across the sea. The red light drained through bronze and silver to a metallic blue against the glare of which only a towering column of smoke rising from the torpedoed oil tanker remained sharp and distinct. 'It reads very poetically, sir,' a petty officer said to the American War Correspondent. 'But what about the poor sods in the water who lost their eyelids in the blast?'

Chapter Eleven

'I don't get it,' Joe Constantine said angrily. 'I just do not get it. You told me yesterday that the fuel allocation had been approved, even if it was only for 750 miles. I was definitely given to understand that this plane was available.'

'Dash it all, you even took us to *see* the plane,' Fortune put in.

'Specifically, I was told it was available as of today. I handed over money. Now you come up with some shit about unforeseen problems. What the hell goes on?' Constantine demanded.

The French official spread his pudgy hands. 'You must understand, Monsieur,' he said evasively, 'that we are not entirely – how do you say? – the free agents in these matters. Technically, there is Vichy to satisfy ... and Vichy in its turn is answerable to the German or Italian Armistice Commissions. I can do no more than my best.'

'Fuck Vichy!'

'If you were to come back, perhaps in a week's time ... ?'

'Fuck the Germans and the Italians too!' Constantine

stormed. 'Give me a straight answer, for Chrissake! Do I get the goddam plane or don't I?'

The hands spread wider. 'Alas, Monsieur, for the moment ...'

'It's nothing to do with the war, sure,' Fortune said. 'We are businessmen, for God's sake. We came to you with a business offer. You accepted the offer. I already cabled home saying we'd have the locations fixed in three days.'

'Mr Grossbreitner will do his fuckin' nut!' Constantine said. 'Mr Grossbreitner is—'

'Monsieur Grossbreitner,' the official interrupted suavely, 'may be, as you frequently point out, the greatest. But I fear that his weight will not balance that of Monsieur Laval, Marshal Pétain and Herr von Schirach.'

'Fuck them all! And fuck you too!' Constantine shouted. 'We'll see about that, mister!' He picked up his briefcase and led the others from the office.

'There's a puppet government and someone's pulling strings,' Fortune said later to Captain O'Kelly. 'If you ask me, sir, the string-pullers are out to stop us overflying a sensitive area.'

'Smell a rat, do you? Don't think it's just the usual administrative cock-up?'

'No, sir. I do smell a rat – a rat called Fritz.'

'Very well. If we're going out to bat on that kind of wicket, it's up to us to send down a few bouncers,' O'Kelly said with a fine disregard for the mixed metaphor. 'The old lion can still pull a few strings, you know. I'll have a word with Robert Murphy right away. If a film company doesn't cut any ice with these beggars, perhaps the combined weight of President Roosevelt and the American Secretary of State – plus a gentle hint threatening a cut in lease-lend supplies – will be enough to counterbalance the gentry they threw at you!'

The old man wasn't boasting. He spoke to the head of the British Mission and then spent three hours at the American consular offices – three hours in which the teleprinter operators and coding clerks, the vice-consul on duty and the cypher office worked harder than they ever had done before. Later that evening, a cigar glowing and fading like a blast furnace as he sucked fiercely at the soggy end, he went back to the building to read over the replies that had come in from London and Washington. He went to a villa on the outskirts of the city to see Robert Murphy's secretary, his briefcase bulging with the teletyped sheets. The secretary drove to the Ministry of the Interior. Lines from the telephone switchboard at the Ministry to administrative offices in Vichy were unusually busy that night, and there were lights burning in the second floor windows of the Hôtel de Ville until the early hours. The next morning, Constantine was summoned to the building and told that the aircraft he had been shown would be made available to him the following day.

He returned to the private field with Mullen and Fortune to make arrangements. Later, apparently by chance, he ran into O'Kelly in the baccarat room at the Aletti. 'Well, blow me down,' the Captain breezed, 'if it isn't Mr Superlative himself! What can I order you, my boy?'

They talked for a little about the Canadian's imaginary film. Constantine was vociferously excited because he had permission to hire a plane in order to look for locations. The name of Grossbreitner loomed large in the conversation. Then they ordered another drink and carried their glasses out on to the terrace, where Fortune joined them soon afterwards. 'All right,' O'Kelly said in a low voice, 'Now here's what you have to do. I heard from Webster last night. He's identified the range as somewhere within a forty-kilometre radius of an oasis in the southern Atlas. It's called El Glouai.'

'Bully for the old war horse!' Fortune crowed. 'I always said there were brains behind that tango-instructor's moustache!'

O'Kelly glared at him for a moment and then went on: 'I'll pass you the full text of the message in a matchbox before I leave. Did you check on the fuel allocation when you went to the aerodrome?'

Constantine nodded. 'It's still 750 miles,' he said glumly.

'Can't be helped.' O'Kelly looked out over the esplanade. Beyond the loop of lights garlanding the waterfront, the sea was like a sheet of black glass. In the far distance, lightning flickered on a cloudbank above the horizon. Faintly, they heard the thunder rumble – or it might have been a salvo from warships hull-down over the darkened ocean. 'You've got to play the balls the way they're bowled,' the old man said. 'So you do what we have already discussed more than once. You forget about any return trip: you fly straight to El Glouai and locate the base. I looked it up on the map at the consulate; you should just about be able to make it on that ration. As soon as you've taken your readings and fixed the position, you turn back and ditch the plane when she runs out of juice, right?'

Constantine and Fortune nodded again. In the mild, humid air, the smoke from O'Kelly's cigar rose straight as a die from the glowing tip.

'As soon as you have a fix on your own position – the place where you've been obliged to make your forced landing – you radio that, plus the range location, to Webster. He'll be cutting across to meet Hawkins and the others from a place called Wadi Elmira. All you have to do then is sit tight and wait for them to collect you.' The smoke spilled wildly as the cigar-end gestured in the dark. 'After that – once you chaps are teamed up together – it's up to Webster. You follow his lead and tear the bally range apart.'

Constantine fished a packet of Lucky Strike from his pocket and stuck a cigarette between his lips. 'When do Hawkins, Chilton and Zygmund take off, sir?'

'Don't call me sir!' O'Kelly hissed. 'At least not here. They leave at dawn. About time too, because it seems the town is getting too hot, so to speak, to hold them.' He handed a matchbox to the younger man. Constantine lit his cigarette and stuffed the box absentmindedly into his pocket. 'Whoever it was that tried to put a spoke in your wheel over the plane,' O'Kelly went on, 'the odds are it was the same lot that accounted for Mackenzie and the American – to say nothing of Webster and the Arabs. Then, because they'd obviously seen Hawkins and the others with Webster at some point, they chucked a bomb at them too. Friendly fellows, what?'

'You figure they know why Major Webster and his team are here then?'

O'Kelly shook his head. 'Not a chance. No – my guess is, they knew Weiss and Mackenzie worked underground. They killed them *to stop them* learning about the base. Because Webster was seen with Weiss quite a bit, they tagged him as some sort of spy – any sort of spy – as well. So they tried for him too. And the same thing goes for Hawkins.'

'But why,' Fortune asked, 'should they heave a spanner

into the works over our plane? Surely they haven't made the connection between us and your man?'

'Absolutely not. It's another case of just-in-case. In case you *might* see something from the aircraft that they wanted to be covered up. And you will, my boy – you will!' O'Kelly chuckled and pitched the end of his cigar over the balcony.

'So who's behind all this action?' Constantine said. 'Krauts or collabos?'

'Both, perhaps. Someone with pull in the administration. But that doesn't mean that they know why we are here – or that they connect you chaps with the miners. They're just covering all the angles, as you people say.'

'Nazi efficiency, O wise one,' Fortune said. 'What yours truly would like to know is: if they're so jolly efficient at eliminating all the evidence, why on earth didn't they have another go at Webster after they'd messed up the first? Or the goodly sarge, for that matter, after he'd dodged the infernal machine?'

'I'd like to know the answer to that one myself,' O'Kelly said soberly.

He went back inside and lost a hundred dollars at the roulette table. Nobody noticed him leave: two Arabs were wagering the whole of the next year's date crop against the turn of the wheel, and the excitement was infectious. As they had arranged, so that none of them should be seen together for too long, he communicated the final part of the briefing to Mullen on his way back to his hotel.

They met as casual acquaintances in the street, and the Ulsterman fell into step with O'Kelly as he strolled towards the Mirarmar. He listened carefully as the naval captain filled him in on the remaining details of the operation, and then, as they stood apparently chatting outside the hotel, he said: 'One more question. We're supposed to be a film crew looking for locations. We fly out, we look at the desert, we fly back. Or that's what they think. So we don't have any guns or anything like that, isn't that right?'

'Right.'

'Hawkins and his friends is miners. Once again, no arms. So how do we attack this desert base at all? How do we get in there and blow the place up, tell me that?'

O'Kelly rarely laughed. He did so now. He looked swiftly

up and down the deserted pavement, and turned around to check that there was nobody on the hotel steps behind them. 'Obviously you don't know this Webster fellow,' he said in a low voice. 'For a start, Hawkins and his crew may be miners, but they will be travelling in a truck. They will be allowed hand guns and rifles to protect themselves against bands of guerillas. Secondly, as miners, prospectors, geologists, and what-not, they'll naturally have their equipment. Besides the drills and bores and suchlike, that will include primacord, detonators, firing pins, fuses, and a limited number of explosive sticks. After all, they have to investigate the rocks and check their findings, don't they?'

'Yes, but . . .'

'As for the rest,' the old man went on, 'that Nazi base is a firing range, isn't it? They're testing these blasted machines packed with some kind of explosive, aren't they? The oasis will be full of the stuff! It's just a question, as you might say, of turning the bally gun against the chap who's holding it. Once you're inside, that is.'

'Oh, surely,' Mullen said slowly. '*Once* we're inside . . .'

'You leave that to Webster,' O'Kelly said. 'All you fellows have to do is pinpoint that oasis, ditch the plane, and call him up on the radio.'

There were just two factors which wrecked this plan. One, Webster's radio was hidden in an orange tree in Wadi Elmira while he himself was a prisoner in Kerim's stronghold; two, when it came to the take-off, Fortune, Mullen and Constantine were not allowed to fly the hired plane on their own. It had to be piloted by a Frenchman, with a French navigator, to ensure that the supposed film crew did not stray from the flight path permitted them by the authorities.

The two maquisards sat astride the lowest branches of a big chestnut growing beside the road. The girl wedged herself into a fork a little higher up. There were four Germans in the patrol: two motorcycle combinations, each with a machine-gunner in the sidecar. One of the grenades missed and bounced off the road to explode in the ditch. The other fell straight into the second sidecar as it passed beneath the tree. There was no need to bother about those two Germans but the maquisards had to waste five shots finishing off the pair in the leading combination. 'Won't they kill more hostages now?' the girl asked. 'They already shot ten and bulldozed the church and the town hall.' One of the Resistance men said they probably would. 'They do it to show that ambushes don't pay off,' he said. 'We do it to show that it's useless shooting hostages.' The girl laughed. 'Mine fell right into the bastard's lap!' she said. 'Wasn't that a fine shot?'

Chapter Twelve

Webster was bewildered as well as angry. Nothing on this show made sense; none of it had ever made any sense. He was like a man in a dark room, knowing that somewhere in the blackness was a lamp, and somewhere else there was a box of matches, but ignorant of the position of either. Very well – now he knew which corner of the room the lamp was in, so to speak. But he still hadn't touched it, nor had he found the blasted matchbox. He didn't even know if he would be able to strike a match when he did find it, and if he did (he reflected ruefully, remembering the circumstances of his capture), there would probably be a squad of armed men waiting for him, blocking his exit from the room!

Webster was a man of action. This hole-and-corner under-cover lark made him nervous. The base was located now – but until that silly young ass Fortune reported, he knew nothing of its size, the disposition of its defences, the number of guards around it, what arms they had, or how the hell he was to overcome them and destroy the place. Could he in any case rely on Fortune to find out those things? Lang had said he was a good man – had got quite shirty in fact when Webster had suggested the contrary – but he'd reserve judgement on that until he'd seen the proof.

Aside from these imponderables, there were a number of specific questions he would like to see answered. Were Weiss and Mackenzie killed because of their association with him, or was the attempt on his life made because of his association with them? How had the killers known that Weiss's body was to be left on the quay, and why, if they did know this, had they left Mackenzie's beside it? Why had they made no further attempt on his own life? Above all, *how in God's name had a German in this remote village known that he was a major in O'Kelly's 'Cosy Corner' show*?

For the hundredth time he cursed his own carelessness. He should have checked that the bloody pilgrim was still out for the count before he left to call the old man up on the radio. The fellow must have freed himself and given the alarm while he was away. That would account for his capture all right. Hassan could have told them his name. Kerim would reasonably enough have wanted to punish an impostor who had tricked his way into the *diffa*. But the CO(S)E Special Services bit ... He shook his head in bafflement. How could they *possibly* have known?

From that unanswerable problem, more urgent questions arose. He had been thinking as if he were still a free agent, planning the assault on the Nazi base. But he wasn't: he was a prisoner in the desert chieftain's stronghold. He was locked in a room on the upper floor, with two huge Nubian guards armed with Stens on the far side of the door. The room was bare, with a single window embrasure above the courtyard where they had dined. Below the window was a third Nubian.

He had been brought here from the lodgings where he was captured. That had been in the early hours of the morning. It was now noon of the following day. The German had said nothing on the way to Kerim's palace. Webster had been brought before no angry chief. Hassan had not appeared. Nobody had interrogated him. Why not?

It all boiled down, Webster thought, pacing the empty room, to a single key question: *if they knew that he wasn't a mining engineer but a fighting man, did they know why he was here?*

If they did, why hadn't they simply killed him? If they didn't, why didn't somebody interrogate him in an attempt to find out why the hell he *was* here? Surely they would want to know why a British officer would bribe his way into a rebel Arab headquarters in Algeria! Unless, of course, Mahmoud Hassan's part in the deception was still a secret. Could the wily contact man have covered up his own involvement – and if so, would he be amenable to a further bribe? They had taken Webster's unloaded gun, but the remaining five hundred dollars was still in a pocket of his stolen robes.

This didn't seem likely. If Hassan hadn't blown the gaff in some way, how had they known his name? Webster stopped his pacing in mid-stride, struck by a sudden thought. Maybe Kerim was waiting for someone else to arrive, some senior colleague of the German's, perhaps, before he was questioned. Yes, that made sense. In which case ... His thoughts were interrupted again. A confused and angry shouting rose from the courtyard below. He went to the window and peered out.

Hassan stood by the Moorish colonnade, gesticulating. In front of him, two guards with slung carbines were attempting to restrain a choleric man in plain white robes who was demanding compensation, retribution, punishment for the guilty ... Webster's Arabic was only good enough for him to get the general drift. He understood even more when, with a start, he recognized the furious man: it was the pilgrim he had knocked out – the owner of the robes he was still wearing.

Clearly the aggrieved traveller had only just been released. Webster sank to the floor and sat with his back against the wall, shattered by the implications of the discovery. He had naturally assumed that his capture was the result of a scene such as he had just witnessed, and that it had taken place the previous night. But if – as was evidently the case – it was *not* because the wretched man had raised the alarm while he was contacting O'Kelly, there was only one other possible explanation: *They had known he was coming and they had been waiting for him.*

The idea, alarming as it was, clarified the issue. Hassan and the chain of contacts who had arranged for him to join the caravan could have given him away. But why would they bother, when they could simply have pocketed the bribes and failed to deliver? And how could they have had any information on his military connections?

Apart from them, there was only one person in Algeria who knew that he was planning a clandestine visit to Wadi Elmira and who could have tipped Abd-el-Kerim off. Céleste Harari.

Christ! Of course! Webster rose to his feet and started excitedly pacing again. If the girl had in fact been a collaborator ... It was the only answer that made sense. She would have known that he was allied with Hawkins and the others because she lived in the same *pension*. She could have been watching them when they took Weiss's body to the quay, and tipped of Mackenzie's killers that it was there. She might even have arranged for some evidence to be planted that would frame them for both murders.

That could be why they hadn't tried a second bomb and why no further attempt had been made on his own life – it was neater to let the French police deal with Hawkins while Webster himself walked into a trap where they could question him undisturbed. The only detail that had been missed was the fact that he'd bluffed his way into the *diffa*. That had simply delayed his capture by a few hours – but in that time he had got through to O'Kelly and hidden the radio, thank God! He hoped to hell that Hawkins and the others had taken off before they were arrested. At least there was a chance that they could liaise with Fortune and wipe out the base on their own.

Webster's mind was racing. All his reasoning derived from the fact that Céleste Harari happened to be living in the *pension* he had chosen for himself and his men. *Happened* to be living there ... ? Wasn't that a bit of a stretch, even for the long arm of coincidence?

As clearly as an old dance tune which refused to be banished from the memory, he heard the words: *I'll be generous too. I'm going to give you the address of a girlfriend of mine ... we were at finishing school together in Lausanne*. Liz Macnamara had suggested that he should get in touch with Céleste.

Macnamara was an Irish name. There were still plenty of Irish nationalists who were resolutely anti-British. Lausanne was in Switzerland, where there was a large German-speaking population. Céleste was a prostitute. Her father, a Moroccan who could easily have been anti-French and certainly anticolonial, had been killed at Mers-el-Kebir – reason enough for any girl to feel antipathetic towards the Allies. If she was a collaborator, was it within the realms of probability – or even possibility – that her Irish friend was an enemy agent?

Forcing himself to remain calm, Webster went over the details of his relationship with Liz step by step. He'd run into her outside the White House, soon after he left O'Kelly's headquarters for the first time. She'd spilled the contents of her handbag, paying off a taxi, *and although she didn't live in the block and said she was visiting a friend, she had in fact cheerfully gone off with him – indeed spent the whole night with him – without once thinking of the 'friend', or phoning to explain why she had never turned up.*

It looked, then, as though the friend was non-existent and that oh-so-casual meeting could have been a plant. She was outside the White House with the sole purpose of engineering a meeting with Webster. So what about the rest of the evening? With a quickening pulse, he recalled the air-raid, the near-miss and the descent into the flat below hers. He saw again, as though each had been spotlit separately, a cupboard full of recording equipment, a powerful ham radio, a half-full whisky bottle and a used glass in a flat that was otherwise neat and tidy as an Ideal Homes exhibition display. *No wonder there were no clothes and no food in the apartment – if it was used only by people who recorded the indiscretions of the men that Liz Macnamara took home to bed in the flat above* ... and then transmitted them to Germany? To enemy agents in Eire?

Was it possible that the place had been wired up in that way? Remembering how Liz had plied him with questions as soon as she knew he was posted, how impatient she had become when he started speculating about the used whisky tumbler, how suddenly she had wanted him to come to bed once he had discovered the radio, Webster thought that it was.

Liz Macnamara worked in War Office records. She could have found out that her mysterious 'oil man from Texas' was in reality a major in a Special Services unit. Dammit, he had *told* her himself that he was going to Algiers! She wouldn't have known why, but she could have alerted Céleste to look out for him. So that extraordinary coincidence of her staying in the same *pension* wasn't so extraordinary after all – she had deliberately staked herself out there and made his acquaintance. Just the way Liz had done. Then she had encouraged him to separate from his companions by arranging the caravan trip with Hassan. And he had walked into it with his eyes wide open. All along the line.

Webster pounded his forehead with a clenched fist in a fury of self-disgust. God, what a clot he had been! What a brass-bound, nickel-plated, hundred per cent cock-up he'd made of the mission! He'd fallen for the oldest trick in the business: they'd caught him – twice! – with what the professionals called a honey trap.

Just a minute, though ... He sat up suddenly. All this explained why he was here, how they had known his name and rank and so forth. But it didn't explain how they had known that he would be available to fall *into* the trap. Not the first one, anyway.

How the fuck had they known that he would be walking down Albany Street at that time on that particular day, so that Liz could pull off her spilled handbag stunt as he passed her cab by the White House? And how had they known he was the kind of character who couldn't resist a bit of skirt on any day?

Again, there could be only one answer. They knew that he had been summoned to the CO(S)E headquarters, and when; and they had had access to his personal dossier.

This meant – there was no getting away from it – that there must be a third crooked link in the chain, and there was only one place it could be. The leak must have come from somebody in Colonel Chard's office.

Webster put the thought from his mind. He would communicate his suspicions to O'Kelly if he ever got out of the scrape he was in. For the moment he preferred to concentrate on the only three rays of hope left to him. One was that they hadn't made the connection – his cover and Hawkins's might be blown, but they still didn't know about Fortune's unit. The second was that he had been able to report the rough location of the base to the old man. And the third was that, apparently, they still didn't know for sure whether or not he even knew about the base.

Kerim would be holding him, for sure, so that some Nazi security man – somebody more important than the officer who had captured him – could come to Wadi Elmira to find out exactly what he did know. The deduction was proved correct almost as soon as he made it. There was a rattle of heavy bolts and the door of his prison swung open. Dwarfed by the two Nubians, a short man in a tan suit and dark glasses stood looking into the room.

'My name is Benckendorff,' he said in English. 'There are a few questions I wish to ask you.'

* * * *

Captain O'Kelly shook his head. 'There's absolutely nothing we can do about it,' he said for the third time. 'The referee's blown his whistle and you have to stick by the decision – that's all there is to it.'

'But Captain, sir,' Joe Constantine protested, 'we *must* be on that plane on our own. I mean, like it stands to reason. With a couple of frogs at the goddam controls, how can we insist on flyin' the ship to this El Glouai dump if they tell us it's off the route?'

'My dear fellow, that's up to you,' O'Kelly said. 'You chaps are supposed to be trained in initiative. Use it.'

'That's all very well, sir and master,' Fortune said, 'but they'll probably search us for arms before we board the kite: they did the last time we went out to the airfield to inspect her. It's a pretty tall order, asking us to hijack the bally plane without a spot of the old bang-bang.'

'I'm thinking maybe we'll have to do them,' Mullen said. 'Come up behind them once we're in the air, and—' He drew his finger across his throat.

'You're out of your mind,' Constantine said. 'Shit – it's not as though they was krauts. These are neutrals, right? Nobody's supposed to know what we're at, right? So if we knock 'em off, what do we do with the bodies? How do we explain to the authorities? It'd be a sure-fire tip-off that we wasn't what we said, wouldn't it? It'd bring us just the attention we was supposed to avoid. Isn't that right, sir?'

'Certainly.'

'So I can't for the life of me see what stops you pulling a few more strings and *make* 'em let us fly that ship on our own,' the Canadian complained. 'After all, you pulled strings to *get* us the sonofabitch. Why couldn't you—?'

'Because it wouldn't *look* right! man,' O'Kelly cut in roughly. 'When are you people going to use your heads? You're supposed to be an advance production unit from a film company on the look-out for specialized locations. It's reasonable to kick up hell if they take away the plane they promised you; it's *not* reasonable to insist on flying it yourselves. If you were a genuine film unit, what difference would it make? You'd be grateful, if anything. It would mean you had two extra pairs of eyes to scan the terrain. In the same way, it's reasonable for them to put two men aboard: it's their country and their plane; they make the rules. A genuine crew would follow them, as long as it didn't mess up their work. And it wouldn't you know – it wouldn't.'

Fortune sighed. 'Point conceded. I guess you're right, sir.'

'All the same—' Constantine began.

'I don't want to hear any more,' O'Kelly snapped. 'If I was to do what you ask, it would be just as much of a give-away that there was something bogus about you as it would if you disposed of the chaps in the way Mullen suggested. Can't you see that?'

'Yeah, but—'

'That's enough. Subject closed. Now you get on that damned plane and work out how to deal with the frogs yourselves. Is that clear?'

In his turn, Constantine sighed. 'Yessir, Captain,' he said resignedly.

*   *   *   *

Webster coughed his way back to consciousness through swirling red mists of pain. It was the third time he had blacked out since they brought him down to the cellar. Benckendorff, the little German in dark glasses, had said his piece first. 'I have been following your movements, Major, with a great deal of interest since the day you landed in Algiers,' he sneered. His voice was dry and rather high-pitched, his English meticulous and unemphatic. 'It was an odd route for a miner to take from London: a so-called liberty ship sailing direct from Galveston.'

'A sea voyage is good for everybody once in a while,' Webster said.

'Doubtless. But a puzzling waste of time for a Special Services officer on assignment, one would think. I myself took a simpler route once I knew where you were coming. There is a reliable submarine service operating from southern Ireland. However, we will let the unconventional method of transport pass. I imagine they put you aboard from a launch or a helicopter.'

Webster said nothing.

Benckendorff continued: 'It was clear from your clumsy efforts to obtain information in Algiers that you wished to visit our friend Kerim. I was anxious to know why, and so, with the help of a few friends, I was able to arrange this for you. Yet in fact, although you tricked your way into Kerim's house, you made no attempt to speak to him. I wonder why that was? And I wonder why you are here with three ruffianly companions, pretending to be mining engineers? Also, I wonder what you have been instructed to do, and precisely why immediately on arrival you sought the company of known saboteurs and spies? It doesn't seem a very friendly way to behave in a neutral country.'

Webster had his answers worked out. It was useless to deny his rank and his trade, futile to persist with the prospecting cover when they knew so much already. The golden rule in such a situation was to tell as much of the truth as you dared ... without blowing the operation. So he told Benckendorff the whole story, exactly the way it had happened, except that he altered the objective. They had been sent, he said, to penetrate the interior and sound out rebel Arab opinion in relation to a possible Allied landing on the Algerian coast. He was giving nothing away: the Germans had already heard plenty of rumours about an invasion, and so far as the London end was concerned, Benckendorff's words simply confirmed the suspicions that had formed in his own mind. Clearly, there *was* a leak – and Liz Macnamara must be a part of it.

For the moment, the important thing was not to let on that he understood German – and thus could have overheard Kerim's remarks at the *diffa*. If he could keep up this pretence, Benckendorff might still believe he knew nothing of the experimental range.

'Let me make myself quite clear,' the Nazi said when he had finished talking. 'I have the means to hurt you. Badly. It does not, after all, require sophisticated equipment.' He flexed

'Ibrahim,' Benckendorff said, judging his timing to a nicety, 'go and fetch the generators. Mustapha – bring me the wires.'

The two Nubians left the cellar. Webster closed his eyes. It is very difficult for a naked and manacled man whose bodily functions are totally controlled by others to maintain his human dignity, let alone keep up a spirit of bravado. For some reason this situation is worsened when the controllers wear uniform. The anonymity of extreme pain soon results in a humiliation so complete that the psychological distance between the torturer and the victim becomes immense, like that of the ringmaster and the lion, the scientist and the rat in the laboratory. It is no longer possible for the victim to answer his tormentors' questions on the same, as it were, social level. Webster knew this. He also knew that this phase is followed, if the torture continues long enough, by an obscene relationship that is almost sexual in its intimacy: the invasion of privacy is after all more complete than anything achieved in a normal encounter between a man and a woman. It was in a vain attempt to stave off this obscenity that he closed his eyes. They were the only organs still under his own control.

'I have already told you,' he said painfully. 'I was sent here with three companions by what is known as the department CO(S)E. We were instructed to pose as mining experts, to penetrate the interior on the pretence of seeking mineral concessions to be developed after the war. That is why we arrived by boat . . . to make the cover more – more credible.'

'You are telling us what we know already,' Benckendorff rasped. 'And you know we know it. Why did you contact the American, Weiss?'

'To find out if he . . . if he knew . . . how I could arrange a meeting with Kerim and . . . the other PPA chiefs.'

'Why should you want to do that?' the German officer asked.

'I *told* you . . . a dozen times. To sound them out about their reactions to an Allied landing. To find out if they would oppose . . . or even help.'

'Yes, you told us that,' Benckendorff said. 'It is an unlikely story. Government strategists do not send serving officers of only junior field rank to conduct diplomatic negotiations. They smuggle in men experienced in such manoeuvres, perhaps with a very senior staff officer to advise.'

'That was to happen later,' Webster improvised desperately.

'I was just to ... to sound them out ... to see if such an attempt was worth making.'

'Then why did you not speak to Abd-el-Kerim once you had bluffed your way into his presence?' the officer asked.

'It was not a suitable occasion.'

'Yet you could have asked the man Hassan to present you, and you could then have arranged a later meeting.'

'I ... it was ... I told you: the situation was impossible. I was disguised as a pilgrim forbidden to speak, and I—'

'Ah, yes,' Benckendorff interrupted. 'Of course. But if you were going to negotiate, you would naturally be prepared to discard the disguise and reveal your true identity, wouldn't you?'

Webster said nothing. His breathing creaked in the silence.

'To do this,' the SS man pursued, 'you would of course have to produce credentials – some kind of document that would establish your bona fides.' He paused, and then added silkily: 'These credentials, Webster – where are they?'

When the captive still made no reply, the officer leaned forward and said something very quickly in Arabic. Webster remained mute. The German repeated the question – if it was a question: the words came out too fast for Webster to be sure – a second and a third time. Webster ground his teeth in frustration. He knew he had lost the round.

'You see?' The officer straightened up and stared at Benckendorff. 'Even the damned Englanders would hardly be foolish enough to send a man whose Arabic is poor to handle delicate negotiations with Berbers and Touaregs! So much for your story, my friend. Now perhaps we can try to find out the *truth* ...'

Webster's eyes were still closed. *'That's right,'* Benckendorff said suddenly in German. *'Hit the swine in the balls!'*

Webster was ready for it: he had been expecting some such ruse. Not a muscle in his body tensed; not a quiver of the eyelids betrayed the fact that he understood. At least the knowledge that he had scarcely any Arabic might support the idea that he was ignorant of German too.

The Nubians came back into the cellar. Webster caught his breath as Benckendorff took two lengths of electric flex from one of them and attached the wires to his penis and nipples with miniature bulldog clips. The steel teeth bit painfully into his exhausted flesh. He was unable to prevent his eyes from opening. The second guard was holding a cast-iron truck generator with a crank attached to the armature spindle. Benckendorff dragged forward a crude wooden table. 'Put it down there,' he said.

When the generator was clamped to the table top, the SS man screwed the free ends of the wires to the terminals. He took hold of the handle. 'For the last time,' he said, 'what have you been sent here to do?'

Webster nerved himself for the agony, trying to imagine the pain so that he would be readier to meet it when it came. 'I have nothing to add to what I have told you already – the truth,' he whispered through set teeth. He had been taught sophisticated techniques of self-hypnosis to cope with situations like this. He could remember none of them. The pressure of the powerful steel clips alone was exceedingly uncomfortable. Almost as though he were an objective observer watching a film, he saw Benckendorff begin to turn the generator handle.

For a moment there was only a fierce tingling in the area of the clips – and then, as the handle turned faster, he suddenly gasped. His chest felt as though it had been ripped open; fire flamed through his loins and seared his belly. A cold sweat broke out all over his body and his breath began to sob. Some time later, his bladder and bowels evacuated themselves.

One of the Nubians giggled. Benckendorff laughed aloud. 'He thinks that's it,' he said conversationally to the other officer. 'Think again, my friend.'

The grinding of the handle rose to a screech.

* * * *

Harry Chilton cursed as he wrestled with the wheel of the half-track. The caterpillars might be fine on the shifting surfaces of the desert, but they were no help at all on the steep hills of a mountain road strewn with limestone chips. The bitch hung out her tail at every single hairpin!

They had left the vineyards and orange groves, the long straight avenues and the rich estates of the fertile coastal strip before the sun was up. But for three hours now they had been grinding through the foothills of the Atlas while the temperature soared and the wrinkled blue sheet of the Mediterranean vanished in the haze behind them. The heat in the cab was insufferable. Chilton's thin bush shirt was dark with sweat across the back and under the arms. Beside him, Hawkins dabbed continually at the beads of moisture rolling steadily down his face from beneath his hair. Zygmund was sprawled in the back with the drills and theodolites and detonators, a rifle across his knees.

'Jesus!' Chilton complained ferociously, pulling into the side to allow a truck full of grinning Arabs to career past in a cloud of dust and small stones. 'We're never goin' to get anywhere at this rate! And what the hell's happened to the officer? He was supposed to call us up at ten.'

Hawkins grunted. He passed a drenched sleeve across his brow and turned his head. 'Try again,' he said.

From the floorboards at his feet, Zygmund lifted a radio that was the twin of Webster's. The effort brought streams of sweat running down his arms. For several minutes as the half-track laboured upwards he fiddled with the dials. Finally he shook his head. 'Not a bleep,' he said glumly.

'Try callin' him up in clear.'

'They said to wait, we should have the acknowledge bleep first,' the Pole said doubtfully.

'Do as you're fuckin' told,' Hawkins growled. 'They also said to make our own soddin' decisions in the field, didn't they? Show a bit of fuckin' initiative, they said. You call the bugger up.'

'Okay,' Zygmund said. 'You're the boss, Sarge.' For another couple of minutes he spoke into the grille of the radio, his fingers sensitive about the controls. But although he paused frequently to listen, straining his ears over the clatter of the motor and the whine of gears, no tinny voice replied from the miniature speaker, no answering bleep shrilled over the air.

Hawkins shrugged. 'Try again in a half hour,' he said.

The road straightened out and ran for several miles across a barren plateau studded with thorn trees. For the first time in over an hour, Chilton was able to change into top gear. In the stifling cab, the smells of hot oil and exhaust fumes gave way to dust thrown up by the wheels, seasoned with the thin, aromatic stink of petrol slopping about in the jerricans lashed to the roof.

'Harry!' Zygmund called suddenly from the back. 'For a little take off your foot, will you? Go slow so the dust it settles some.'

'What the hell for?' Chilton shouted.

'I don't know, but ... I want to check. I think somebody follows us.'

'Blimey, you ain't half shifty, Ziggie!' Chilton laughed. 'Of course there's some cunt followin' us. And others ahead of us. We ain't the only blokes usin' the road, you know!' But he slowed down until the half-track was going almost at walking pace. Gradually, the yellow dust subsided behind them.

'Yes,' Zygmund yelled. 'I see his windscreen flash in the sun before. Soon after we start climbing. Now I see him good.'

'What makes you think he's followin' us?' Hawkins asked.

'Is a 328 BMW for one thing,' said Zygmund, the sports car fan. 'He can go much, much faster than us if he wants. But he prefers to keep his distance. He is already there twenty, twenty-five miles.' He was holding a pair of field glasses to his eyes now, balancing himself against the swaying of the truck.

'Second,' he said after a pause, 'the man he sits in the passenger seat is holding a Parabellum across his knees. Also, the windscreen is not all that flashes in the sun. This is the coupé version of the car, and there is a dammed great radio aerial sticks through the roof ...'

The last thing that Willi Kunstler saw was a Tiger tank. It was perched on the lip of a dune forty feet above him. They had been advancing with the Panzers behind a smoke screen rolling across the desert, but two squadrons of Englander armour had outflanked them and driven in from the north. The tank was spinning around to meet the threat when it was caught on the sharp ridge of sand. The last thing Willi heard was a sound like the slamming of a giant steel door somewhere in his skull. The tank erupted in flame and plunged down the steep slope. The last thing Willi tasted and smelled – it was only for a thousandth of a second – was the oil on the caterpillar track. And the last thing he felt was pain.

Chapter Thirteen

Webster lay on the bare floor of his prison, watching the light fade outside the window embrasure. The black-and-yellow robes had been taken from him – presumably to be returned to their owner – and they had thrown a plain white shift into the room when they carried him back from the cellar. But the cotton garment was not warm enough to stop him shivering in the cool air of the evening. Unless, he thought wearily, it was a reaction to the tortures he had suffered. His throat felt as though he had swallowed molten lead, and every nerve, muscle and sinew in his lean body was aching. Yet he was astonished to find that, apart from a redness around the site of the clips, the ordeal had left no visible marks on him. So much pain, and so little to show for it!

He tried to wrench his mind away from his predicament. But there was nothing else to think about. Benckendorff had revealed, during the interrogation in the cellar, that he must have been on Webster's trail before he even left London. This confirmed Webster's suspicions that there must be a spy somewhere in Chard's organization – a spy sufficiently well placed to know that he was being seconded to O'Kelly's unit, but not well placed enough to find out why. The knowledge was interesting, but there was nothing he could do with it now.

With the information he had given them, it was just possible that Hawkins and the others might go ahead and succeed in destroying, or at least severely damaging, the base. Their main weapon would be surprise. It was therefore vital, absolutely vital, that he must not give away the true object of their mission. Once the Germans knew that he was aware of the existence of their secret range, they would warn the garrison and any chance of a surprise attack would be reduced to nil. He must therefore hold out against the worst that Benckendorff could do, will himself to silence until he had provoked them to an excess that would finish him off. It was the most he could hope for now.

For even if he broke, there would be no chance for him, no reprieve as a reward for betrayal, no prisoner-of-war camp when he had given them what they wanted. The Geneva Convention did not apply in the sombre shadows of undercover warfare like this. He was on a clandestine assignment on neutral territory and he could expect no mercy from his captors. The Nazis, too, were in a position as illegal as his own ... but this time they were calling the tune. It was up to him to stop the record playing through to the end. He hoped he would be able to find the strength. After the indescribable agonies of the electric current, at times he doubted it. It wouldn't be long, in any case, before he found out. 'Leave him for an hour,' Benckendorff had said when they dumped him back in the room. Fifty minutes of that hour must have elapsed already.

Pushing himself upright into a sitting position, he cocked his head and listened. Here in the interior of Kerim's palace, the everyday noises of Wadi Elmira were muted by distance. But he could hear the cries of barkers in the market, the tramp of a sentry's feet, a jingling of harness as someone rode along the narrow street outside the stronghold. Nearer at hand he could distinguish a murmur of Arab voices, the splashing of the fountain in the patio below.

And something else.

He frowned. He had been subconsciously aware of all those other sounds for some time, but now there was an extra component. What was it? How long had it been there? Where was it coming from?

For a moment he couldn't even separate it from the others: he just knew that an additional noise had manifested itself.

Then suddenly – it was very faint – he had it: a surreptitious slithering sound punctuated by soft, barely discernible thumps. But where?

He concentrated on the noise, trying to exclude all the others. Yes! It seemed to be coming from the direction of the window!

Webster rose silently to his feet and moved across the empty room. It was dark outside now, but in the diffused light reflected from the chambers off the courtyard below he could see a length of heavy rope dangling in front of the embrasure.

It hung down almost to the sill and it terminated in a double knot the size of his fist. Every now and then the rope twirled and lowered itself a few inches so that the hempen knot bumped against the rough sandstone of the embrasure. As he watched in amazement, the rope swung slowly to and fro, scraping the knot back and forth along the sill, making the noises he had heard.

Somebody, somewhere above, was trying to attract his attention!

Seizing the rope, he tugged it once. Immediately, the swinging motion stopped and the rope hung still. Webster hauled himself cautiously up on to the sill and leaned out. The Nubian guard below was squatting with his back to the wall, his gun across his knees. Webster twisted his head and looked up. He had of course checked as soon as he was locked in the room. Between the window and the parapet of the roof there was a ten-foot stretch of sandstone unbroken by any ornament or projection. Only now, the line of the parapet was interrupted by a head and shoulders silhouetted against the stars.

The rope twitched impatiently several times. The knot rose upwards for twelve inches in a series of small jerks. The message couldn't have been clearer if it had been sung by a boy from Western Union in a Hollywood film. Climb up. Escape. For God's sake pull your finger out and get on with it. And a happy birthday to *you*!

Webster pulled hard on the rope. It was rock-solid. The unknown rescuer must have turned it around a chimney or some other projection on the roof. Who the hell could it be? Mahmoud Hassan, belatedly earning his bribe? It didn't seem likely. From what Benckendorff had said, the Arab must have been part of the plan to lure him to Wadi Elmira. And if he wasn't he would probably be dead by now, executed for double-crossing his master. Who else then? Webster was damned if he could think of anybody. Nobody but O'Kelly even knew that he was in Kerim's fortress town. But what the hell – *somebody* was offering him a way out! The tunnel, which had been completely black, now showed a pinpoint of light at the far end. He darted back into the room.

There was a loose tile in one corner and he had secreted his five remaining hundred-dollar bills beneath this before he was taken to the cellar. Stowing the money in the waistband of his robe, he climbed up on to the sill and grasped the rope again.

The Nubian was still nodding over his carbine. Webster was barefoot. If he could make those few yards of sandstone without a single sound, without dislodging the smallest fragment, before the torturers returned to find his prison empty...

He shrugged. If he couldn't, he would be a sitting duck. But even that was better than what lay in store for him if he remained in the room. Swinging himself out over the void, he braced his feet against the wall and began hauling himself up towards the parapet.

The ascent took him six minutes and five seconds – three hundred and sixty-five seconds, each one of which seemed like a day, the sum of which seemed even longer than a year. Every silent inch was a major achievement, a triumph of determination and muscular effort over fatigue and the laws of gravity. By the time he swung a leg over the parapet and subsided, panting, on the flat roof, his shoulder muscles were shrieking for relief and the balls of his feet were raw.

As soon as the thundering in his temples had quietened down, he raised his head and looked at his rescuer. There was no Western Union cap but it was certainly a boy.

The slight figure stealthily coiling up the rope was that of Ali, the Arab urchin who had been looking after Alastair Mackenzie.

Webster gasped. 'How the devil...?'

Ali laid a finger across his lips. Jerking his small head imperiously, he stole away to the far side of the roof. Webster rose to his feet and limped after him. The boy was paying out the rope over another parapet. Below, Webster could just make out a huddle of smaller buildings, more flat roofs, and then a raised walk edged with battlements. 'Ali!' he whispered fiercely. 'How the hell did you—?'

'Sssssssh!' the boy hissed. 'Very dangerous.' He waved a hand at the battlements. 'Soldiers walk there on patrol, yes? We wait until they pass. Then we go down.'

'Fine, fine, fine. But what are you *doing* here? How did you know that I—?'

'I come from Wadi Elmira,' the boy said in a low voice. 'After they have kill my master I cannot stay in the city. I come home.'

'Yes, but how did you—?'

'I am in same caravan with the *effendi*. I see what happens. Small boy can go many places, hear many things. The *effendi* is a friend of my master, so I help.'

'As simple as that,' Webster mused. 'My God, life would be simpler if more people ...'

He broke off as Ali grasped his shoulder and forced him to duck down behind the parapet. From over the wall they heard the tramp of booted feet and the clink of equipment as a patrol marched along the battlement. When the footsteps had died away in the distance, the boy rose silently. 'We go,' he said, indicating the rope.

Webster swarmed down and found himself on the roof of a mud-walled shack overlooking a narrow alley. The sweet stench of vegetable refuse rose to his nostrils. As the boy joined him at the edge of the roof, a confused hubbub broke out somewhere behind him. Voices shouted in Arabic and in German. Feet clattered on a stone stairway. Benckendorff must have returned and found that the bird had flown. It gave Webster some pleasure to imagine the Nazi's bewilderment on finding that his prisoner had vanished from a locked room with guards at the window and door. But he didn't have long to relish the thought.

'Quick!' Ali urged. 'They call back that patrol from the other side of the palace. Very soon they guess how you escape. We go, yes?'

'We go,' Webster agreed hastily. Together they dropped into the alley. Already, footsteps of the returning patrol racing along the battlements at the far end of the lane were audible.

Ali led the way across a broader street, through a deserted courtyard, and into another alley at the end of which Webster could see the flaring lights of the market. Over the clamour of the crowd there he heard another outburst of shouting behind them: the patrol must have discovered the rope.

He glanced desperately around him. The pursuit couldn't be far away. Two things were essential: he must recover his radio, and he must find some means of transport to get him out of Wadi Elmira. He peeled a bill from the thin wad beneath his shift. 'Ali,' he said, 'this is American money. It is worth a great deal of piastres. Many, many piastres. If I give it to you, do you think you could hire, buy or steal a horse for me? I must go away from this place very quickly.'

'*Si, si, effendi*,' the boy nodded eagerly. 'Behind the mosque there is a jacaranda tree. From the lower branches you can cross the wall without passing the gate. Below is a *wadi*. I will wait for you there in one hour.'

'That's my boy!' Webster thrust the bill into the youth's hand. 'One hour is fine. I have something else to do first. If I am not there in two hours, do not wait. It may be dangerous.'

'Very well, sir. Be careful of the patrols when you cross the wall. One passes each fifteen minutes.' There was a gleam of teeth in the dark and the boy was gone.

Boots pounded on the cobbles of the courtyard they had just crossed. Webster sprinted for the end of the lane and melted into the crowd eddying around the fringes of the bazaar. The water torture had effectively removed his false moustache but his skin was still stained. Nevertheless, without a djellabah or a burnouse to cover his head, his features, with the thin chevron of hair on his upper lip, would be an immediate give-away the moment anyone got a good look at him. Keeping as far away from the naphtha flares as he could, he threaded his way between *fellaheen* and their black-veiled women, hoping to lose himself among the stalls. Somewhere behind him there was a commotion as the soldiers erupted into the throng. Over the shuffling of feet and the cries of haggling merchants and customers, he could hear voices raised in argument and shouts of protest.

Hands gesticulated, fingers wagged, palms were upraised in the suffocating press over displays of fruit, vegetables, cloth and hardware. He had almost worked his way around to the far side of the market square when three shots rang out above the heads of the crowd.

There was a screaming and a stampede as everybody fought

to get away from the centre of the bazaar. A huge stand of copper pots and pans near Webster toppled over. 'Stay where you are! Don't leave the market!' a strident voice shouted over the clangour of metal and the furious protests of the stallholder. 'This is the military. There is a foreign spy here and we wish to catch him. Stay where you are – you have nothing to fear.'

Feeling as if he had suddenly been exposed in the glare of a searchlight, Webster slunk around behind the stall and made for an alley twisting away into the shadows. 'Over there!' another voice yelled. 'Look – on the far side of the bazaar! Quick! After him!'

He looked swiftly over his shoulder. The owner of the hardware stall, his arms full of cooking utensils, was dancing up and down, trying to free a hand to point at the fugitive. Beyond, advancing rapidly down an aisle between the striped awnings, a group of soldiers led by the three Nubians came running.

Webster himself broke into a run and plunged down the dark lane. A fusillade of shots exploded behind him as he gained the shadows. Slugs spurted up the dust between his lacerated feet. Fragments of plaster stung his face as another chipped the wall by his shoulder and whined off into the night. Panting hoarsely, he dashed around the first bend in the alley. Ahead were the lights of another crowded square. He swerved aside into an unlit, evil-smelling entry that was choked with garbage, ran up a flight of stone steps, crossed a wider street and hurried through an archway into a maze of twisting lanes beyond.

Behind him, the sounds of pursuit increased. There had been plenty of people in the street he crossed to point out the route he had taken. Putting on an extra burst of speed, he skirted the bulk of the mosque, ran down a second flight of stairs, and found himself in a narrow thoroughfare lit only at the far end by a small flare. All around him a faint murmur of voices behind closed shutters stirred the evening air. He halted, the blood pounding behind his eyes. Footsteps. Shouts. The sound of music rising and falling in the distance.

'Why do you not come inside, stranger?' a soft voice intoned at his ear in heavily accented French.

Webster swung around. There was a small click. In the

upward-directed beam of a pencil flashlight, brown flesh quivered. The tiny circle of illumination revealed a woman's breast, the swelling contours held towards him by silver-tipped fingers, the nipple and aureola purplish in the dim light.

'By Jove!' Webster exclaimed. He had seldom seen anything more suggestive, more overtly and obscenely erotic, than that naked breast shamelessly exposed against the dark. Below it, a tight swathe of diaphanous material sheathed belly and hips; above, a hint of white teeth, the highlight on a full lip, shone through the gloom. He hesitated. The hunters were only a block away. Already heavy feet were scrambling down the last winding flight of stairs.

He made up his mind. 'Done,' he said huskily. He stepped towards the doorway in which the woman was standing. The light vanished. A door creaked open into blackness. Webster brushed past her and stood waiting as she closed it.

In the airless dark of the passage, the odour of some cloying, exotic cosmetic washed over him. Outside, footsteps scraped to a halt. He heard the voice of Mustapha, one of the Nubians: 'A foreign pig ... tall, no beard, in a white shift with no head-dress ...'

A woman mumbled a negative.

'But he must be here somewhere! He can't have got away. The far end of the alley is blocked.'

'He could be anywhere,' another Nubian cut in. 'You know where we are? This is the street of the—'

'It does not matter what street it is,' Mustapha interrupted. 'We shall post sentries at the entrance and search it house by house. The foreigner must be captured at all costs.' The footsteps died away.

The prostitute, whose breath had hissed in sharply the first time Mustapaha spoke, now moved past Webster towards the rear of the building. Soft flesh brushed the back of his hand. In a low voice, she said: 'This way.'

Light stabbed the dark as she switched on the flashlight and shone the beam at the floor behind her to show him the way. Webster shook his head. An electric pocket lamp in a Berber hill village in the middle of the Sahara! He wondered if it had found its way there from one of Seymour Weiss's lease-lend consignments. He followed the woman up a flight of stone stairs. Apart from the clip-clop of her slippers and the swish of garments against her naked flesh, they mounted in silence. At the top of the stairs he saw a poorly lit hallway with a number of curtained doorways leading off it. The illumination was provided by a primitive lamp: a simple wick floating in a small bowl of oil. There was another in the tiny room into which she showed him. The place was no more than eight feet square, furnished only with rugs and cushions strewn across the floor. As she went to draw heavy drapes over an arched window embrasure, he closed the door and leaned his back against it while he tried to regain his breath. His lungs were bursting and the torn soles of his feet hurt like hell. 'I am sorry,' he panted. 'I only want ...'

She turned to face him. She was voluptuously built, the bare breasts heavy on her chest, her soft belly shadowed under the transparent skirt. With a start of surprise, staring at the kohl-fringed eyes and full lips, he recognized Yemanja, the dancer from the caravan.

'So! It is you!' she breathed. 'I knew we were fated to meet again. Yet you tell me that you only want ...?'

Webster cleared his throat. It seemed to be a night of unexpected meetings. But was this one going to be a help or a hindrance? 'You are running away, are you not?' Yemanja said. 'It was you that Mustapha and Ibrahim and the soldiers were chasing? This is no concern of mine: I have no love for the guards or the military, especially those Nubians, who are brutal men. So why do you not stay here with me? See ... am I not beautiful? Come. Sit beside me and I will send for some refreshment.'

Webster swallowed. 'Yemanja,' he said, 'I cannot.'

'How – cannot? I wish it. You also are beautiful. You have a strong but kind face, *effendi*. You are different from the Nubians and the other men I meet: here I am forced by Abdul Mohammed of the camels to take whoever chooses to stop. Let me for once make a choice of my own. Do you not find me seductive?'

'I think you are beautiful,' Webster said truthfully.

'Then if I please you, why do you reject me?'

'It is not a question of rejecting. There are things I have to do. A companion awaits me. Yemanja, I didn't recognize you when I stopped outside. I—'

'Why would you, my friend? How could you recognize that which you will not see? Each night on the caravan journey it was the same thing: you refused to look at what I have to show. Well, here we are alone. Perhaps you can find time to look now!' Raising her skirt, she thrust forward her pelvis and smiled. Below the shaven triangle at her loins, pink flesh, ritually circumcised in childhood, pouted outwards like an open mouth.

Christ! Webster thought distractedly. My God, I've got to get out of here! Fast! Aloud, he said: 'I have told you: it is not a matter of desire; it is a matter of time ...' But suddenly she was pressed against him, her hands drawing aside the shift, feeling for his genitals, her fingers crawling knowledgeably over his flesh, caressing, massaging. 'See!' she cried triumphantly. 'You do desire me! Your manhood—'

Abruptly she tensed, stopping in the middle of her sentence. From below a persistent hammering echoed up the stairway. 'The soldiers!' she whispered. 'They said they would search every house!'

Gently, Webster put her away from him. 'I am sorry,' he said again. 'That was what I was trying to say.'

'No, you are right. You must come this way.' Yemanja ran to the window embrasure and pulled aside the drapes, her eyes wide with alarm. 'Nobody saw you come in. So far as they know, I have been here alone all the time. Out here is a flat roof. Beyond is an alley that leads back to the mosque without crossing the lane in front. You must go.'

He thrust another of his hundred dollar bills into her hand. 'Take this,' he said. 'Perhaps one day you will be able to buy a little freedom with it.' The hammering had stopped and there was the sound of many voices from below. Webster swung a leg over the window sill. He turned back to the girl. 'You are very desirable and very kind. I am grateful. If there is ever anything I can do ...'

'You know what you can do!' Yemanja said.

He grinned, leaning inwards to kiss her briefly on the lips. The next instant she was all over him, devouring him with wet-lipped kisses, her body pressed against his chest, her hands cradling the back of his head. Once more he disengaged himself. 'The soldiers,' he reminded her in a whisper.

'I had forgotten.' She was panting. 'But I will not forget

you. The next time you have occasion to visit Wadi Elmira . . .'

'It'll be a pleasure,' Webster said. 'Believe me, this is the first time in my life that I . . .' He looked deep into her eyes for a moment, and then jumped lightly on to the flat roof and ran to the edge. The curtain dropped over the window.

The alley was about fifteen feet below. The jump jarred him from head to heels, and even barefoot he seemed to himself to make the devil of a noise. But nobody appeared to have heard; no voice questioned him and no footstep advanced. He waited a moment, listening, and then limped away in the direction of the mosque.

The beaten earth road behind it was deserted. Just before he reached the square where he had hidden the radio, he saw the back of a sentry silhouetted against the sky on top of the perimeter wall. But he had gained the safety of the orange trees before the man turned at the end of his beat.

Mercifully, the radio was still in its hiding place and the old truck still parked nearby. Should he take a chance and try to call up O'Kelly? No – it was long before the time when the old man would be listening in. Far better to get out of here while he had the chance. Holding the radio beneath his shift, he hurried back to look for the jacaranda tree. Half an hour later, he was slithering painfully down the dried-up bed of the *wadi*.

It took him some time to find the boy, but at last a faint whinny from the far side of a huge boulder led him to the place. The horse was saddled, and there was a djellabah and burnouse flung across its back. 'Ali,' Webster said fervently, 'you're a treasure!'

'*Effendi?*'

'It does not matter. I am grateful. Tell me – do you know of the oasis called El Glouai?'

'I have heard men speak of it,' said the boy. 'But I have not been there. It is very far: beyond El Golèa, on the trail to In Salah, where they make flames come out of the earth.'

'Can you tell me how to get to that trail from here? It is very important.'

'I think so, sir. You must follow this *wadi* until it joins the river which flows on the other side of the town. You will have to lead the beast, for it is too rough to ride and would in any case make much noise. The river makes a ravine and after that it crosses a plateau with thorn trees. You follow the river until the far side of the plateau, where you will find a caravan trail leading away and over the mountains. Beyond the pass, you descend – and there you will see the track that goes towards El Golèa and the south.'

'How far is it to that track?'

'Perhaps one day's ride; perhaps a little less,' Ali said. He hesitated, and then added: '*Effendi* ... I did not have to pay for the horse. It will not be missed until tomorrow morning.' Webster felt a crumpled bill thrust into his hand.

'Keep it, Ali,' he said. 'Perhaps your parents ...?'

'I have no parents.'

'Oh, God!' Webster said. On an impulse, he drew out the remaining three bills and gave them to the boy. 'Take these,' he said. 'Go away from here. Go back to the coast. Perhaps with this money you could start some kind of business, maybe a stall in a bazaar. You must in any case stay away from evil men. It is difficult for you to understand, but what you have done for me will perhaps one day right a great wrong. I will not forget you, Ali.' He reached up and took the horse's bridle.

'Allah go with you,' the boy said.

As Webster and his mount walked slowly away down the dried-up river bed, the waning moon rose above the rim of the *wadi*. In the pale, unearthly light, two tears glistened in Ali's eyes and splashed to the dusty stones at his feet.

PART IV
Desert Victory

'There wasn't much left of Kiev when we did get there,' Klinger said. 'The XVth Panzars had gone in ahead of us and what the Russkis had left standing they knocked down. It was just hundreds of acres of rubble buttressing an occasional end-wall. You could see the smoke for forty miles. I remember the remains of one tall house. About five floors up there was still a bathtub hanging from the brickwork by its pipes ... and in the tub was a skinny old woman, naked as the day she was born and yelling blue murder! It was freezing cold and she must have been there for hours. Weiderhaus stood up in the turret as we rolled past and picked her off with a single shot. It was the prettiest piece of sharpshooting I ever saw. When we got nearer the centre, where the raids had been heaviest, the streets were cluttered with bodies that had fused with the tarmac in the heat. I can tell you, that was damned inconvenient.'

Chapter Fourteen

It was late afternoon before they were certain. More than an hour had passed since they had seen another vehicle in either direction. But still the smart little BMW coupé kept its distance, rather more than half a mile behind now. Zygmund had seen, as they drove across a shelf of bare rock, that the man in the passenger seat was keeping them under observation too with a pair of powerful field-glasses. That clinched it. 'All right, Chilton,' Sergeant Hawkins said. 'How long would it take the bleeders to catch up if we stopped?'

'We're averaging twenty,' the driver said. 'That's a mile every three minutes. If they're more'n half a mile away – I reckon a minute and a half, sarge. Two at the outside.'

'It's not much,' Hawkins grunted, 'but it'll fuckin' have to do.' He climbed into the back with Zygmund and began sorting through the mining equipment stowed on the floor. He spent five minutes giving precise instructions to the Pole and Chilton and then, as the trail levelled out along a twisting ravine, he shouted: 'All right – let 'er go!'

Chilton trod fiercely on the accelerator pedal. The whine of gears rose to a scream. The half-track slewed wildly from side to side, its motor roaring, as tyres and caterpillars scrabbled on the stony surface.

At the far end of the gulch, the track looped down towards a barren moonscape of crumbling rock dotted with vast piles of stones. Beyond this the jagged crests of another range of hills gnawed at the sulphurous sky. 'Right,' Hawkins shouted through the choking dust. 'Next hairpin. We should be all of two minutes ahead now.'

He busied himself with lengths of wire and sticks of explosive. There was a firing pin between his teeth. He raised a hand to signal that he was ready, and Chilton changed down, changed again, and braked. The half-track broadsided around the U-bend in a shower of pebbles. As it slowed in the lee of a ten-foot boulder beside the trail, Hawkins dropped off the tailboard into the dust. The half-track continued on down the hill.

Hawkins gouged frantically at the shaly surface of the road. The sun pounded down on his bare head. When he had scooped out a shallow depression, he packed in the explosive, paid out wire to a hollow beside the boulder, and then dashed back to scatter stones over the traces of his work. He could already hear the snarl of the BMW's exhaust when he returned to the hollow, wiping the sweat from his eyes with the back of his hand.

The driver of the little sports car changed down as he braked for the hairpin. Tyres screeched. The BMW careened around the bend. Hawkins raised his head briefly to confirm the car's position, then ducked back as he touched the naked ends of two wires together.

The thunderclap of the explosion started reverberating echoes from the rock wall above at the exit from the ravine. A huge cloud of yellow dust mushroomed up from the road. Further away across the dead landscape, buzzards flapped angrily into the air above the picked white bones of a desert rat.

Hawkins waited with his arms crossed over his head until the shower of stones and fragments of hot metal had died away. Then he scrambled to his feet and walked back to the road.

Beside the raw crater in the shale, the twisted remnant of

the BMW lay on its side. The charge had gone off between the front and back wheels, splitting the vehicle almost in two. The driver had been blown through the windscreen and an immense smear of blood, glistening with portions of human brain, varnished the crumpled bonnet. The other man must have been killed by the blast. He lay several yards away, apparently unmarked – a small, neat man with a moustache, whom Webster would have recognized as one of the four extremist officers pointed out by Weiss. Nobody could have recognized the driver.

Chilton drove slowly back up the hill in low gear. He stopped the half-track and got out. Small flames licked the paintwork of the savaged sports car, and one of the rear wheels was still slowly turning. Chilton nodded his head several times. 'Nice work, sarge!' he approved.

Zygmund shouted suddenly, excitedly, from the cab. 'Come quickly, come quickly! I just got Major Webster on the radio!'

*   *   *   *

Charles G. Fortune heard the voice crackle over the speaker with a pang of alarm. The racket from the three engines of the Macchi-Castoldi was deafening, and it was only because he was leaning forward between the pilot's and navigator's seats that he caught the intercepted message at all. Delannoy, the navigator, was fiddling with the radio dials ... and suddenly Webster's unmistakably English voice was struggling through the static.

'... found myself in the hands of the krauts ... tricky little SS bastard by the name of Benckendorff ... apparently been following me ever since I was briefed in London ... call up the Captain and ask him to get the Special Branch on the job ...'

The voice became momentarily unintelligible. Delannoy, who had started at the mention of the German colonel's name, nudged the pilot and spun the dials. The voice returned, swelling and fading through the interference.

'... to get away from Wadi Elmira ... heading for the trail that leads to El Golèa ... wait for you there and you can pick me up some time tomorrow ... only give you ... approximate position, but at the moment I'm—'

The message was cut off in mid-sentence as Delannoy flipped a switch and jammed the earphones over his head. He picked up a pencil and started scribbling hurriedly on a pad strapped to his knee. Fournier, the pilot, glanced at him once and then reached for his own cans.

Fortune could see that the navigator was copying down map references and figures. Evidently Webster had been captured and had escaped. Now he was calling Hawkins to report his position and arrange a rendezvous. But why should this interest two Frenchmen who had been detailed to fly a film crew out over the desert to search for locations?

Fortune and his two companions had not met Fournier and Delannoy until after they had been searched at the airfield by men of the gendarmerie who had checked their papers and permissions. The attitude of the two French flyers was stiff but correct, though neither the fast-talking Joe Constantine nor Fortune himself with his carefully contrived Irish neutral's blarney could get behind their formal façade. They strapped themselves into the seats in front of the controls, discussed the route that Fortune had worked out and checked with the authorities, and blocked any conversation not directly related to the flight. It was the same after take-off. Fournier and Delannoy stared woodenly ahead as the plane roared south, as uncommunicative as a pair of dummies. They were in any case as alike as two peas in a pod: short, compact, muscular men with hard, lined faces and military moustaches (Webster would have recognized them as the remaining pair of the four ex-army extremists).

Fortune had very carefully chosen the first site they were to pretend to examine – a rock-strewn plain separating two parallel escarpments. According to O'Kelly's large-scale maps, it had the twin advantages of being eminently believable as the scene of a Biblical epic, and falling only a short distance away from the land route Hawkins must take to reach the El Glouai oasis. They had still not decided how to handle the situation once they got there. The other locations they had been permitted to include in their flight plan were all way off the route to the German range. Now there was an additional complication: it was essential that the French must be prevented from discovering that there was a belligerent raiding party on their territory, but it looked as though Webster's overheard message could tip them off to exactly that. Fortune backed out of the greenhouse and returned to the cabin to discuss the new development with Mullen and the Canadian.

The plane rattled and shook and vibrated as it ploughed through the turgid atmosphere, occasionally yawing or dropping with a sickening lurch as they encountered air pockets over the sun-baked ridges of the Atlas. Beyond the circular ports, a waste of brown gullies, bluffs and saw-toothed peaks slid slowly past beneath the wing. After a brief conference at the rear of the small cabin Constantine went forward and tapped Delannoy on the shoulder. 'How long before we reach the first location?' he shouted.

The navigator was transmitting. He spoke tersely in the headset, thumbed up a switch, and then turned his head enquiringly. *'Pardon?'*

'How much longer before we're over the first location?'

Delannoy glanced at his watch. 'Fifteen minutes, Monsieur. Perhaps a little longer. There is a great deal of turbulence today.' He turned back to the radio.

Before he returned to the cabin, Constantine heard the next few words the navigator spoke. *'Herr Benckendorff? ... Yes, it seems that the man is heading east. He gave his present position as ...'* Delannoy reached for the pad on his knee and read off a string of names and numbers.

Constantine gasped. The man was speaking in German ... and he was obviously reporting everything he had heard, including Webster's whereabouts, to some Nazi unit in Algeria!

'No, no,' Delannoy said. *'A routine job flying some fools from Hollywood out to a film location ... Two hundred miles away from your base. Do not worry ...'*

The Canadian scrambled hastily back to the others. 'Those two sons-of-bitches must be collaborators,' he said when he had told them what he heard. 'Of all the frogs to be lumbered with!'

'At least it confirms the fact that the flipping base is there,' Fortune said. 'And that it's your actual jack-booted Hun that we have against us. I say "us" – they don't realize there's a connection between the Major's lot and our little show?'

Constantine shook his head. 'Our cover holds. As far as they're concerned, we're just a trio of stupid showbiz bums. The guy made that clear, thank God.'

'What will we do now?' Mullen asked. 'Sure we'd be better off goin' back to me original idea and doin' the fellers in.'

Fortune frowned. The idea didn't shock him but its politics could be puzzling. 'Whatever happens,' he said, 'they told us that we must knock off no frogs. Upsetting the international applecart an' all that. But these blokes are collabos, helping the Boche work *against* the French if you take the long view. They're in the same league as bally fifth columnists. I dunno – but I'd say that puts them on the same footing as the Nazis themselves so far as we're concerned: it sort of changes things.'

'Will we kill them then? Dear knows it would make life the easier. Or maybe we should just tie them up and leave them be.'

'You're joking!' Constantine said. 'We're unarmed and each of them has gotten himself a Mauser pistol stashed in a shoulder holster. I saw when the pilot was getting aboard.'

'So it's back to the ould one-two?' Mullen said.

Fortune grinned. 'Yes, its back to the ould one-two,' he agreed.

Two minutes later, he was leaning over Delannoy's shoulder. 'Hey, Mister,' he said, 'would you be after comin' back to the cabin a minnit? One of my boys – Mr Mullen it is, the wee one – he's been took bad. He's queer and sick. I'm afraid we may have to turn back. Would you come and take a gander at him? I fear it may be an appendix, you know.'

The navigator shook his head. 'It is against the rules,' he said. 'I regret, Monsieur, but the aviation regulations are formal on the point: they require a pilot *and* co-pilot to be present at the controls at all times. At all times.'

'But this is an emergency, man!'

'You will have to deal with it yourself. If you decide it would be best to turn back, tell me and we shall do so at once.'

'I tell you the poor feller's sick!' Fortune shouted.

Delannoy shrugged. 'I am desolated, Monsieur ...'

Back in the cabin, uncharacteristically for him, Fortune swore. 'Silly bugger wouldn't buy it!' he complained.

'So?'

'So if we can't separate 'em, we'll have to take 'em together somehow – though at the moment I'm blessed if I can see how.'

Constantine touched his arm and pointed at the side of the cabin. The plastic soundproofing that jacketed the stressed skin of the fuselage was webbed with a complex of electric cables, control conduits and circuit-breaker boxes. Just aft of the flimsy door, one of these boxes – which had once presumably controlled some auxiliary equipment – had been disconnected. From the bakelite casing protruded a nine-inch length of metal conduit about a quarter of an inch in diameter. There was no wire in the tube, which had a slightly thicker aluminium collar round its free end. Fortune sat back in the canvas-and-tubular-steel seat and raised his eyebrows. The Canadian held out a fist, extended his forefinger and thumb, and crooked the thumb joint to mime the shooting of a pistol. Fortune grinned, suddenly catching on, and pushed himself upright.

It was very cramped in the greenhouse over the controls. Delannoy was studying a sectionalized map folded into a perspex cover. Fournier was staring ahead through the whirling disc of the central airscrew as he banked slightly to correct a compass reading. Below them now was a limitless expanse of yellow sand, ridged into dunes like a photographic blow-up of the foreshore exposed by a receding tide. Fortune pressed the cold ring of the conduit collar against the back of the pilot's neck. 'Your hands on your head, please,' he said loudly, 'and not a move until we have taken the gun ...'

What followed happened in less than a minute, though it seemed a great deal longer to those involved. Feeling what he believed to be the muzzle of a gun against the top of his spine, Fournier tensed and then slowly began to raise his hands. Mullen and Constantine were supposed to throw themselves bodily on Delannoy, pinion his arms to stop him from drawing, and drag him backwards out of his seat. But the navigator must have sensed some movement, a reflection perhaps in the glazed cover of his map, and he was half twisted around before they reached him. His hand flashed between his lapels and reappeared holding the Mauser. The heavy automatic roared in the confined space of the greenhouse. Mullen cried out. Slammed backwards by the impact of the 9-mm nickel-jacketed slug, he cannoned into Fortune and threw him off balance as Constantine fell on Delannoy.

Fournier half rose from his seat and grabbed for his own

gun. Fortune struck at his head with the conduit tube, but the metal was too light to stun him: the best the Englishman could do was to slash again at the pilot's gun hand. The pipe struck him on the wrist bone, and Fournier yelled with pain. The pistol dropped from his nerveless fingers.

Constantine was grappling furiously with Delannoy, wrapping his arms about the French collaborator as he seized his wrist and tried to shake the Mauser from his grasp. Mullen was on the floor. Fournier came out from behind his controls to tangle with Fortune.

The tail of the pilot's jacket caught in the control column as the two men closed, jerking it abruptly back. The Macchi-Castoldi's three engines screamed and the plane's nose lifted in a forty-five degree climb.

Overbalanced by the sudden change in elevation, Fortune and the pilot shot backwards together and fell into the passenger cabin. Mullen slid across the floor and ended up against the bulkhead. Constantine and Delannoy tumbled away from the navigator's chair, still wrestling for the gun.

The airscrews bit into the atmosphere as the plane clawed its way higher. But without the extra boost to support the climb, the speed dropped and the Macchi-Castoldi stalled. The nose dipped and they twisted into a spin.

Two muffled explosions sounded from the tangle of bodies between the seats. Delannoy choked and went limp. Panting hoarsely, Constantine fought his way out from beneath the dead weight of the navigator's body. He hauled himself into the pilot's seat and seized the controls.

On the floor of the cabin, Fortune tried every unarmed combat trick that he knew to worst the wiry Frenchman. But Fournier was tough. He traded judo lock for judo lock, chop for chop, and nerve grip for nerve grip. As the plane whirled into its spin, he freed one arm and brought the flat of his hand down in a murderous blow to Fortune's throat. Fortune almost blacked out as the blood supply to his brain was temporarily cut off. Fighting for breath, he slid away across the steeply canted floor. Fournier levered himself upright and took a running jump at the fallen man's belly. Fortune drew up his knees ... and then straightened his legs at the moment the pilot landed. His heels lodged in the pit of Fournier's stomach, hurling him across the cabin to smash against the door. At the same time, the plane's corkscrew spiral twisted that side of the cabin to the underneath. The door burst open and Fournier dropped into the void.

His wild cry was lost in the shriek of wind. The alto whine of the Macchi-Castoldi's dive was approaching the soprano, and now it was topped by a high, thin descent of air whistling through the bullet holes in the unpressurised skin of the fuselage. They had been flying at around eight thousand feet – two thousand above the highest mountains on their route. By the time Constantine, wrenching fiercely at the control column and rudder bars, had pulled the aircraft out of its lethal spin, the desert was less than nine hundred feet below them.

Fortune dragged himself forwards as the engines roared and they settled back into a steady climb. The bullet that had winged Mullen had passed through the fleshy part of his upper arm without touching the bone. The wound was painful and messy without being dangerous. Fortune patched him up with the plane's first-aid kit, and made him as comfortable as he could in the cabin, and then went up into the greenhouse to take over the controls from the Canadian. 'She's as heavy as lead, but she handles okay,' Constantine said, sliding into the navigator's seat. 'Can't say I'm happy about the gas situation though.'

'Not to worry,' Fortune said. 'I'll save some by using the centre motor only – if it's strong enough to row this old tub through the air. It'll cut down our speed, but we'll go further. First, though, let's locate the bally trail we have to follow – and for that we'll have to climb a bit more.'

'What are we going to do with the stiff?' Constantine jerked his thumb over his shoulder at the body of Delannoy, which was still crumpled on the floor behind the navigator's seat. 'Chuck him out to give the buzzards another meal?'

Fortune looked shocked. 'Good God, no! Couldn't do that, old boy. Bury him in the sand when we've run out of juice and ditched this crate. Say a few words and all that. Wouldn't be Christian just to ... to throw him away, would it?'

Constantine grinned and shook his head. These bloody limeys! They were in the middle of a total war; the guy was an enemy, a buddy of the Nazis; he would have rubbed them out with no compunction ... and all this kid could think of was giving him a decent burial!

They were at three thousand feet when they spotted the trail – a paler smear snaking among patches of thorn cactus on the far side of a rocky ridge that sheltered the location they had been supposed to visit. A camel caravan wound its ant-like way among the scrub. Even from this height, the shadows of the beasts were iron-sharp on the baked ground. In the distance, a hint of dull green and a group of mud-coloured buildings broke the monotony of the mud-coloured landscape.

'El Golèa,' Fortune said briefly on the intercom. 'Another hour, and we'll be at In Salah. El Glouai should be soon after that.'

'We're gonna run out of gas even sooner.'

Fortune studied the gauges. He shook his head. 'No, no. Once we get there, we'll make an eighty-kilometre cast, pin-point the base, and then fly back as far as we can towards Hawkins and the boss.'

'They said we only had enough for seven-fifty.'

'I know, old boy. But as I said, we can economize by cutting out the wing motors as soon as we reach five thousand feet. It's easier work for the old girl when the atmosphere's thinner.'

It was just before they made that height that they were buzzed by the German. He came in from behind, and the first they knew of it was a shadow over the greenhouse followed by a sudden lurch as the Macchi-Castoldi flew into a blast of hot exhaust gases. Then they saw the silhouette of a fighter pulling out of its pass into a steep climbing turn ahead. Fortune swore as he fought the stick. 'Me. 109,' he said. 'Nobody ordered fighters!'

The Messerschmitt levelled out of his climb fifteen hundred feet higher up and away to the east. He flew back past them before turning to dive into his second pass. A German voice rasped peremptorily in the headsets. They were approaching a restricted area. No overflights were permitted. They must return to their authorized flight path immediately, or take the consequences. 'Warning us off,' Fortune said. 'We have to turn back or he'll fire third time round.'

'Fuck him. Shake him off.'

'That's not so easy, old lad. The 109's very fast. More than twice our speed, for a start.'

'You can try – a clever boy like you!'

'Fuck you too!' Fortune said equably. 'Look – Mullen's properly strapped in, isn't he?'

Constantine glanced over his shoulder. 'I guess so.' The fighter buzzed them again and rocketed up into the sky.

'Right. Now, I didn't expect they'd have a fighter umbrella out here in the back of the beyond ... and if they have, I bet they're not going to waste veteran Luftwaffe men staffing it. I'm going to take a chance on that and try an old trick on this chap. If he *is* a new boy, I hope he'll fall for it. Now fasten your own belt and hold tight, eh?'

The Messerschmitt, seeing that the Italian plane was making no attempt to turn back, flew around behind them for the third time. Again the German gutturals crackled in the cans.

Fortune hauled back the throttles and pushed the Macchi-Castoldi's nose hard down. The German pilot anticipated the manoeuvre but turned a little earlier and a little steeper than he should have done. Fortune nodded in a satisfied way and flung the three-engined transport to port, banking into and underneath the fighter, forcing him to tighten his turn still further. But the 109, already in a power dive, was going too fast. His wings canted vertically for an instant as tracer sprayed harmlessly past them on the right, and then he levelled out and climbed again to start a fresh attack.

Fortune continued downstairs in tight spirals. The German circled about five hundred feet above them, slowing down in a gentle curve outside their radius. 'What's the idea?' Constantine asked. He had twisted around in his seat and was apprehensively watching the fighter over his shoulder.

'Temptation, old bean, temptation. Get thee behind me, and all that.'

'You mean you *want* him on our tail?' The Canadian was incredulous.

'Provided he's going slow enough, yes. We already made him realize he overcooked it on the first turn. Now he's easing off more still. And that's the aim of the operation – make him lose height and speed before he comes in for the kill.'

'But ... ?'

'Hang on and you'll see.' The Macchi-Castoldi was below a thousand feet now, staggering through the hot air over a dust bowl surrounded by a rim of bare rock. Fortune put his hand on the lever controlling the flaps. 'Grab this,' he said.

'When I give the word, shove her down all the way, hard and quick. Right?'

Constantine swallowed. 'Right, squire.'

Fortune banked extra steeply, then suddenly levelled out and flew for a pass gashing the rock wall at one side of the dust bowl. The Messerschmitt half-rolled and dived in for the final attack, approaching in a wide curve that would place him immediately behind the three-engined plane. Fortune turned into and under him yet again, but this time the German pilot was ready for it: he was flying slowly enough to follow them all the way, tightening his diving turn, easily holding the Macchi-Castoldi.

Fortune levelled once more and hauled back the throttles. The 109 slid behind their tail-plane, still in a shallow dive. Ragged holes suddenly appeared in the slower plane's starboard wing, advancing inexorably towards the cabin.

'Flaps!' Fortune yelled.

Constantine slammed down the lever. The effect was exactly as if he had stamped on a brake pedal. Flying into a wall of air, the old plane shuddered, and then lurched upwards straight into the Messerschmitt's path.

Involuntarily the German pilot reacted as Fortune had expected. He snatched back the stick, instinctively, frenziedly, at the same time flinging the fighter into a sharp turn in an automatic attempt to avoid the obstacle.

The 109 reared up like a frightened horse. But it was already down almost to its stalling speed. The nose dropped, the wing slid away, and then the machine was plunging earthwards as it stalled out.

They saw a helmeted figure fighting the controls in the cockpit. Blue smoke streamed from the fighter's exhausts as the pilot applied full boost and tried to dive out of it. But he had less than 800 feet to go. He decided he couldn't make it. The cockpit canopy spun away in the slipstream, followed by the parachute leaders. He was still only halfway out when the 109 hit the deck. There was a vivid flash and then a cloud of yellow-black smoke rolling across the dust. 'Well ...' Constantine said, 'that's one outa the way! Let's hope they don't have no goddam squadron!'

Apparently they didn't. Perhaps the fighter wastage in Europe was too serious for the High Command to detail more than one expensive aircraft to act as deterrent in a place so far away from the battlegrounds. At all events, no more Messerschmitts buzzed them as they continued on their way.

Fortune took them up to five thousand feet and then cut the two outboard engines. The plane clattered slowly on. They passed over the oil derricks and natural gas installations at In Salah and swung southeast for El Glouai – a smudge of brownish green at the mouth of a ravine in the foothills of the Mouydir Mountains. The base – whose very existence they had at times doubted – was easier to find than they had expected, for the southern half of the circle centred on the oasis was clearly ruled out; the terrain was far too hilly for an experimental firing range. In fact the ridge that it lay beyond was due east of El Glouai.

They circled three times while Constantine made a plan of the site – a handful of palms around a collection of huts and tents by the side of what looked like an aircraft hangar. In front of this larger building there was a short length of railway track and a group of small, cockpit-less monoplanes. Beyond, the sand desert rolled in hot waves towards a purple horizon.

There were sandbagged machine-gun and mortar emplacements around the site, and mounted tribesmen patrolling the track over the ridge, but they could see no signs of artillery. The dun metal of trucks and armoured cars gleamed dully in the sunlight between the trees. A double line of oil drums stretching away to the north marked the strip from which the ill-fated Me. 109 had taken off. There was no sign of another.

'Hold it a minute, squire!' Constantine called out as Fortune banked to turn back. 'Something's goin' on down there.'

'Fuel's pretty low now,' Fortune warned.

'The hell with it. Just one more circuit – and look!'

One of the miniature planes had been manoeuvred on to the railway track. They could see the minute figures of men around it. Others ran out to stare up at the strange aircraft. As they watched, flame stabbed the air behind the projectile. It shot along the rails, swooped into the air, and flew off across the desert, still trailing fire and smoke. 'Must be some kind of launching ramp,' Constantine said. 'But the goddam ship's on fire! What the hell are they playing at?'

'We'll jolly well find out,' Fortune said. 'I'm going to follow the thing.'

The pilotless plane levelled out at about two thousand feet. Fortune was three thousand feet higher – but although he used all three engines, shoved the throttles forward, and put the Macchi-Castoldi into a shallow dive, the tiny machine streaked away from him. 'She must be doing three or four hundred miles an hour!' he exclaimed blankly as the twinkling spot of fire vanished into the haze. 'Even a Spit or an F.W. 190 would find it hard to keep up with that. What kind of engine can that be?'

'Search me,' the Canadian said. 'All I know is, I'd sure hate to be part of an assault unit trying to make a landing if there was a coupla hundred of those babies, loaded with H.E., falling outa the sky every hour!' There was a bright flash on the surface of the desert about ten miles ahead. 'Thar she blows!' he added. 'You figure we ought to mosey on out there and see if she made the target – assumin' there is one?'

There was. A ghost city had been built on the sand. Over an area more than half a mile square the shells of office blocks, houses, apartment buildings and warehouses had been constructed in brick and stone and concrete and wood. Much of it had been destroyed by blast: twisted girders raised skeletal arms from the rubble heaped against shattered walls. For two miles around the site, the desert was pockmarked with huge craters.

Constantine was busy taking notes. 'I guess they're checking out the explosive effect on different types of structure,' he said. 'Doesn't look as if they're all that accurate yet – not with all those misses around.'

Fortune said: 'I'm turning back now. We're on the last few gallons of juice.' As he banked for the turn, Constantine yelled and pointed down through the greenhouse window. A winged shadow plummeted earthwards below them. From the centre of an undamaged six-storey block on the far edge of the site, a burst of black smoke veined with flame erupted. The walls of the building trembled, slid downwards, and then collapsed in a column of dust that boiled out and swelled through the empty streets. They could hear the thump of the explosion over the racket of the three radial engines.

'Yeah,' Constantine drawled after a moment. 'Like you said, we better go back now.' He shook his head. 'Jesus! The *force* of the motherfucker! They must be packed full of Göring's hottest explosive!'

Fortune cut to a single motor again and flew on a diagonal course that would intersect the trail from In Salah. Slowly, the fake city, and then the base away to their left, vanished in the haze.

The radio was still tuned to the frequency on which Delannoy's contact and the Messerschmitt pilot had spoken. A few minutes later, a harsh voice vibrated in their headsets. '*Delannoy? Here is Colonel Benckendorff. We picked up your man not far from El Golèa. He was riding a stolen horse and he was unarmed. I have to return to base, so I am obliged to take him with me in the armoured car. I have yet to find out whether he knew about the base ... but I will. In the meantime you had better warn Algiers of the possibility ... Curtet and Pellétier are still tailing the other three in the half-track, I presume?*' The voice paused, and then resumed on a questioning note: '*Delannoy? Are you receiving me? Please acknowledge ... Delannoy? Calling Delannoy in the Macchi-Castoldi F-EBQN ...*'

Constantine cut the switch. 'Shit!' he said disgustedly. 'That's all we need: the Major in the krauts' hands again! What are we gonna do now?'

'Fasten our belts and sit tight,' Fortune replied. 'We're out of fuel.'

The central motor spluttered, faltered, gave a loud bang, and then caught again. Fortune jockeyed with the throttles and put the nose down. But a little later the engine coughed once more and then choked into silence. The spinning disc of the airscrew slowed until they could distinguish the separate blades. Beyond them, an inhospitable wilderness of shale rushed towards the plane. 'How far east of the trail are we?' Constantine asked uneasily.

'Fifteen or twenty miles,' Fortune said.

The sun was dropping into the belt of purple mist over the mountains to the west. Long shadows stretched across the desert from a line of irregular hillocks in the shale. Wind moaned through struts and wires as the aircraft sank lower.

'Hold on,' Fortune said. 'This may be a rough one.'

'Germany calling . . . this is Germany calling . . . You are listening to the stations Hamburg, Köln and DJA. Here is the news in English . . . After the disastrous Malta convoy action in which the British navy lost HMS Manchester, HMS Eagle and HMS Cairo to units of the German Mediterranean fleet, strong forces of Luftwaffe bombers escorted by fighters last night destroyed oil installations and munitions factories in the Thames estuary without loss. The people of Britain are asking how long this waste of life and material can last. But there is worse to come . . . the Fuhrer's first Vergeltungswaffen are ready to spread terror and destruction in the cities of Britain. Remember the name – Vergeltungswaffen or V.1 – the secret reprisal weapon devised to avenge the senseless bombing of innocent German civilians by the murderers of the RAF and the USAAF. Remember the name . . . and remember as you quake in your useless shelters that this powerful new weapon will enable the valiant flyers of the Luftwaffe to remain at home with their families while death rains on you from the sky . . .'

Chapter Fifteen

There was no glasshouse on the secret German base in the desert. The worst they could do for Webster was lock him in a disused storeroom and station guards with machine carbines outside the window and door. He was furious at his recapture, mystified by the speed of it, and apprehensive at the certain knowledge that Benckendorff would return to the attack very soon. 'You are intelligent enough to know that, now you have seen this place, you will never leave it alive,' the German said. 'But before you die, I intend to find out whether you knew of its existence before – and, if so, who else has been told. Specifically, I want to know if your three friends, at present being followed in a south-easterly direction by French colleagues of ours, are heading this way. And if they are, what they – and you – are supposed to do about it.' Benckendorff opened a flat box of cigarettes, selected one, and lit it. 'Are you simply spies?' he asked. 'If so, why was it necessary to send four of you? If not, I fail to see the point. Surely the British, even the British, would not be so foolhardy as to attempt *sabotage* of a guarded base with a miserable quartet?'

Webster said nothing. He was dying for a cigarette himself.

'Suppose that you have in some way stumbled upon this secret,' the German continued. 'It will do you no good, for you are all under surveillance and you will simply be eliminated. If your presence in the region is a coincidence, and you are in fact on some other espionage mission, the result will be the same. We cannot afford the risk that stray gossip might compromise this, the latest and greatest of the Führer's plans for the victory of the Reich. In any case, I shall have to know whether or not your superiors are aware of the existence of an experimental station in this area.'

'Since the area is neutral, the base – whatever it is – must surely be illegal,' Webster said, playing for time.

Benckendorff laughed. 'There are many things – especially in wartime – dubbed illegal by some but acceptable to others,' he said. 'The extortion of information by forcible means, for example. Victory goes to the strong, and it would be ludicrous to ignore that fact because of an outmoded regard for the namby-pamby rules of the so-called Geneva Convention.' He paused and then added softly: 'You would be well advised to remember that, my friend. It applies particularly to a situation such as ours, where there is no chance of any ... transgression ... ever being found out. No chance whatever.'

Webster remained silent. When they started boasting, there was always the possibility that some crumb of information might inadvertently be dropped.

'I shall therefore find out from you – or from the others, when they are brought in – the answers to my questions. In the meantime, you are privileged to witness one of the proving stages of a weapon that should hasten the establishment of Greater Europe.'

'What-ho!' Webster said with a levity he scarcely felt.

Benckendorff walked to the door. 'Think very carefully, my friend, before you decide to remain stubborn. Your decision will govern whether your death shall be swift and merciful or long-drawn-out and exceedingly painful.' The door opened and closed. A key grated in the lock. Webster heard the click of heels, a murmur of German, and then the SS man's footsteps receding down a concrete passage.

There was no point, Webster knew, in thinking over what Benckendorff had said. There was nothing he could do about it anyway. For the moment, his trained saboteur's mind had plenty to occupy it in pondering the logistics of the mission – or what remained of it. For the barred store-room window looked out on the hangar in which the 'radio-controlled pilotless planes' Webster had come so far to see were actually assembled. And if he leaned his head against the glass and squinted sideways he could make out the launching ramp beyond a row of palms.

It was a long concrete structure, shaped rather like a giant ski, furnished with rails which tilted upwards at the far end – presumably, Webster thought, to lift the missiles into the air as they were catapulted off. Seen in close-up, the machines themselves were surprisingly small, not much more than twenty feet long, with a wingspan of about fifteen feet. The fuselage was cigar-shaped, with stubby, squared-off wings sprouting from the centre. What appeared to be the engine was a long, waisted tube mounted above the rudder. So far as Webster could see, there were no control surfaces on the wings, nor was there any landing gear. Mounted on the cross-braced wooden trolleys which ferried them to the ramp, the machines were only chin-high to a man of average height. They looked, in fact, more like winged artillery shells than pilotless aircraft.

Soon after Benckendorff had left him, Webster saw one of the missiles with the inspection plates along one side of the fuselage removed. There were servo controls in the tail, and a master gyro fed from spherical bottles of compressed air amidships. The centre-section housed a fuel tank, and ahead of this was the cxplosive compartment. Furnished with an impact fuse, he estimated that this would have about the same effect as a 1000-lb bomb – although if the missile were programmed to approach the target in a shallow dive, the lateral blast effect would be considerably greater than that of a conventional bomb falling almost vertically. In any case it would be a formidable, indeed a terrifying, weapon used in built-up areas or against a heavy concentration of troops.

But were they in fact programmed in any way? The reports had spoken of radio control, but Webster could see no sign of receptor aerials, no trace of radio installations or control linkages among the simplified mechanics. Watching with increasing astonishment as three of the devices were launched, he noticed that such control surfaces as there were appeared to be pre-set. That the fuel was carefully metered suggested some kind of automatic engine cut-out that would stall them and allow them to fall to earth at a predetermined time after take-off. In which case, of course, with so many variables out of the launchers' control, they would be wildly inaccurate, almost random, in terms of specific targets.

'Bloody things are blacksmith all the way,' Webster mused. 'Built down to the cheapest price and the hell with any kind of accuracy. Not that the buggers couldn't put the wind up civvy street.'

He frowned, concentrating on the drill around the launching ramp. Although the personnel staffing the base were not in uniform, they fell into three distinct categories: soldiers, in unmarked bush jackets and shorts; overalled mechanics working on the project; and a group of about half a dozen scientists and technicians. The colonel who had been at the *diffa* in Wadi Elmira – his name was Stahl, Webster had discovered – was in charge of the military. The supremo nevertheless appeared to be a civilian: a tall, thin, balding scientist with thick-lensed spectacles. This man, together with Stahl and three of the technicians, grouped around the first missile as mechanics manoeuvred it on to the ramp. There was some kind of conference as last-minute adjustments were made, and then a whistle shrilled. All except two of the mechanics scattered and took refuge in shallow bunkers scooped from the sand on either side of the ramp. The whistle blew again. The two mechanics were busy about some kind of electrical machine that had been wheeled up to the rear of the missile. There was a sudden clattering roar from the nearer end of the ramp, and a stabbing burst of flame. The remaining mechanics ran for cover.

Webster's eyes were wide. He could make neither head nor tail of the strange tubular motor, which seemed to have no moving parts. Yet the forked tongues of fire emitted at the back of the tube were receding along the rails. The missile was moving, gathering speed.

But the pulsating brilliance of the flames dimmed and then

died. The machine lurched once or twice and then slewed sideways, jammed across the ramp at the foot of the incline at the far end. The men emerged from their bunkers and there was another discussion around the stalled projectile. A flat-bed truck equipped with a crane backed up and lifted it on to a trolley; then it was wheeled back into the hangar. A second took its place at the foot of the ramp and the launching process was repeated.

This time, the missile accelerated the full length of the ramp, rose into the air over the uptilted tip, dipped momentarily, and then gradually gained height as the shattering detonations of the mysterious engine propelled it out over the desert. The hard, wavering drone of the motor finally faded and died. A few minutes later there was the thump of a distant explosion. At once Stahl, the head scientist and two other civilians piled into a jeep-like truck and drove out over the desert in the direction taken by the experimental machine. It seemed likely, Webster thought, that they had gone to check the accuracy of the shot.

It was dusk by the time they returned and the third missile was launched. Webster was now certain that there was no radio control, and that the machines were not in fact catapulted into the air: they left the ramp under their own power, rather like a carrier-borne plane from its flight deck.

A bar of flamingo pink separated the darkening sky from the purplish haze over the rim of the desert. The glow at the third machine's tail dwindled in the thickened air . . . and then suddenly it dived straight into the sand when it was only a few hundred yards beyond the end of the ramp. A vivid orange flash silhouetted ramp and watchers – and then there was a thunderous, flat explosion that shook the building. Webster grinned. 'One out of three,' he said aloud. 'That's amateur night at the pier-head!'

'Even one out of ten would have a certain deterrent effect on a sea-borne landing,' a voice said behind him. 'However, in less than a week we shall be able to guarantee nine out of ten!' Webster swung around. Benckendorff was standing just inside the open door with two armed guards at his back. 'Now that the trials are over for today,' the Nazi said, 'I would like to continue the little conversation you so discourteously broke off when you were Kerim's guest at Wadi Elmira.'

Webster dug his nails into the palms of his hands. He had heard the drone of an aircraft an hour ago, but had assumed it was the return of the Messerschmitt he had seen take off earlier. Even if by some miracle it had been Fortune and the others, they would still have to ditch the plane and rendezvous with Hawkins's unit before any advance on the base was made. That advance was the only hope for him now ... and he knew he couldn't expect it before the following afternoon. Could he hold out that long under Benckendorff and his torturers?

* * * *

As soon as the all-clear sounded, Commander Lang walked into the back room of the house in Regent's Park and asked the telegraphist: 'Any more signals from the Captain, Ford?'

Ford eased the headset from his ears and allowed the aluminium hoops to subside around his neck. He looked up from his dials and screens and pilot lights. 'What was that, sir?'

'The Captain. Have you any more news from Algiers?'

'No, sir. There was a message relayed from Gib, but it was just a confirmation of the stuff we had from Captain O'Kelly direct.'

Lang sighed. 'I suppose I'd better act on it, then,' he said. 'I'd really have preferred something a bit harder to go on; it'd be terrible to put up a black just because this fellow Webster's got a bee in his bonnet about the way he was rumbled.'

'Yes, sir.'

'There's nothing else? No standby-for-an-important-announcement signal? Nothing from the gents at the Mission?'

'Not a sausage, sir.'

Lang nodded, and then sighed again. He went back into his office and read O'Kelly's message, which encapsulated Webster's suspicions, for the tenth time. He reached for the scrambler phone and asked for an unlisted number.

Late that afternoon, he sat behind a desk in a fourth floor office above the rush-hour traffic on Victoria Embankment. The man sitting beside him, whose name was on the door of the office, was a Superintendent in Scotland Yard's Special

Branch. On the far side of the desk, Colonel Chard paced angrily up and down the green Ministry of Works carpet. 'Balderdash!' he snorted. 'I never heard anything so ridiculous in me life. What a lot of tommyrot!'

'I'm afraid there can be little doubt, Colonel,' Lang said with an assurance that was largely assumed.

'Rubbish! Why, she's been with me since—'

'Since when, sir?' the Special Branch man asked quietly.

'Well ... Since the beginning of '34, actually.'

'Just so. Soon enough after Hitler came to power.' Superintendent Rawlins was a large, slow, heavy man with exceedingly penetrating eyes. A man who spoke seldom but whose few words were weighed with care. A man whose every word carried its full burden of meaning.

'But I can't believe it. I—'

'The person in question did have access to the reports you made? Specifically with regard to possible candidates for Commander Lang's formation?'

'Well, yes. I mean, naturally. But—'

'The possible destinations ... the postings of such candidates, would be on file, then? But not necessarily the reasons for those movements? Is that right?'

'Of course. What they did with them ... it wasn't my show. I mean, I vetted them and that was that. Sometimes I knew ... a word to the wise and all that. But none of it went into the files. Obviously.'

'Let me get this clear,' Lang said easily. 'To take the case in question: the fact that Major Webster was in line for some secret job, and that this job would take him to North Africa, would be on file? Such a file would be freely available to the person we suspect? But none of your reflections on the nature of Major Webster's work in North Africa – assuming he got the job – would be quoted in it? Is that roughly the situation?'

Chard cleared his throat. 'Yes, but I still don't—'

'And if our suspect happened to have a confederate in War Office Records,' Rawlins said in his turn, 'and orders on file there confirmed that Webster had indeed been sent to North Africa, then that would itself confirm that he must have been taken on by O'Kelly's cloak-and-dagger outfit, right?'

'I suppose so. Yes.'

'Which would be enough reason, I suppose, for an enemy agent to put Webster under observation, even while he was still in London,' Lang added in his lazy drawl. 'Especially when it was noticed that he had stopped wearing uniform.'

Chard flushed. 'I don't know anything about that. This is ... Dammit, man, she's been working with me gettin' on for eight years!' He turned to the window and blew his nose violently.

'It comes hard on blokes like that,' Rawlins said to Lang as the squad car sped south across Battersea Bridge soon after darkness had fallen. 'It's an expensive luxury to keep these days, trust is.'

'Yes,' Lang replied. 'It's funny nobody thought to check the refugee immigrations against the official changes of name at Somerset House.'

'Well, we can't do everything, sir, can we?' the policeman said comfortably. 'But we usually get around to it in the end.'

The house was a semi-detached Victorian villa in a cul-de-sac off York Road. Doors, windows and brickwork alike had been blackened by a century of smoke blowing down from the railway embankment that blocked off the far end of the street. Lang surveyed the weed-grown front yards, the identical tiled paths, separated only by a sooty privet hedge, that led to the twin front doors, and the grimy window bays that flanked them. ' "If you know of a better 'ole ...",' he quoted softly.

The iron railings fencing in the properties had been removed for war salvage, but there was still a rusty gate at the entrance. They pushed it open and walked up the path.

A fat woman in blue railway porter's uniform opened the door. 'First floor right, dear,' she said in answer to Rawlins's query. 'Though you'd be lucky to find a second floor in this dump, wouldn't you?' She shook with asthmatic laughter. 'Sooner one of 'is bombs blitzes the place, the better I'll be pleased! I could do with a few quid of War Damage, and that's a fact. Put in a proper lav, fix the leak in the outhouse, lick of paint on the bleedin' windows – that'd be a bit of all right, wouldn't it?'

'Thank you, madam,' Lang began. 'If we could—'

'Not but what it'd do *me* any good,' the woman said. 'Not

while the old man's on nights, anyways. But what I always say is, you got to take the rough with the smooth. Every cloud has a silver linin'. I mean it stands to reason, doesn't it? Though I wish them painted-up tarts at the Food Office would turn out the silver linin' on me supplementary rations for the old man. I mean you got to build them up, haven't you? It's hard work, specially on nights, with 'im sendin' over the blitz regular as clockwork. They deserve the extra, if I do say it myself. But you try and get it; you try and get it! Did you see what butter's down to this month? Well, I ask you! They said on the wireless—'

'Quite so,' Rawlins said firmly. 'Thank you, madam. No – there's no need to announce us: we'll just go up and knock on the door.'

The knock was answered by a faded blonde of about forty-five. She was drying her hands on a flowered overall and there was a patch of soapsuds at one side of her chin. 'Elsie Potter?' Rawlins said formally. 'I am a police officer and I have to tell you that I have a warrant to search these premises.' He produced a document from his breast pocket.

'*Sheisse!*' exclaimed Miss Elsie Potter. '*Ich bin drin!*' She turned hurriedly and tried to slam the door in their faces.

Rawlins blocked the move with a heavy boot, and shouldered her back into the room. 'I have reason to believe,' he said, 'that you are in fact a certain Ilse Pütter, born in Limburg in 1897 and accepted in this country in 1934, when you claimed falsely to be a refugee.'

'*Geh zum Teufel,*' the woman snapped. 'Go to the devil!'

Lang closed the door and leaned his back against it. The room was cheaply furnished, with oilcloth covering the table and cracked linoleum in a parquet pattern on the floor. The air was heavy with the smell of sausages frying on a gas cooker which stood beside the wash basin.

'For certain irregularities under the Registration of Aliens Act,' the Superintendent pursued, 'I would be empowered to take you into custody by virtue of Regulation 18B. There are, however, one or two other matters which require investigation first.'

The woman compressed her thin lips. 'I am under arrest?'

'Let us say that I shall require you to accompany me to the police station.' Rawlins's stare was flinty. 'The niceties are not always observed in the case of spies in wartime, but I can caution you that anything you say will be taken down and may be used in evidence.' From another pocket, he took out a small notebook and pencil.

Ilse Pütter switched off the gas, removed the sausages from the pan and placed them on a sheet of brown paper to drain. She sat down on a kitchen chair, crossed her legs and lit a cigarette.

Lang called up the two men from the squad car and the search began. She had been very clever. The cover of a secretary who found it difficult to make ends meet in wartime was perfect. There was not a single item in the whole shabby apartment – not a book, not a trinket, not a scrap of paper or an article of clothing – that betrayed the slightest interest in, or connection with, Germany. They had even begun to have doubts – at least on the spying charge – when Lang discovered the Everyman edition of Thackeray's *Vanity Fair*.

Some of the pages were uncut, and it had evidently never been read right through. But if it was allowed to fall gently on to the table it invariably opened either at page 17 or at page 47. Both the leaves were dog-eared and slightly yellower than the rest.

'The usual simple cypher,' Lang said wearily. 'Almost impossible to crack unless you have the key. The person at the other end has the same edition of the same book. A page is selected, and the message is just a series of numbers identifying which letters, on which lines, go to make up the text. You get no help, trying to decode it through the length of words, because it's transmitted in equal groups of four or five figures, with a pre-arranged sequence to indicate where the spaces come.'

'I know the technique,' Rawlins nodded. 'All we have to do now is find the receiver and transmitter.'

Ilse Pütter was munching one of the sausages. She didn't look up.

There was a small box-room leading off the apartment, one end of which had been partitioned off to make a clothes closet. In the ceiling was a trapdoor which had been used, before the house was turned into flatlets, to gain access to the loft. Rawlins stood on a chair and pushed up the wooden flap. It opened easily, and a rope ladder tumbled through to hang at his feet.

The transmitter was balanced on a couple of planks laid across the joists. It was fairly simple – not powerful enough to reach Germany, but quite powerful enough to exchange messages with Dublin. A low-power electric bulb hung from a nail above the transmitting key. Rawlins and Lang climbed back down into the closet. 'All right,' the policeman called. 'That'll do for now. Let's go.'

A Black Maria was parked behind the squad car outside the house now. The chatelaine, still in her porter's uniform, had already adjusted to the situation and was profiting from it. 'I always did say,' she confided to the knot of curious neighbours grouped around her front door, 'that there was something fishy about that one. No better than she ought to be, if you ask me. Why, to think that I've got her under-the-counter fags at Foster's off-licence up the road more times than I can remember! ... *Yah! Dirty foreign bitch! Why don't you go back to Adolf and 'is bleedin' Dachshunds?*'

'You can see it in 'er face, can't you?' one of the neighbours said. 'Shifty!'

'Some kind of fifth columnist, I shouldn't wonder.'

'Yer. Know that old dog down the road? Mongrel's always 'angin' around outside Number Fifteen? Well, I saw 'er kickin' 'im the other day. Straight up – kickin' the shit out of the poor bugger!'

'Gettin' honest workin' folk in bad with the law!'

'They want to put her kind up agin a wall, don't they?'

Rawlins stood with the woman by the open doors of the Black Maria. 'We know about some of your accomplices already,' he said. 'The Irish one in Records, for example. You might make it easier for yourself, if you'd like to tell us about the others.'

'Piss off, flatfoot!' she spat out in German. 'You'll get nothing from me.'

The Superintendent shrugged. 'Take her away,' he said. The Alert had just sounded and the streets were greasy with rain.

* * * *

Chilton dragged himself to the crest of a low ridge – one of a series of parallel outcrops that looked like wrecks which had foundered in a sea of sand. For fifty miles around, the lines of dunes rolled inexorably in from the horizon, a scorching wilderness of troughs and peaks drained of all colour by the pitiless, white-hot glare of the sun. And in the whole bleached expanse not a living thing moved, not a blade of grass or a spine of vegetation showed. Chilton cursed. Sweat dripped from his chin, crawled between his shoulder blades and slid off his wrists. He stumbled back down the rocky slope and ducked in under the awning stretched out from the roof of the half-track. 'Bugger-all!' he said curtly.

Hawkins and Zygmund were lying on the sand, smoking. 'We got food and water for one more meal,' the sergeant said. He flipped the fag-end away and watched the smoke rise steadily into the super-heated air. 'After that it'll be too bleedin' bad.' Zygmund was too hot to say anything.

Seven hours had passed since the truck had stalled. They had run into trouble early in the morning: a stone holed the radiator on a slope of shale, and before they knew what was happening the engine had boiled dry. They patched it up with chewing-gum and insulating tape, but the overheating had already done the damage. An hour later, Chilton discovered that he had missed the trail somewhere, and while he was driving around trying to find it again, a main bearing went. He coaxed the thumping motor another mile or so to the west ... and then something seized solid in the heat. The half-track ground to a halt with a stench of fused metal, leaving them stranded a good seventy-five miles short of El Glouai, marooned in an ocean of scalding sand.

Fortune had contacted them on the radio early the previous evening, reporting a successful forced landing with one man wounded. According to the position he gave, they were still fifty miles short of the ditched plane. 'A fine thing!' Zygmund said bitterly. 'Three men stranded in the desert with a broken-down truck; three more in an aeroplane she has no fuel – and one of them wounded already; the officer in the hands of the Germans! This is an assault team we are supposed to be?'

'Ah, pack it in, Ziggie!' Chilton began.

The Pole turned towards him. 'And all,' he said levelly, 'because some ignorant *schmuck* he cannot see the road in front of his face.'

'If it was that easy to see, why didn't you fuckin' suss it

out yourself?' Chilton said angrily. 'You was sitting beside me, wasn't you? If a route's that clear you should bloody notice when we leave it.'

'Most times, it is the driver who watches the road,' said Zygmund.

'You can piss off, mate! Any case, the soddin' rad was fucked *before* we lost the trail.' Chilton swung around and addressed Hawkins. 'And I can't see why we don't fuck off out of here and find the bastard again. She can't be more than ten or fifteen miles at the outside. At least we'd stand a chance of bein' picked up then. Why don't we do that, Sarge?'

'Because it'd be the quickest fuckin' way to die,' Hawkins snapped. 'You walk a couple of hours in that sun an' you've had it.'

'So we start an hour before sunset, when it's cooled off a bit, wait out the night, and then walk another hour after dawn, before she's too high in the sky.'

'In a pig's arse!' Hawkins said. 'How far do you think we'd get in an hour over this terrain? These ain't no dunes behind Blackpool bloody beach, man – there's thousands of square miles of the fucker. You'd be walkin' in circles before you made a mile.'

'We got a compass.'

'Oh, yes, we got a compass all right. There's plenty of skeletons picked clean by the vultures had compasses too, I'll bet. I'm tellin' you: the desert's on its own. They know what they're doin' when they tell you never, ever leave your bleedin' transport if you get stuck. They can fuckin' see you from the air then. But a man on his own, two men, three men ... ? Be your age, Chilton!'

'So who the hell's flyin' around lookin' for us? Are you goin' to call up the frogs on the radio?' Chilton was scowling sulkily. 'As far as they're concerned we're just a bunch of bloody miners got lost.'

'And blow the operation? Leaving the officer in enemy hands? Looks like the sun got to you already!' Hawkins sounded scandalized. 'No, I've got other ideas. But first the soddin' engine has to cool off. At dusk—'

'I still think we should be *doin'* something, not just sittin' here on our backsides!' Chilton burst out.

Zygmund said: 'So if you are so crazy for action, Chilton,

why do you not go on out and rustle up some game, eh? You heard what the Sergeant said: there's only enough in the canteen for one more meal. We're relying on you for the next. You can even borrow my gun: you may not be able to see a road, but you could hardly miss a herd of gazelle should they stampede among these dunes. Or perhaps you prefer a wild turkey? a serpent? a nice fat trout, maybe?'

'Why, you dirty little . . .!' Chilton lumbered towards the Pole with an open clasp knife in his hand.

Hawkins sprang to his feet. '*That man!*' He used his full parade ground authority. 'Stop that! Both of you! Can't you bloody see, you stupid cunts – this is what the heat does to you? And we're under cover here. Can you imagine what you'd be like after an hour out in that?' He threw out an arm in a furious gesture at the blistering landscape.

The bonnet of the truck trembled in the blazing heat. Zygmund and Chilton eyed one another, breathing heavily.

'All right,' Hawkins said. 'Chilton – shut that fuckin' knife and give it to me. Now siddown and shuddup. You, Zygmund, go on up to the top of that bluff again, and see if you can see anything.'

Zygmund shrugged and wiped a sweat-soaked shirtsleeve across his forehead. He pushed himself upright. 'For this,' he said sourly, 'I gave up a nice cool prison cell in Cracow!'

* * * *

The caretaker was quite positive. Miss Macnamara – something important in the ATS, wasn't she? – had left the day *before* yesterday. No, so far as the caretaker knew, she hadn't been due for leave. She'd had a forty-eight only last week, and she'd gone back to Ireland for ten days in January, the lucky girl.

'She must have been tipped off,' Lang said to Rawlins. 'And that means there must be *another* leak somewhere. I'll swear the Potter woman was taken completely by surprise when we went there tonight.' He turned back to the caretaker, a wispy, frail woman peering myopically through thick-lensed spectacles. 'This particular trip – the day before yesterday – must have been unexpected, then?'

'Certainly was.' The woman stared past them at a bus,

crawling with hooded headlights in the direction of John Barnes. The thin beams of illumination struck wavering reflections from the rain-wet surface of Finchley Road. 'They was phoning all day yesterday from her office, asking where she was.'

'She hadn't even told them she wouldn't be in? It must have been something urgent, then,' said Rawlins.

'I dare say. Perhaps she'd had bad news. You never can tell, can you? Or maybe she'd found somewhere else. She was bombed out of her last place, you know: down in the city somewhere, it was.'

'She didn't leave a forwarding address? She didn't say where she was going or anything?'

The caretaker shook her head. 'Paid up to the end of the month, like a good girl, and off she went.'

'Just a minute,' Lang said. 'Do you mean to say that she's gone for good? I thought maybe she was just away on a trip.'

'No, no. She took all her things and went. It's a furnished flat but she had quite a lot of stuff. A little van came and took it away. Ever so nice, the driver was. He—'

'Was there anything on the van?' Rawlins interrupted. 'The name of a removal firm, or anything like that?'

She screwed up her thin face in the effort of concentration. 'I don't think so. I think it was ... Yes, I'm sure it was a plain van. It was a funny thing, too, the way Mr Meredith had to leave the very same day. Lucky for him the van was there. As I was saying, the driver was ever so nice: he offered to take Mr Meredith's things too.'

'Mr Meredith?'

'Gentleman on the third floor. He had the flat below Miss Macnamara's. Travelled in wirelesses and things like that, Mr Meredith did. I think he had important government contracts; leastways, his living room was always covered in wires and valves and batteries and suchlike. A job it was for the girl, cleaning and dusting, I can tell you.'

Rawlins cleared his throat. 'Madam,' he said, 'I have to tell you we are police officers. Special Branch, Scotland Yard. With your permission, I should like very much to look over those flats.'

The woman's mouth opened and closed. 'Goodness gracious me!' she exclaimed. 'Well, I never did!'

As they had feared, the search was fruitless. It had been the same story when, immediately Lang had received O'Kelly's signal, they had turned over the wrecked Chancery Lane flats where Webster and Liz Macnamara had spent the night. 'Picked clean as a whistle,' Rawlins complained. 'Not a single blasted thing left that couldn't be found in a thousand furnished flats all over bloody London.'

'They were warned, that's all,' Lang said. 'And even if we have no proof, at least we know that Webster's hunch must have been right.' In each of the two blocks, holes had been bored between the upper and lower flats which were just big enough to accommodate a microphone lead.

'A fat lot of good that does us,' Rawlins grumbled. They were standing on the pavement a hundred yards up the hill from Finchley Road underground station. The rain was heavier now, drumming on Lang's umbrella, splashing up around their feet. A Beardmore taxi executed a U-turn and slowed as it drew level with them. 'Cab, sir?' a hoarse voice enquired. 'If you're goin' back into town, that is.'

'A gift from the gods!' Lang enthused. 'Do you know the Savage Club, off Carlton House Terrace?'

'We'll find it, sir. Just you hop in out of the rain.'

'I suppose she'll be safe back in Ireland now?' Rawlins said as they sank on to the shabby seats.

'I would think. She'd have had the right travel documents and permits laid on. Her father was killed by the Black and Tans, you know. I was able to get confirmation of that in half an hour,' Lang said. 'I do wish people who might have a grudge were vetted more thoroughly before they were given security-sensitive jobs like hers.'

'We can't do everything,' Rawlins replied irritably. He had eaten nothing since a light breakfast before he caught the 7.50 train from Surbiton to Waterloo. 'And the mysterious Mr Meredith?'

'The eavesdropper? The chap who listens in on the indiscretions spilled into Miss Macnamara's bed? He'll lie low for a bit, I imagine. Probably somewhere in the north. Then he'll start up again somewhere else. With another girl. We're bound to catch him in the end.'

It was nearly eleven o'clock when they paid off the taxi: he had dropped them at the nearest corner he could find to the

Savage. 'It's a funny old life all right,' the cabbie said, pocketing his fare. 'You can go for years an' you don't see the same geezer twice – then you get yourself a co-hincidence like tonight.'

'Like tonight?' Lang asked absently. He was busy buttoning his wallet back into his hip pocket.

'Pickin' you gentlemen up twice,' the driver explained. 'Once in York Road, and then again up Finchley. You never know, do you?' He chuckled gustily and reached behind him to put up his flag.

Rawlins and Lang walked the hundred and fifty yards to the club. It was very quiet in the dark. The rumble of traffic in Piccadilly was muted and they could hear wind in the trees. Although the All Clear had not sounded, the raid must have been a long way away, perhaps at the mouth of the Thames estuary.

They were halfway up the steps to the main entrance when both of them were struck by the same thought. 'My God!' Lang exclaimed suddenly. 'In both places! And a genuine cabbie ...?'

'... would have known at once where this place was!'

'A prowling taxi would be the perfect cover ...'

They turned and ran back through the rain to the corner. But the Beardmore cab and its driver had already disappeared.

* * * *

Fortune and Joe Constantine lay panting on the hard shale beneath the plane. There was a two-day stubble on their chins and the skin over their cheekbones shone whitely in their gaunt and blistered faces. It was more than thirty-six hours sincc Fortune had brought them down in the stony wilderness – two nights and one day of unrelenting hell, with no food, no water, and only the negative news on the radio from Hawkins that he was stranded fifty miles away. Now the sun was nearing its zenith on the second day and conditions were worse than ever.

Fortune wished they had buried the body of the Frenchman further away or that they had had the strength to scoop a deeper grave from the stony surface of the desert. The patch of shadow under the Macchi-Castoldi was too narrow, too near the hot metal of the fuselage, too subject to the reflection and refraction of sunlight off the shaly ground to be called shelter or even shade. But it was paradise compared with conditions in the open. The heat rose in numbing waves from the rocky floor of the depression, thundered down from the brassy sky, seared their hands each time they touched the aircraft.

Inside the cabin it was even worse. The temperature was over 150° Fahrenheit, the furnace air too suffocating to breathe. Kit Mullen stumbled through the open doorway and dropped to the ground. Although Fortune kept on changing the dressing, the wound in his arm was hurting like hell. Also it had begun to smell bad, and that embarrassed him when the others were near. On his back in the dusty shale (he must have fallen over – how strange!) he gazed sightlessly into the sky and listened to the music of an organ. At some other time that day, swaying, he stood holding on to the rudder, looking over a great field of grass rippling in the wind. 'Come on there, Billy!' he mumbled through cracked lips. 'Help push the boat out on to the lough, you! Else wee Seamus McBride'll be out there afore us, and the salmon are runnin' today.'

The organ music was louder now. Could it really be the pounding of blood through his own veins? He shook his water bottle. Empty. Screwing up his eyes against the blinding light, he stared over white-capped waves and watched the hills on the far side of the depression tremble in the sun. Fortune was shouting in the greenhouse. It seemed that a man called Hawkins was on his way.

It was so cold in Stalingrad that you dare not lift the goggles away from your eyes: if they watered, the fluid froze at once and you couldn't close the lids. Without a roof over our heads we couldn't even take a leak, because the stuff turned into an icicle before it hit the ground. Klinger swore that you could break off a man's prick like a dry twig in conditions like that. I wouldn't know, but I saw a fuel tanker caught by the Russki artillery the first time we tried to cross the Volga. She went up like a torch about half way across, and even that wasn't enough to melt the depth of ice covering the river. For the first time since the war began, we were hoping for the order to attack: at those temperatures, the warmth from the engine inside a Tiger was the only thing that kept you alive.

Chapter Sixteen

Zygmund saw it first. He slithered down the rock waving his arms. 'Sergeant Hawkins!' he called. 'Sergeant! There's a dust cloud over to the east!'

Hawkins was explaining for the tenth time why it was useless to call O'Kelly on the radio. 'For a start it's against orders to call Algiers in clear before the end of the op,' he said patiently. 'Except for the officer, that is. Too much risk the frequency'll be monitored, see? And that'd bugger up the whole shoot. Apart from that, it'd do no soddin' good: by the time the Captain could fix anything, it'd be too late.'

'Fuck the op,' Chilton growled. 'They could send a plane, couldn't they?'

Zygmund staggered across the sand. '... a dust cloud over to the east,' he panted. 'Perhaps two miles ... beyond the next ridge ... and heading this way already.'

Hawkins stared. He grabbed the field glasses and toiled up to the crest of the rock promontory. Zygmund and Chilton followed. For a long time the sergeant concentrated, fiddling with the focus wheel in the aching light. 'I'll be damned,' he said at last. 'A kraut convoy, that's all! A Panzer tank and three trucks. They must be runnin' in supplies from some Afrika Korps depot in Libya.'

'You mean they're on their way to our bloody firin' range?' Chilton asked.

'They must be. And that means the garrison'll be expectin' them.' For once the NCO sounded almost excited. 'You two – I have an idea: we're goin' to win ourselves a lift, but we'll have to move like greased bloody lightnin' to make it. Now here's what you lazy sods have to do ...'

Hastily, he outlined his plan. They raced back to the half-track, scooped up primacord, gelignite and rifles and dismantled the tripod of a theodolite so that each man could have a baton with which to sweep away his own tracks. Then they hurried back to the crest and down the other side. If the convoy kept on the same course, it would pass between the ridge and another outcrop sixty yards away. 'You take the far side, Chilton,' Hawkins ordered. 'Take your cue from me, and then set 'em off when you like, only for God's sake don't fuck up the tank, right?' Chilton nodded and strode away. In the distance they could hear the steady whine of the approaching vehicles.

When they had done what they had to do, they retired to the two facing crests and concealed themselves in depressions eroded from the weathered rock. The noise of the convoy grew louder. The dust cloud mushroomed against the desert sky. Then the tank bucketed into view over the rim of the nearest dune and headed for the trough between the two ridges. There was a green pennant at the tip of its whipping aerial; a goggled officer with a strap over his Afrika Korps cap lolled in the open turret. The three caterpillar trucks followed close behind.

When the tank was halfway along the trough, Hawkins yelled: *'Now!'*

Primacord explosive fuse burns at the rate of 18,500 feet a second. With a shattering roar, the first of the gelignite sticks exploded out of the sand in a fountain of flame and black smoke fifty yards ahead of the Panzer. It was followed by two more, slightly closer, and then three of Chilton's nearer the other crest. The effect was exactly as though the convoy had run into an unexpected medium artillery barrage. Before the shattering concussions of the explosions had died away, the tank had slewed to a standstill in a shower of sand. The officer scrambled out of the turret and dropped to the ground.

Cautiously raising the field glasses hanging around his neck, he began to climb the further ridge. He was followed by a man from each of the trucks, and then a sergeant from the roasting interior of the tank. 'That should leave two of the buggers in the Panzer, and a driver in each truck.' Hawkins whispered. 'Unless they ain't supplies but reinforcements for the base.'

'I like a man who's optimistic,' Zygmund murmured.

'Anyway, let's hope they'll be too scared to notice the shells don't whistle on their way,' Hawkins said. He exploded three more sticks and Chilton followed with another couple. The officer, the sergeant and the three men threw themselves flat on the slant of rock. You learned to do that quickly enough in desert warfare. The drivers of the trucks jumped out and lay on their faces beneath their cabs. Hawkins nudged the Pole and the two men stood up and raised their rifles. At the same time the wiry silhouette of Chilton rose into view on the opposite ridge.

After the roar of the explosions, the crackle of shots sounded as inoffensive as the guns in a pheasant shoot. The puffs of smoke hung in the hot, heavy air while the echoes rolled away across the dunes. One of the soldiers lay dead on the ground; the sergeant jerked, twisted, and then slid down the slope on to the sand in a cloud of dust; Chilton had accounted for the man under the nearest truck. Methodically, they reloaded and fired again.

The officer was halfway to his feet, his revolver drawn and aimed at Chilton, when Hawkins's shot took him between the shoulder blades. He spun around and crashed to the rock as Chilton picked off the second truck driver and Zygmund killed another soldier. The third man was hurling himself desperately down the slope towards the shelter of the tank. Chilton whirled around and fired a third time. The bullet slammed the German against the armour plate. He subsided slowly, leaving a scarlet smear down the yellow steel side of the Panzer.

At that moment a revolver shot cracked out from the back of the third truck. The driver had seized the opportunity to drag himself up over the tailboard and find temporary cover. Chilton ducked hastily as the slug chipped rock fragments from beside his feet and screamed off into the glare. The

German fired two more shots at the opposite ridge. Hawkins and Zygmund dropped to the ground and raised their rifles, hearing the heavy-calibre bullets whine over their heads. But the man must have crawled forward inside the truck and operated the starter, for the engine rumbled suddenly to life and the vehicle lurched into motion, zigzagging backwards in a shower of sand churned up by the caterpillars. The windscreen erupted in a fountain of toughened glass as Hawkins and the Pole blasted off together. Sheltered by the armoured scuttle, the Afrika Korps man continued reversing. When he was a hundred yards away, he braked, shoved the lever into first, and sent the truck careening along the defile between the two ridges.

'That's his mistake,' Hawkins muttered. 'Bleeder should've turned around and bloody run for it.' The engine roared; the gears screeched in protest. They saw the man, crouched low over the wheel now, as the truck flashed past the tank. Then Hawkins picked up the ends of the three remaining Primacord fuses. The trio of detonations sounded as one, blowing the truck over on its side. Something flopped out of the smoke with flames licking its limbs and threshed around on the sand. Chilton fired a single shot and the thing lay still.

Hawkins signalled for quiet. Once more three bolts were pulled back and then slammed home in the breech. Drawing a bead on the tank turret, they waited.

Slowly the dust settled. The smoke blew away and the stink of cordite dispersed. They became aware once more of the relentless hammering of the sun, the tremble of heat over the hull of the stalled Panzer.

Minutes passed. And then, with infinite caution, the head and shoulders of a man appeared over the rim of the turret. He looked straight at Chilton, crouched just below the further crest, rifle at the ready ... and ducked frenziedly back. But he was half a second too late. Three guns spat flame and the German's head disintegrated in a cloud of blood and bone splinters. The carcase dropped back inside the tank.

Soon afterwards, a gun barrel to which a piece of white rag had been tied was thrust into view above the turret. Hawkins looked at Zygmund. 'Drop the gun and come out slowly with your hands above your head,' Zygmund shouted in German.

Hawkins banged a new clip into the magazine with the palm of his hand. He shook his head. 'Poor little sod,' he said as a pale-faced youth hauled himself out of the turret. 'It's a stinkin' bloody war, all right. Still, we're on a search-and-kill op and we can't take no prisoners – and it's better'n bein' left to die of hunger and the heat.'

The boy's knees were shaking. Holding his hands high, he jumped from the Panzer's track-guard to the sand. Hawkins pressed the trigger.

Half an hour later, the convoy was under way again, one truck short. Hawkins, who had served with an armoured brigade before Dunkirk, piloted the tank, Chilton drove the first truck, and Zygmund, resplendent in the officer's cap and goggles, brought up the rear.

They had salvaged as much of the dead men's uniforms as was still wearable and then radioed Fortune that they were on their way. Once they had picked up the other three, each truck would have a driver and mate – and Zygmund could play the rôle of the officer in the turret, answering any questions in German when they ran into the outer ring of Abd-el-Kerim's patrols. There were even papers and documents and orders in a steel cubbyhole beside the driving levers of the tank.

'That's what I like to see,' Hawkins approved before they set off. 'Efficiency without the bull, the way that only Fritz can do it!'

Jean-Jacques Simondi cracked a little too easily. We'd been stuffing electrodes up some woman they'd caught parachuting into the Pas de Calais, and we put him in the cell next the interrogation room so that he could hear her screaming. That was supposed to soften him up, but we were surprised to see him go to pieces the moment he saw the sweat-stained straps on the table, the mess on the floor, and Heinz's whip rack. After all, he was supposed to be tough: he was the head of this whole ring. Maybe he was put off because the place still stank after the woman. Anyway, he started blabbing right away, said he couldn't bear the indignity of physical pain, that there was no need to behave in an uncivilized manner, and what did we want to know. Unfortunately, the stuff he gave us was all phoney – and while the Gestapo were checking, the rest of his cell went to ground. That was too bad for Simondi. The commandant was mad, so he gave him to Klaus for those experiments on human endurance. This time he told the truth, but he got the indignity just the same. And Klaus kept him alive a long time.

Chapter Seventeen

The attack on the secret proving range staffed by the unit referred to by the German High Command as Flakregiment XII was brief but bloody. Because it took place on neutral territory, where neither attackers nor defenders had any right to be, the action never made the headlines, and it appears in no official history of the war. Yet if the results had gone the other way, the effect on the Normandy landings – and thus on the outcome of the war itself – could have been decisive.

Hawkins and his hijacked convoy picked up Fortune, Constantine and the injured Irishman an hour before dusk. Following Fortune's precise directions, they swung out across the dunes in a wide arc that would bring them in to the base from the north-east. Then, when they still had ten miles to go, they halted for the night in a *wadi* that split the desert floor.

They started again soon after daylight. As Fortune and

Constantine had predicted from their aerial sketch plans of the area, they were able to approach to within two miles of the oasis in the lee of a rocky spur which ran out from the ridge to the west of the base. On the far side of this spur, they knew, Kerim's patrolling tribesmen would be deployed across their path, and they would be in full view of the Germans defending the base.

Fortune, who had naturally assumed command in Webster's absence, stopped for a last-minute briefing. 'All right, chaps, this is the way we'll play it,' he said. 'I want Sergeant Hawkins to keep on at the controls of the tank, of course. Zygmund, you stay in the turret and play the bored Nazi officer for all you're worth if we get stopped by the tribesmen. Chilton can drive the first truck, with Joe up alongside. I'll take the second myself, so that I can look after Mullen.'

He glanced swiftly at the Irishman. Once on the move and away from the shaly depression, his delirium had vanished. But they all knew his wound had turned gangrenous; his temperature was still high, and he was very weak. For the moment, there was nothing they could do about it.

'We'll drive in very close formation,' Fortune resumed. 'And for goodness' sake don't any of you utter when Ziggie's swopping funny stories with the wogs. If there's any trouble I'll weigh in with a spot of the old Hunnish myself.' He spun round the aerial map on the sand so that they could all see it. 'With the armament they have, there's only one way to do it: come in as close as possible, head-on, in line ahead. Then knock out the bally mortars and the machine-gun nests surrounding the place.'

Hawkins said: 'Permission to speak, sir?'

'Yes, Sergeant, of course.'

'Knockin' out your machine-guns and your mortars, sir, we'll be circlin' the oasis, won't we? Well, it's just that in that formation your trucks'll be like sittin' ducks to anythin' stronger than rifle fire.'

'Yes, that's true.' Fortune frowned. 'As soon as we turn the tank to start the enfilade, then, we'd better junk the trucks. Mullen can get into the Tiger's cabin with the sergeant. Chilton, you hop up into the turret: Zygmund will need you to help operate the seventy-five anyway. Lieutenant Constantine and myself will give our celebrated impersonation of the

PBI: we'll stalk along in the lee of the tank, firing at anything that moves.'

'And after we done the machine-guns and the mortars, sir?'

'Normally,' Fortune said, 'the next step would be to blast the hutments to hell with the turret gun, then fire on the hangar where they store these machines and send the whole bang shoot sky-high. With a gun that can outdistance anything they have, it'd be a piece of cake. But there are two reasons why we can't do that. One, we have to have sight of the paperwork, photograph the blueprints and suchlike, and we don't know which building they're in; two, they've got Major Webster somewhere in there, and we don't know where he is either.'

'So what do we do?' Constantine asked.

'We'll have to go in at close quarters – hand to hand if necessary.'

'Yeah, but ... Shit, man, there's only *five* of us! Five that's fit for action, that is. I don't know how many they got in there, but wouldn't it—? I mean, wouldn't there be a better chance of success if we waited until after dark and snuck in kinda secretly?'

'No,' Fortune said – and Webster would have been astonished at the authority and decisiveness in his voice – 'The only place to hide up during the day is behind this spur. And that would mean we'd have two miles of desert to cross in the dark. On foot if we didn't want to warn them that we were coming. Plus the one trump card we have – the 75-mm turret gun – would be left out of the pack. Apart from which, we might be spotted by Kerim's patrols while we were waiting. I'm sorry, old lad, but it's simply not on.'

Constantine nodded. 'You're the boss.'

'We'll take a gamble,' Fortune said. 'Although there's damned few of us, we'll gamble on our superior fire power. If we're lucky, we should be able to spread enough alarm and despondency with the old seventy-five to even the score a bit before we go in. We'll have a jolly good try anyway.'

'Supposing we can't locate the Major even if we do get in close?' Constantine asked.

Fortune began folding up the map. 'There are no Queensberry Rules in this game,' he said soberly. 'We get him out if we can. But the mission comes first. If searching for him looks like spoiling the show, then we don't search. Fullstop.

That's the way he'd play it himself, and that's the way it has to be.' He cleared his throat, and looked around the circle of attentive faces. 'No more questions? All right, chaps – let's go!'

The lightweight Afrika Korps uniforms had been shared out as evenly as possible. A private's shirt and pants were the only ones big enough to fit Hawkins. The officer's shirt had been too bloodstained to salvage, and Zygmund had to be content with the cap, the goggles and his own khaki bush shirt. Fortune found that the German sergeant's clothes were his size – but he must remember to keep facing any tribesmen who stopped them, because there was a bullet hole in the back of the shirt. The others wore drivers' fatigues, except for Mullen, who draped a spare sergeant's shirt over his shoulders to hide his wounded arm.

Climbing up on to the hull of the tank, Sergeant Hawkins muttered: 'Fuckin' marvellous, isn't it? The officer's dressed as a sergeant, I'm got up as a private, and the unit's commanded by a clerk from the bleedin' Pioneer Corps!'

He lowered himself down through the turret and into the driving seat, thumbed the fan switch, and started the 300-h.p. V.12 Maybach engine. Zygmund settled himself up above, and then Fortune's voice came through on the radio, ordering the convoy to move off.

Fifteen minutes later, the Panzer tipped over the crest of the promontory and ground to a halt by a group of mounted Berber warriors barring the way. The trucks pulled up with their engines idling. A fierce-looking tribesman reined in his horse beside the turret. Wordlessly, he held out his hand. Zygmund was lounging indolently against the armour-plate. He pushed his sand goggles up over the peak of his cap. 'I suppose you want to see these?' he said in German, holding out the papers they had found.

The Arab took them in silence and looked them over. 'Why do you not follow the usual trail?' he demanded haughtily. His German was correct but heavily accented.

'A sandstorm.' Zygmund matched arrogance with disdain. 'We made a detour to try and avoid it. Not worth trying to find the route again afterwards, not in this godforsaken country.'

A few yards behind the tank, Chilton and Constantine sat

and sweated in the cab of the first truck. The sun was only about twenty degrees above the horizon but already it was insufferably hot. 'Blimey!' the Cockney muttered, 'I wouldn't want to find meself on the wrong side of one of them blokes! Shoot first and ask questions afterwards, I reckon. And as for what their wimmin do! Did you ever hear—?'

'The boss man said not to talk,' Constantine warned in a whisper. Chilton leaned outboard and spat into the hot sand. He mumbled something under his breath and relapsed into silence.

'According to the papers there are three trucks,' the Arab said to Zygmund. 'I can see only two.'

'I told you – a sandstorm.' The Pole sounded more bored than ever, as if he could only just bring himself to answer such banal queries from a man of inferior race. 'We lost contact. Either he'll come in later, or he bought it. No point wasting time looking for him. They said this stuff was urgent.'

Impassively, the horseman handed the papers back and nodded. He pulled his capering mount away a few yards and waved the tank on. Zygmund raised a languid hand to the peak of his cap. '*Raus!*' he called into the interior. The convoy jerked forward and rolled down the hill. As it gathered speed, the Berber drew a pistol and fired a green Very light into the burnished sky.

'Christ!' Hawkins was staring through the slit in the steel windscreen. Even in the harsh sunlight, the star-shell cast a livid tinge over the collection of huts grouped around the palm trees a mile and a half ahead of them. 'I hope to hell that means we passed the bloody test!' He could see men gathered around a miniature winged shape on a ramp. Others manned the scooped-out emplacements on the perimeter. Above an intervening swell of dunes, the sinister black shapes of half a dozen vultures hovered.

They had breasted the rise and dipped down the far side when Zygmund's voice cried excitedly behind the sergeant's shoulder: 'Holy God – there's some poor *schmuck* he's staked out there on the sand!'

Hawkins squinted sideways through the slit. By the iron-hard shadows of the waiting birds, he saw a naked figure spreadeagled on its back, the wrists and ankles lashed to pegs driven into the ground. 'It's an old Foreign Legion punishment,' he called back. 'The say half a day will send the poor sod ravin', and by sunset, if he's still alive, he'll be out of his bleedin' mind for good. You can trust the krauts to—' Abruptly his words choked in his throat. His great hands closed on the levers, and the tank skidded to a standstill in a cloud of churned up sand. The man staked out under the merciless sun was Webster.

'Bastards were going to leave me there until it was dark,' he gasped when Fortune and Constantine had jumped down from their trucks and cut him free. He rubbed a raw patch on one wrist. 'I held out on the water and the electricity all day yesterday, but another couple of hours of this damned sun and I'd have told 'em all they wanted to know!' His hawk face, grey with a three-day stubble, was lined with fatigue and even at this early hour his lean, bronzed face was flushed an unhealthy pink from over-exposure to the fierce heat.

'Good God!' Fortune was pale. 'Hop into the tank, sir. There are some Boche overalls in the back. If you don't mind, we'd better get on with the job: they'll certainly be watching from the base, and they'll have twigged by now; no genuine Afrika Korps patrol is going to stop to pick up a prisoner from the sand!'

'I'm afraid your right.' Webster jerked his head towards the oasis. A mile away across the sand, men were running for the sandbagged perimeter emplacements, and an aldiss lamp winked urgently from the nearest hut. He scrambled into the overalls that Zygmund handed down from the turret, wincing as the rough material grazed his inflamed skin. 'What's the score, young Fortune?'

'Circle the oasis out of range of the machine-guns and knock out the emplacements,' said Fortune. 'After that – now that we know where you are – we can blast the rest to hell. D'you know which huts the boffins are in?'

Webster nodded. 'The two long ones built like an L on the far side of the hangar. Better leave them if we can. But it may not be so easy, you know. They've got a mobile 50-mm PAK hidden among the trees, and three armoured cars. I know – they caught up with me in one!'

'We spotted the armoured cars from the plane,' Fortune said. 'Two Sd-Kfz-222s – lightweight, four-wheeled jobs – and one of those hump-backed, eight-wheel 231s. Eight tons of strength-through-joy, with a 20-mm cannon and one Spandau MG.34 that fires seven point nine two ammo at a rate of knots.'

Webster was looking at the young man with a new respect. There was very little of the irreverent, silly-ass attitude that had so angered him visible now. Perhaps Lang had been right after all! 'The PAK field gun has a range of a thousand metres,' he said. 'The cannons in the armoured cars rather less. What have you got in this bus, and how fast can she circle the base?'

'Two MG.34s and the old seventy-five,' Fortune replied. 'But she's a Mark IV: almost 25 tons and a top speed of under thirty. Think we can make it?'

Webster grinned. 'Press on regardless!' he said.

Fortune raised a finger and touched his forelock. 'Better climb aboard, cock – I mean, sir. We don't want to miss the connection, do we?'

They helped Mullen to squeeze through the hatch and stow himself gingerly in the rear of the cramped and stifling cabin. Webster followed and began to check the two Spandau machine-guns. Zygmund and Chilton settled behind the big gun in the turret. Sergeant Hawkins sent the tank rolling forward, with Fortune and Constantine lying flat on the hull behind the turret.

The aldiss had stopped signalling. Three puffs of smoke blossomed among the trees surrounding the hangar. A hundred yards ahead, three orange flashes sent up fountains of sand. The explosions were inaudible over the roar of the V.12 at full throttle. 'Cannon from the armoured cars!' Webster yelled. 'Zygmund, wait until you see the flashes from the PAK, and then aim for that.' The Pole nodded. With Chilton's aid, he had already slammed the first of the 75-mm armour-piercing shells into the breech.

Soon there was a larger, darker puff of smoke from beneath the palms, a brighter flash and a heavier blast among the cannon shots fifty yards to the Panzer's left. Webster looked over his shoulder. 'Righto, boys: "Let battle commence"!' he quoted gleefully.

The long barrel of the tank's seventy-five belched flame and recoiled. Inside the bucking cabin, the detonation was deafening. Zygmund and Chilton fired again and again, watching the shellbursts among the distant trees. Tongues of crimson licked the underside of a smoke cloud billowing up among the huts as they scored a direct hit on one of the armoured cars. 'Wacko!' Webster shouted. 'Let the buggers have it!'

The gunners in the two remaining cars were becoming more accurate now, their shots interspersed with the flatter bursts of mortar bombs and an occasional thump from the PAK. A sudden steel hail beat on the armour-plate as they drew within range of the perimeter emplacements. Hawkins swung the tank to the right and began circling the site. The turret gun traversed, shooting at the sandbagged hollows surrounding the oasis while Webster, aided by Mullen using his good hand, enfiladed the defenders with the two Spandaus. Fortune and Constantine dropped off the hull and ran on the lee side of the Panzer, stopping every now and then to loose off a short burst of automatic fire with Schmeisser machine-pistols originally carried by members of the convoy.

One of the machine-gun nests erupted in a ball of flame; men spilled from another and lay on the sand as bullets from the two Spandaus found their mark. When they had travelled in a wide arc around half the base, the remaining two armoured cars came out of hiding and started circling with them, inside the perimeter, firing as they went. Through his field glasses, Zygmund could see the crew of the PAK feverishly slewing the wheeled 50-mm gun around to keep them within its field of fire. A near-miss shivered the hull of the tank. 'You should excuse the thought,' the Pole called, spitting sand from his mouth, 'but a couple of shells inside that hangar would really take care of those krauts!'

Webster was in his element. The hell with the burns on his skin, the fatigue and the scars that the torturers had left – this was action, the way he always wanted it, and the days of hesitation and intrigue were over. 'You'd blow all the paper-work we need to hell!' he shouted. 'No, Ziggie – for God's sake lay off the missiles in there ... but there's one on the launching ramp. When those armoured cars are within a hundred feet, let them have it!'

Zygmund leaned down and gave him the thumbs-up sign. They were now opposite the southern extremity of the oasis, with the squat bulk of the hangar hiding the huts. But the gun layer with the PAK crew was improving his aim. They saw the gun recoil as flame stabbed the air in front of the barrel. The next moment their view of the base dissolved in a whirlwind of smoke and sand and fire. The Panzer lurched and slewed broadside on. Stones and shrapnel rattled across the armoured shield. The next shellburst was behind them, and so was the one after that – although the second was near enough to rock the hull. Flat on his face in the sand, Fortune shook his head to stop the ringing in his ears. 'Bracketing us,' he said to Constantine. 'I don't care too much for that.'

Wrestling with the levers to steer the tank around a crater, Sergeant Hawkins watched the next salvo advancing towards them. One, two, three, an overshoot that caused Fortune and the Canadian to drop hastily to the sand again, five – and then the world disintegrated in a roar of flame and a hot blast of smoke that whipped past the turret as the Panzer screeched to a shuddering halt. Choking, Webster dragged himself out of the hatch and dropped to the ground. The plating on the port side was buckled and seared. The screen was pitted. Three of the guide wheels had been blown off, and the caterpillar track lay in fragments at his feet. Astonishingly, nobody seemed to be hurt.

'All change here!' he shouted. 'All right, chaps, this is the terminus! We'll have to—' But his words were drowned in the thunder of the seventy-five. One of the armoured cars had neared the ramp and Zygmund was following orders. Through the vanishing smoke, Webster saw a spasm shiver the surface of the desert. An incandescent fireball bloomed momentarily at the edge of the site; a gigantic explosion shook the ground. When the tornado of dust and sand had subsided, a scene of devastation was revealed. A huge crater had been blown at the near end of the ramp, and around its edges lay chunks of concrete, twisted rails, the burning and mangled remains of the armoured car, and a scatter of formless bundles that might once have been men. Three of the huts had lost their roofs and windows. The doors of the hangar were crumpled as though they had been squeezed by a giant fist.

Before Webster could take it all in, Zygmund and Chilton fired again and the field gun that had crippled them disappeared in a maelstrom of flame and flying metal. The remaining armoured car, the heavy, eight-wheeled Type 231, seemed to have been put out of action, either by a near-miss or by the blast when the missile exploded. They could see the crew scrambling out and heading for the bunkers. The barrel of the cannon pointed uselessly at the sky.

The seventy-five in the tank's turret bellowed once more, then Webster was yelling: 'All right, chaps, this is it! This is where we go in and finish it off!'

There were smoke canisters in the Panzer. Hawkins set them off and threw them out on the sand. As the black fog boiled out and rolled slowly towards the base, they grabbed rifles, revolvers and machine-pistols, and left the shelter of the tank. Webster led Constantine, Hawkins and Chilton towards the hangar, while Fortune and Zygmund circled around to approach the site from behind the remains of the ramp. Mullen was propped up in the turret with instructions to fire an occasional burst over their heads from one of the Spandaus.

Advancing behind the thick screen of smoke, all Webster could hear over the clatter of the wounded man's gun were sporadic bursts of mortar fire and a single carbine shooting blindly into the dark. When he judged that they were almost on the perimeter, he motioned the others to spread out and edge around to come in from behind the hangar. The smoke was thinning here. Gradually, the outlines of the base took shape again. The mortar emplacement was well-sited beneath two palms between the hangar and the research department. The lone rifleman was perched on the gantry along which the hangar doors had once slid, firing over the top of the smoke-screen towards the stalled Panzer.

Webster dropped on one knee and drew a bead on the sniper. His P.38 cracked out once, twice. The man jerked half upright, folded up, and plummeted to the ground. But the shots had drawn the attention of the mortar crew. They saw one of them hunched up behind the sandbags, dropping the shell down the barrel before he ducked out of sight. The explosion was uncomfortably close, showering them with hot sand. Again there was a blur of movement in the dugout. The four of them fired as one. But the mortar crew were too well entrenched to be caught. A faint puff of smoke emerged from the squat, canted barrel and Webster and his men threw themselves flat as the detonation of the shell split their ear-drums and fragments of searing metal scythed through the air above their heads. Off to their right, somebody shouted a command in the smoke.

Each of the attackers was carrying a couple of improvised grenades, fashioned by Chilton from short-fused sticks of gelignite. 'Go on firing to make them keep their heads down,' Webster gritted, unhitching one of these from his cartridge belt. 'I'm going to try to put those sods out of business.'

Hawkins, Chilton and Constantine lay on their bellies and kept up a withering fire while their leader crawled forwards across the sand. When he was fifty yards short of the emplacement, Webster rose to his feet, ran a short way, dropped, ran again, and threw himself flat for the second time. There were revolver shots from behind the sandbags now – the bullets kicked up sand around his prone figure – but a man who had once been picked to play for his county because of his outfielding could throw further than the accurate range of side arms. He lifted himself on to one elbow, his free arm swung up and over, the gelignite stick spun through the air ... There was a blinding flash a few feet above the mortar barrel.

No hostile fire greeted Webster and his men when they walked warily across the perimeter line two minutes later. Even the staccato rasp of Fortune's Schmeisser, which had been sounding from somewhere beyond the smokescreen, was stilled.

Prowling through the shafts of sunlight penetrating the yellow cordite fumes, they saw nothing around them but destruction. The acrid stench of explosives was overlaid by the sweet and sickly smell of death in the blistering heat. Bodies lay twisted in grotesque attitudes by the smashed machine-gun emplacements. Less identifiable bundles of cloth and flesh strewed the craters torn by the Panzer's seventy-five. Here and there, wounded groaned and writhed on the bloodstained sand. 'What the hell are we going to do with *them*?' Constantine asked.

Webster was wearing a Mauser pistol looted from the Nazi tank captain. He loosened it in its holster. 'I hate to say this,' he replied grimly, 'but this is an assassination mission. It's also highly illegal, and nobody must be left alive to rabbit about it. In the circumstances, there's only one thing we *can* do ...'

Later, Fortune appeared out of the murk, walking a little unsteadily. One side of his face was blackened and his shirt was torn. 'Had a bit of a barney with the crew of that Type

231,' he said. 'They'd been issued with those new plastic grenades. It got pretty noisy at one point, and I'm afraid Ziggie may have bought it.'

'Good God! Where is he?' Webster asked. 'What about the Hun?'

'They ... won't be lining up for the next issue of grenades,' Fortune said. 'Ziggie's over on the far side of the ramp.'

The Pole was lying face down among a litter of reinforced-concrete fragments. Webster turned him over gently. His face was paper-white, his right leg was clearly broken, and the clothes on that side of his body were hidden by caked blood and sand. After a cursory examination, Webster stood up. 'He's still alive,' he said. 'He may just be concussed by the blast; the wounds may not be as bad as they look. We'll see when we've cleaned up a little. There must be a first-aid room in this place. In the meantime, let's get him out of the sun, under those trees over there.'

They were lowering the unconscious man to the ground in the shade beneath the palms when they were surprised by a volley of revolver shots from the window of a hut that served as cookhouse. Chilton ran up to the window and flung one of his home-made grenades in through the glass. The hut collapsed in a roar of brown smoke and a belch of flame. A little way beyond, they found the body of Colonel Stahl. He had been caught in the open when the missile exploded. He lay on his back, his feet together and his arms at his sides just as though he had been blown over standing at attention. The fingers of his right hand grasped the butt of a service revolver. There were still razor-edged creases on the short sleeves of his neatly pressed bush shirt.

'So far, so good,' Joe Constantine said. 'Just so long as those goddam Arabs don't charge us from the hills!'

Webster raised the field glasses slung around his neck. He had seen the horsemen gathering on the promontory before the smoke canisters were released. Now, as he watched, they wheeled away and galloped back towards the ridge. He let out his breath in a sigh of relief. 'They don't want to know,' he said. 'It's not their war ... and I should think they'd be pretty keen not to get involved in a fight between what looked like two different sets of Jerries. Especially if they weren't quite sure which side they were supposed to be on.'

In a drawing office adjoining the research department, they found the only defenders left alive on the base – a couple of mechanics and three scientists led by the tall, thin man who seemed to be in charge. 'You vill of course respect the Geneva Convention,' he said. It was a statement rather than a question. 'Ve haf the right to be make prisoner of war, isn't it?'

'Brother,' said Webster, 'you don't have any rights, and you know it. You're engaging in warlike activities in a neutral country: you're belligerents violating that neutrality. If you carry out a military operation in civilian clobber – which you are, planning mass deaths out of uniform – then as far as the Geneva Convention goes, you're in the same category as spies. And you know what happens to them.'

The scientist's eye glittered behind his thick-lensed glasses. '*Ach, so*,' he began, 'it is thus that the so-called civilized—'

Chilton was the one to see the movement reflected in those pebble lenses. He whirled around with an inarticulate cry. Colonel Benckendorff, his face contorted with rage, was standing in the doorway with a Luger automatic trained on Webster's back.

Chilton hurled himself at the SS man as the gun spat flame, taking the slug that had been meant for Webster full in the chest. The impact of the heavy-calibre bullet flung him back a yard and a half, and he crashed to the floor. Before the ringing detonation of the shot had died away Webster himself had fired from the hip. One of the smoked discs of Blenckendorff's sun-glasses vanished. He crumpled and fell, with blood pumping out through the empty frame.

Webster crouched on the floor between the two casualties. The German was dead but there was still a flicker of life in Chilton. Gently, he supported the little man's head on his knee. The eyes opened. The chest heaved. Webster bent his head to catch the whisper of sound that drifted from the dying man's lips. 'Back ... in the Smoke ... if you make it, go down ... Prospect of Whitby ... have a short one for me, if ... bleeders ... haven't blitzed it ...'

Webster swallowed. 'We'll make them doubles, old lad,' he said. 'And you'll be there too. Now don't you worry ...' But Chilton was past hearing. His eyes filmed over. Blood bubbled slowly from his slack lips. His head lolled sideways.

White-faced, Webster laid him down and rose to his feet.

'As I was saying,' he snarled at the frightened Germans, 'you know what you can expect.'

'Major,' Constantine said unexpectedly, with a sudden note of urgency in his voice. 'Look, you can't . . . not in cold—'

'Lieutenant!' Webster's voice was sharp as a whiplash. 'Do you have that miniature camera you brought along for your film stunt?'

'Why, sure. But—'

'Then get out of here!' Webster shouted. 'That is an order. Take Fortune and start photographing any documents or blueprints of those missiles that you can find. Now get on with it. Sergeant Hawkins and I have some work to do.'

For a moment the Canadian hesitated. And then, 'Very good, sir,' he said woodenly. Followed by Fortune, he strode from the room. They heard the shots as they pulled out the first filing drawer in the adjoining laboratory. Soon afterwards, they discovered that Mullen was dead: he had been killed by a single shot from the sniper whom Webster had tumbled down from the gantry outside the hangar.

Zygmund was still unconscious. They located the first-aid hut, put his leg in temporary splints, and found, when they had sponged down his clothes and cleaned the wounds, that most of his injuries were superficial lacerations. The severest damage had been caused by blast from the grenade. They made him as comfortable as they could on a camp bed, and then set about burying the dead in shallow graves scooped from the sand at the foot of the promontory.

Bareheaded and grimy, Webster eased the overall collar away from his neck. He cleared his throat. 'Kit Mullen . . .' he said as they stood in the sun. '. . . and Henry Chilton.' Once more the voice rasped in his throat. 'Greater love hath no man than this, that he . . . that he should lay down his life . . . for his friend. God rest their souls in peace,' he finished huskily. He turned and strode away.

They were halfway back to the base when the torrid silence was shattered by the sound of an engine being raced. A jeep-like scout car careered out of the hangar, skidded around in a half-circle churning up showers of sand, and then accelerated away from the oasis in a cloud of dust. 'Stop him!' Webster yelled. 'Christ! That's one of the junior boffins. I remember seeing him when I was locked up. Must have been hiding somewhere among the missiles. He may have taken ... Couldn't we—?'

Fortune shook his head. 'Not a chance, guv. We don't have the rifles with us, and he'll be halfway to El Glouai by the time we've got to the trucks and started one. Anyway, he's faster than they are.'

Webster stared after the vanishing scout car with his hands on his hips. 'I suppose you're right,' he said. 'Bad show. Dash it all – if that chap should get back to Germany ...' He shook his head.

'Not to worry. After all, we can't hope to kill the project absolutely stone dead,' Fortune said reasonably. 'I mean, there'll be stacks of brains back there who know the principle of the thing. Bound to be. And the factories making the bits, they're going to have their own blueprints, aren't they? All we can hope is that our fleeing friend hasn't legged it with too much experimental data. That way we can at least be sure that we've delayed the operation.'

Fortunately, the sole survivor of the Flakregiment XII group manning the base seemed to have been too frightened to think of anything but escape. So far as Fortune and Constantine could tell, the graphs and plans and sheets of figures they had laid out to photograph remained untouched.

There were twenty-three of the sinister-looking flying bombs in the big hangar, and parts for a dozen more crated around a rough assembly line. The trucks that Hawkins had captured were loaded with wing sections and spare propulsion units. They found a variety of experimental fuses on the workbenches but no signs of radio or electronic equipment to guide the machines. Fortune seemed to be familiar with the principles of the crude jet engines, whose heating elements were fuelled with low-grade aviation spirit. Beneath the palm trees, they unearthed a huge tarpaulined dump stocked with tanks and jerricans – and enough explosive, as Constantine remarked, to blow the Atlas mountains into the sea.

When they had run the two trucks into the base, offloaded the cargo, and packed them with jerricans of fuel, they wheeled one of the missiles up to each of the huts, soused the research department with petrol, grouped the remaining flying bombs in the centre of the hangar and began preparing a complicated system of time fuses under Webster's direction. Then they drove the trucks back to the rocky spur, parked them on the far side and waited. 'Blimey,' Hawkins said admiringly. 'When she fuckin' goes up, she's goin' to make the blitz look like a kid's firework on November the bleedin' Fifth!'

She did. The sun was at its blinding zenith when the first flash sent one of the huts roaring skywards. Before the shattering detonation had rolled across the desert to their ears, another and another erupted in holocausts of flame. And then they were stunned by a colossal explosion as the missiles in the hangar tore the site apart and sent a towering column of black smoke marbled with fire thousands of feet up into the air. By the time the ear-splitting reverberations had died away and the smoke had dispersed, all that was left of the secret base was a blackened and burning waste of sand from which the charred stumps of trees emerged like the ribs of a long-dead ship.

That's a hell of a reward from a grateful Fatherland! After 103 missions and 15 enemy aircraft destroyed, they put you on some damfool posting in the Baltic ... Seconded to a Flakregiment of all things, attached to some research station tracking pilotless missiles out over the sea. Well, they can make planes without pilots, but they still need us to tell them where the bastards get to! At least we'll still be flying the trusty old Dorniers – but it's hardly the treatment a hero of the Luftwaffe expects. I mean, the Baltic! Whoever heard of a place called Peenemünde in the Baltic?

Chapter Eighteen

Captain Seamus M'Phee O'Kelly's voice was faint, struggling its way through the static. 'Very well,' he said, 'I am satisfied' – it was the nearest he ever came to praise – 'although it's a pity about the chap who got away. Never mind: we'll have to bite on the bullet over that one. But you fellows had better stay away from Algiers. The frogs dare not complain, because it would mean admitting they'd allowed belligerents to make use of neutral territory; nevertheless, there's a neat frame-up waiting for you over the killing of Weiss and Mackenzie. My advice is: head northeast and link up with our people in Libya. I'll arrange things so that there's a welcome laid on, all right?'

Webster pressed the *Send* manual. 'Yes, sir. Thank you. And just in case we run into trouble, let me brief you on the main points, then you can at least pass on the principles.' He picked up the paper on which Constantine and Fortune had summarized their findings.

' "The flying bomb",' he read out, ' "is twenty-five feet long with a wingspan of sixteen feet. With a full fuel tank and a 2000-lb high-explosive payload, it weighs a little over two tons. The prototypes at El Glouai were not – repeat not – radio-controlled: they explode on simple impact and where they explode seems of little importance. A pre-set cut-out stops the engine and then they just drop. We estimate that they have been designed for terror effect rather than for accuracy. According to our observations over their test target, there is no penetration, but lateral blast damage is considerable." They can bloody well say that again,' Webster added. 'Christ, the blasted things go off like—'

'All right, all right,' O'Kelly interrupted testily. 'You can cut out the histrionics, man. We know it's a dangerous weapon. Is there any information on the manufacturing end in Germany? Intelligence will want to know, so that they can alert undercover agents to watch the factories and brief Bomber Command to sort out the suppliers.'

'Yes, sir. They called this proving-range stunt Project Thunderbird, but the operation as a whole is code-named V-1, which seems to stand for *Vergeltungswaffen*. The work-number is FZG-76, and the development is handled by the Fieseler airframe company, with engines supplied by Argus. The motor's ingenious and hellish simple. Fortune says it's what they call a pulse jet – if that means anything to you. The examples we saw here shoot off a ramp, but we found drawings showing that they plan to adapt Heinkel 111 bombers and fire them from those. If they put them into large-scale production, it could make the home front – or any invasion preparations – pretty noisy. At the moment, though, they're suffering a high wastage on take-off. I'd say almost fifty per cent never get properly airborne. That could prove dangerous for the ground crews in the long run. They've got a lot more homework to do before the project's a going concern, if you ask me.'

'Especially now that your lads have scotched this particular experiment. One final question now: did you find anything on the administration of the project in the Reich? Every single detail helps Intelligence and their monitors at Barnet to interpret intercepted radio traffic.'

'Can do,' Webster said. 'It was all down in black and white. They even had a pay office out here!' He glanced down at the paper again. 'Fieseler and Argus come under the German air ministry. But the actual operation of the project is controlled by the army: the 66th Korps, under Lieutenant-General Erich Heinemann. It seems that this is a special formation designated to handle all V-weapons – whatever that means. The unit we destroyed was Flakregiment XII, an offshoot of the 155th Flakregiment, which Heinemann is training to operate the missiles. The top dog here was a Colonel

Stahl, but the 155th as a whole is commanded by another colonel, name of Wachtel.'

'Right, I've got all that. Anything else?'

'By God,' Webster said impertinently, 'you fellows want jam on it, don't you? No, there's nothing else – except to remind you about the two girls: Céleste Harari in Algiers; Liz Macnamara in War Office Records, London. Those bitches damned nearly upset the apple-cart!'

'There was a third,' O'Kelly said. 'Your hunch was right. She worked in Chard's office. Apparently she tipped off somebody called Benckendorff to tail you while you were still in London.'

'The gentleman – the late gentleman – was kind enough to tell me that himself.'

'Yes? Well, one of the birds has flown, but at least she can't operate any more for the moment. Another one's already in the cage. I'm attending to the North African one myself.' The old man's voice faded and then came back again strongly: 'Now for God's sake get the hell out of there before I have the French ambassador and General de Gaulle and Admiral Darlan and probably even the American State Department on my tail at the same time! Is that clear, Webster? Push off!'

'Sir,' said Webster, 'it'll be a pleasure!'

So they pushed off. The original plan had been to head northeast in the two trucks. But then Fortune reminded them that the flying bombs had been fuelled with low grade *aviation* spirit. This would certainly have made the trucks go like a bomb, Fortune said, but if they could ferry enough out to the stalled Macchi-Castoldi, he could probably coax the machine into the air and get them across the border into Libya a hell of a sight quicker. 'It's four hundred miles to the bally frontier,' he pointed out, 'and perhaps another three or four hundred before we meet up with the Eighth Army, across the Tassili N'Ajjer and the great sand desert. I fancy most of us would rather avoid the kind of conditions we'd find there. Also we could find Uncle Irwin Rommel on the way ... and in the way.'

'Behind that vacant expression,' Webster said, 'there are brains at work. Hands up all those who want to shell out five bob for a nice game of circuit-and-bumps in the pretty aeroplane?'

They piled into the trucks and left the desolation of the wrecked base behind them. No tribesman barred their way to the stranded plane, but by the time they got there the sun was sinking below the shaly horizon. Exhausted by the drama they had lived through, dessicated by the intolerable heat of the day, they slept fitfully through the chill desert night. An hour after dawn, Fortune had already dismantled and cleaned the aircraft's carburettors. By the time the sun reappeared, he was seated beside Constantine at the controls. Zygmund, semi-conscious now and muttering feverishly, was strapped into an improvised stretcher between Webster and Hawkins in the cabin.

The engines were reluctant to fire. Three times they coughed, caught, and then choked into silence. As the airscrews creaked to a halt, the old plane quivered and swayed. A puff of hot, dry wind had moaned across the depression, raising swirls of dust from the shale.

Webster glanced at Fortune. The young man's face was set in a worried frown. 'Trouble?' Webster called. 'It's unlike you to be down-in-the-mouth. What is it? Ropey ignition?'

'Trouble all right,' Fortune replied, 'but not with the engines – they're a little cold, perhaps a trifle damp after the night, but they'll be all right. No: weather trouble.' He nodded at the windscreen in front of the greenhouse.

Webster stared ahead and whistled softly. 'I see what you mean,' he said. The sun had hauled itself up over the rim of the desert, but instead of blazing down from a blue sky, it was visibly dimming, retiring behind a veil of dun-coloured mist that thickened as they watched. The plane shuddered again as a stronger gust blew across the stony terrain.

'Bad weather,' Fortune said. 'Maybe sandstorms. And this is very low-grade fuel. Poor octane rating. I'm worried that we might not have enough power to clear the bluff.'

For the third time wind scoured the depression, stirring the dust higher than the Macchi-Castoldi's wing. Fortune stabbed at a starter button and jockeyed with the throttles. The port motor burst into life with a clattering roar, the starboard just afterwards. It took three more attempts to get the centre propeller spinning, but finally they were taxiing down a relatively level stretch of ground to swing into the rising wind. They could hear it howling through the wires over the uneven beat of the engines.

Fortune pushed the throttles home and held the plane against the brakes, checking mixture controls, flaps, airscrew pitch, engine and oil temperatures. When the needles flickered on to the red lines marking the dials of the temperature gauges, he flipped off the brakes and the aircraft surged forward. They bumped across the rough ground, gathering speed.

The sky had turned an ominous sulphurous yellow. The broken ground racing past was grey and shadowless. As the motors bellowed and the whole plane vibrated crazily from nose to tail, they felt themselves slewing sideways – then the land fell away – the plane bounced ... lurched drunkenly into the air ... bounced again ... and again ... and finally, after more than twice its normal run, staggered up into the sky. The rocky wilderness dropped slowly away beneath them.

It was a rough trip. The engines coughed and misfired, labouring under an over-rich mixture to compensate for the low-grade fuel. The oil overheated and began to lose its viscosity. There were pockets of turbulence all over the desert as the heavy air was swirled around by the cool wind pushed ahead of the storm front approaching from the north. Lurching, yawing, sometimes sinking hundreds of feet like an express lift, the Macchi-Castoldi flew sluggishly eastwards parallel with the front. It took Fortune half an hour to persuade her up to 2000 feet. After that he tried every trick in the veteran pilot's repertoire: he put her on the shelf, he played with the flaps, he boosted and feathered and boosted again – but he could not coax the crate a foot higher than 2800 feet. At this altitude they gingerly skirted the 6000-ft peaks of the Tassili N'Ajjer and droned out over the trackless immensity of the great Sahara sand desert.

The storm front was closing fast now. The sky was boiling with browns and purples shot through with livid patches of greenish yellow. Ahead and to the south, dunes bleached of all colour melted into the leaden sky. Webster looked apprehensively over his left shoulder. 'No chance of winding her up above those clouds?' he asked.

Fortune shook his head. 'Not this old kite – there's not enough power; not with this fuel. And they're not clouds, sir and boss: there's the daddy of all sandstorms on the way. I'll have to put her down before I find myself flying blind and kill us all.'

'And then?'

'We sit out the storm and start again.'

A few minutes later – they had been airborne just over two hours – they flew into the fringe of the storm. Streamers of brown tinged with violet whipped past the greenhouse. The sky darkened frighteningly and the plane was tossed about like a leaf in a gale. Fortune swore and threw them into a dive.

They flattened out a hundred feet above the ground. The dunes had disappeared and they were over a huge saucer-shaped crater several miles in diameter and bounded by a ring of bleak cliff faces. Webster and Hawkins grabbed Zygmund's stretcher as Fortune kicked the aircraft into a vertical bank and headed upwind. Small whirlpools of dust were already obscuring the rocky floor of the crater before he dropped them down.

It was the roughest landing Webster had ever experienced. Every nut and bolt and spar in the tri-motor shuddered and groaned as she hit the deck, bounced alarmingly, and then trundled to a standstill in the lee of a pile of enormous boulders stacked at one side of the depression. As soon as Fortune cut the motors, they could feel the fuselage tremble under the howl of the wind. 'Come on, chaps – everybody out, please,' the young man yelled. 'The frogs have prepared the crate for this: there's engine covers, guy ropes, everything, stowed in the back of the cabin. But for God's sake hurry!'

They bailed out and secured the Macchi-Castoldi as well as they could in the screaming gale. The sky was dark as night and the air loaded with whirling grit, stinging the skin, choking the nostrils. By the time they piled back into the cabin, the full fury of the sandstorm was upon them. The howl of the wind rose to a screech; visibility was reduced to nil in the billowing clouds of dust; the whole plane bucked and leaped as each maniac gust surged past. For an hour and a half they shivered in pitch blackness while the windblown sand drove its way into each nook and cranny, every tiny interstice in the machine and its occupants. Then, quite suddenly, it was over. The wind dropped. The sun appeared. The plane cast a dark shadow on the ground, and the storm was just a tall pillar of slate-blue turbulence receding to the south.

But there was plenty of evidence that it had been there. Fine-grained grit was sifted over the cabin floor. It ticked and trickled from every surface at the slightest move; it had penetrated their clothes, their hair, their eyebrows, their fingernails. It clogged their nostrils when they breathed. And it had found its way beneath the canvas cover and put the port engine out of commission.

Fortune dismantled the carburettors again and checked everything he could think of. But the motor still obstinately refused to fire. Finally he attempted to take off with the starboard and centre motors only. The plane bumped along the crater floor, just made its take-off speed, and rose sluggishly into the air. He dragged the stick back into his stomach and slammed the throttles on full boost ... but the labouring airscrews were not biting into the heavy atmosphere enough to pull the machine up over the wall of cliffs surrounding the depression. He was forced to bank, turn around, and try the other way. Again the Macchi-Castoldi lacked sufficient power to lift it over the barrier. He landed and tried a longer run. The plane climbed crazily up to fifty or sixty feet but would go no higher.

Three times Fortune brought her down and took off again, with no better result: the encircling ring of rock, several hundred feet high, held them captive as effectively as prison bars. When they had bounced to a standstill for the third time, Webster called quits. 'Forget it, lad,' he said. 'You'll use up all the blasted fuel. Cut the starboard engine: we'll go ahead on one.'

'On *one*?' Fortune clearly thought Webster's reason had gone. 'But ... my dear old squire and mentor ... if I can't get her high enough into the air on two ... ?'

'Who said anything about the air?' Webster replied.

The pilot stared at him blankly. 'You've left me behind, O king.'

'We can't make it *over* the damned cliffs,' Webster explained, 'so we'll have to go around them. There's a breach in the wall, over to the southeast. A pass or canyon or gulch, or whatever they call them in Westerns. It's wide enough to take a plane. We'll save fuel by using only one engine – and we'll go along the ground.'

'You mean ... ?'

'The hell with the expense!' Webster grinned. 'We'll taxi home!'

And that was exactly what they did. With the heat increasing uncomfortably in the cabin, and the dry clatter of the half-power motor racketing too loudly for conversation, they trundled through the gorge and out across the desert beyond. The plane bounced and shuddered over the rough ground. They had to keep the greenhouse and the ports closed up because of the choking dust raised by the slipstream. At times Fortune was forced to cut in the second motor to make a slope or lift them across a patch too rugged for the undercart. But in a little over four stifling hours they had travelled another hundred miles.

It was then that they came up against the second obstacle: a narrow ravine twisting through a range of low sandstone hills. There was a trickle of muddy water at the bottom of the *wadi*, and a flat, rocky shelf at one side that could pass as a track. But the sheer wall of the defile was too near the trail to allow the plane through: the Macchi-Castoldi's wingspan was too wide.

Webster was in the grip of some manic elation. Against all odds, they had finally made it! Major Webster reporting successful completion of exercise, Captain, sir! Nothing could stop them now. 'Not to worry, not to worry,' he crowed, looking at Fortune's dismayed face. 'So we'll take off the flipping wings and go swanning through without, all right?'

Suddenly Fortune laughed. 'Wacko!' he said, mimicking Webster's own voice. 'Who needs wings on a taxi anyway?'

Once more they piled out of the plane, armed with hacksaws and spanners. Under Fortune's direction, they dismantled struts and bracing wires, unscrewed plates and sawed through dural formers, control cable conduits and fuel pipes. The outer sections of the wings, carrying the pods and their heavy radial engines, collapsed on the stony ground. Left with only the centre-section and its integral fuel tanks, Fortune started the surviving motor and took them through the ravine and on over the sand desert on the far side of it.

Sergeant Hawkins closed his eyes. 'If ever I wanted to do in me soddin' RSM,' he said, 'all I'd need would be to enumerate the King's fuckin' Regulations we done up on this bleedin' trip!'

Fortune was singing at the controls. 'Ve haf vays of makink you fly,' he carolled, pounding the stick with one fist. 'Ladyss und chentlemen, ve are hopink you are zis flight enyoying.

Heer iss your kapitan, Charles G. Fortune, and the G stands for—'

'Good show,' Webster cut in. 'Good show, good show, and a gong if you're lucky!'

An hour and a half later, they were sighted by the Long-Range Desert Group patrol sent by O'Kelly to search for them. 'Good Christ!' the young 8th Army lieutenant exclaimed, looking back at their spidery, wingless, insect-like transport as he led them to the personnel carrier. 'Good Christ – now I've seen everything!'

'Brother,' said Webster, thinking of the still more curious craft whose production he and his companions had delayed – but only delayed – 'you ain't seen nothing yet!'

EPILOGUE

England - 1944

June 13th, 0415 hours – exactly a week after the first wave of British, American, Canadian and French invaders had established their bridgehead in the Normandy landings. Captain Seamus M'Phee O'Kelly sat in an underground bunker at a secret defence HQ near the south coast. Above, the night was loud with the thunder of anti-aircraft batteries and the howl of diving night-fighters. Here, in a cloistered silence broken only by the hum of electronic equipment, girls in WAAF uniform plotted the course of strange new missiles launched on London from the Pas de Calais. The public were to call them buzz-bombs or doodlebugs; Hitler dubbed them reprisal weapons or V.1's. In the first sixteen days of the terror campaign, more than two thousand were to be fired across the British coast. But on that first night only four got through the defences. They fell at Swanscombe, Sevenoaks, Cuckfield and Bethnal Green, where six people were killed.

A fair-haired subaltern with a sandy moustache came into the bunker. 'Just been up top to have a dekko,' he said breathlessly. 'Saw a couple of the things streaking over. Going like a bat out of hell! At first I thought they were Jerry night-fighters on fire ... flames coming out of the ruddy tail and all that! I never saw anything like it in my life!'

O'Kelly took his eyes off the green blips moving across the ground-glass radar screens. 'Young man,' he said, 'if it hadn't been for a certain undisciplined and disrespectful infantry major and his disreputable companions, you'd have been only too familiar with the things for a year or more. Because of that officer, Jerry's plans were knocked for six: he had to re-start a whole research programme in the Baltic and they couldn't get the damned things ready before D-Day. If they had – if the major hadn't succeeded – why, there might not have been any invasion at all!'

NON-FICTION

GENERAL

☐ Guide to the Channel Islands	J. Anderson & E. Swinglehurst	90p
☐ The Complete Traveller	Joan Bakewell	£1.95
☐ Time Out London Shopping Guide	Lindsey Bareham	£1.50
☐ World War 3	Edited by Shelford Bidwell	£1.25
☐ The Black Angels	Rupert Butler	£1.35
☐ Hand of Steel	Rupert Butler	£1.35
☐ A Walk Around the Lakes	Hunter Davies	£1.50
☐ Truly Murderous	John Dunning	95p
☐ In Praise of Younger Men	Sandy Fawkes	85p
☐ Hitler's Secret Life	Glenn B. Infield	£1.50
☐ Wing Leader	Johnnie Johnson	£1.25
☐ Me, to Name but a Few	Spike Mullins	£1.00
☐ Our Future: Dr. Magnus Pyke Predicts		95p
☐ The Devil's Bedside Book	Leonard Rossiter	85p
☐ Barbara Windsor's Book of Boobs	Barbara Windsor	£1.50

BIOGRAPHY/AUTOBIOGRAPHY

☐ Go-Boy	Roger Caron	£1.25
☐ The Queen Mother Herself	Helen Cathcart	£1.25
☐ George Stephenson	Hunter Davies	£1.50
☐ The Queen's Children	Donald Edgar	£1.25
☐ Prince Regent	Harry Edgington	95p
☐ All of Me	Rose Neighbour	£1.00
☐ Tell Me Who I Am Before I Die	C. Peters with T. Schwarz	£1.00
☐ Boney *M*	J. Shearlaw and D. Brown	90p
☐ Kiss	John Swenson	90p

HEALTH/SELF-HELP/POCKET HEALTH GUIDES

☐ Pulling Your Own Strings	Dr. Wayne W. Dyer	95p
☐ The Pick of Woman's Own Diets	Jo Foley	95p
☐ Woman X Two	Mary Kenny	90p
☐ Cystitis: A Complete Self-help Guide	Angela Kilmartin	£1.00
☐ The Stress Factor	Donald Norfolk	90p
☐ Fat is a Feminist Issue	Susie Orbach	85p
☐ Related to Sex	Claire Rayner	£1.25
☐ The Working Woman's Body Book	L. Rowen with B. Winkler	95p
☐ Woman's Own Birth Control	Dr. Michael Smith	£1.25
☐ Allergies	Robert Eagle	65p
☐ Arthritis and Rheumatism	Dr. Luke Fernandes	65p
☐ Back Pain	Dr. Paul Dudley	65p
☐ Pre-Menstrual Tension	June Clark	65p
☐ Migraine	Dr. Finlay Campbell	65p
☐ Skin Troubles	Deanna Wilson	65p

REFERENCE

☐ What's Wrong with your Pet?	Hugo Kerr	95p
☐ You *Can* Train Your Cat	Jo and Paul Loeb	£1.50
☐ Caring for Cats and Kittens	John Montgomery	95p
☐ The Oscar Movies from A-Z	Roy Pickard	£1.25
☐ Questions of Law	Bill Thomas	95p
☐ The Hamlyn Book of Amazing Information		80p
☐ The Hamlyn Family Medical Dictionary		£2.50

GAMES & PASTIMES

☐ The Hamlyn Book of Brainteasers and Mindbenders	Ben Hamilton	85p
☐ The Hamlyn Book of Crosswords Books 1, 2, 3, and 4		60p
☐ The Hamlyn Book of Crosswords 5		70p
☐ The Hamlyn Book of Wordways 1		75p
☐ The Hamlyn Family Quiz Book		85p

FICTION

GENERAL

☐ Stand on It	Stroker Ace	95p
☐ Chains	Justin Adams	£1.25
☐ The Master Mechanic	I. G. Broat	£1.50
☐ Wyndward Passion	Norman Daniels	£1.35
☐ Abingdon's	Michael French	£1.25
☐ The Moviola Man	Bill and Colleen Mahan	£1.25
☐ Running Scared	Gregory Mcdonald	85p
☐ Gossip	Marc Olden	£1.25
☐ The Sounds of Silence	Judith Richards	£1.00
☐ Summer Lightning	Judith Richards	£1.00
☐ The Hamptons	Charles Rigdon	£1.35
☐ The Affair of Nina B.	Simmel	95p
☐ The Berlin Connection	Simmel	£1.50
☐ The Cain Conspiracy	Simmel	£1.20
☐ Double Agent—Triple Cross	Simmel	£1.35
☐ Celestial Navigation	Anne Tyler	£1.00
☐ Earthly Possessions	Anne Tyler	95p
☐ Searching for Caleb	Anne Tyler	£1.00

WESTERN BLADE SERIES

☐ No. 1 The Indian Incident	Matt Chisholm	75p
☐ No. 2 The Tucson Conspiracy	Matt Chisholm	75p
☐ No. 3 The Laredo Assignment	Matt Chisholm	75p
☐ No. 4 The Pecos Manhunt	Matt Chisholm	75p
☐ No. 5 The Colorado Virgins	Matt Chisholm	85p
☐ No. 6 The Mexican Proposition	Matt Chisholm	75p
☐ No. 7 The Arizona Climax	Matt Chisholm	85p
☐ No. 8 The Nevada Mustang	Matt Chisholm	85p

WAR

☐ Jenny's War	Jack Stoneley	£1.25
☐ The Killing-Ground	Elleston Trevor	£1.10

NAVAL HISTORICAL

☐ The Sea of the Dragon	R. T. Aundrews	95p
☐ Ty-Shan Bay	R. T. Aundrews	95p
☐ HMS Bounty	John Maxwell	£1.00
☐ The Baltic Convoy	Showell Styles	95p
☐ Mr. Fitton's Commission	Showell Styles	85p

FILM/TV TIE-IN

☐ American Gigolo	Timothy Harris	95p
☐ Meteor	E. H. North and F. Coen	95p
☐ Driver	Clyde B. Phillips	80p

SCIENCE FICTION

☐ The Mind Thing	Fredric Brown	90p
☐ Strangers	Gardner Dozois	95p
☐ Project Barrier	Daniel F. Galouye	80p
☐ Beyond the Barrier	Damon Knight	[illegible]
☐ Clash by Night	Henry Kuttner	[illegible]
☐ Fury	Henry Kuttner	80p
☐ Mutant	Henry Kuttner	90p
☐ Drinking Sapphire Wine	Tanith Lee	£1.25
☐ Journey	Marta Randall	£1.00
☐ The Lion Game	James H. Schmitz	70p
☐ The Seed of Earth	Robert Silverberg	80p
☐ The Silent Invaders	Robert Silverberg	80p
☐ City of the Sun	Brian M. Stableford	85p
☐ Critical Threshold	Brian M. Stableford	75p
☐ The Florians	Brian M. Stableford	80p
☐ Wildeblood's Empire	Brian M. Stableford	80p
☐ A Touch of Strange	Theodore Sturgeon	85p